## *He had no idea who had sent the bikers . . .*

"Hawk!" Pollock cried. Mike looked up to see a tire iron swinging at his head.

Mike fell aside and took part of the blow on his shoulder. The iron glanced off and smacked the gang's leader a stunning blow on the forehead. The attacker, a bear in a dirty fur coat, fell forward with his own blow. Mike's left-handed chop at the top of the spinal column left him stunned and paralyzed where he lay.

At the same time a chain swung from the other side, and Hawk allowed it to coil painfully around his arm in preference to letting it circle his neck. Yanking the chain loose, he used it to whip its owner across the kidneys.

Three down, but it was a fight he couldn't win . . .

*Also in the HAWK series
from Jove*

**THE DEADLY CRUSADER
THE MIND TWISTERS
THE POWER BARONS
THE PREDATORS
CALIFORNIA SHAKEDOWN
THE SEEDS OF EVIL**

# DAN STREIB
# HAWK

# THE DEATH RIDERS

A JOVE BOOK

Copyright © 1981 by Dan Streib

All rights reserved. No part of this publication
may be reproduced or transmitted in any form or
by any means, electronic or mechanical, including
photocopy, recording, or any information storage
and retrieval system, without permission
in writing from the publisher.

Requests for permission to make copies of any part
of the work should be mailed to: Permissions,
Jove Publications, Inc., 200 Madison Avenue,
New York, NY 10016

First Jove edition published March 1981

First printing

Printed in the United States of America

Jove books are published by Jove Publications, Inc.,
200 Madison Avenue, New York, NY 10016

# 1

*Urgent!*

The frantic plea for immediacy was scratched across the number-ten white envelope in brazen red letters. A bold, thick stroke of pen underlined them.

International airmail and special-delivery stamps with white and blue arrows of urgency had been affixed to the upper-right-hand corner, one of them cocked as if applied in a terrified rush. Closer to the return address extra stamps sent further distress signals to the mail handlers whose fingers had flipped the message through its long, meandering odyssey.

*Please Forward Immediately.*

The second plea on the bottom left-hand corner also was underscored. It spoke of life and death.

The original address had been scratched out and another written in. Then another address and another. Postmarks crowded together, tracing the letter's jet trail to Chicago, New York, to Italy, and finally the hot, steaming Caribbean islands.

More postage had been paid along the way.

The plea for haste had aroused men to brief flurries of activity. One receiver dispatched the sealed message by motorized courier. A second forwarded it on the run to the nearest post office. A third gave up his lunch hour hastening its journey.

Each resented the extra effort. The addressee had won no loving cups among the jaded news bureau chiefs who played general delivery for the wandering journalist. The unwilling couriers forwarded the letter pragmatically; each was indebted to the receiver. To eschew their tenuous link with him was to sever the thread that sporadically drew floods of front-page banner news from the well of world tears.

They resented him because they admired him.

But the letter's rush had occurred on other days, in other places.

On the sun-washed island of St. Lucia the pace slowed to a crawl. In the deep valleys filled with orchids, hibiscus, and hundreds of other exotic blooms, the word "urgent" was an anachronism. Such jolts to the tranquility were a jarring and unwelcome discord. The inhabitants moved slowly through the heat, even on banana-ship day when the women heaped the island's principal export onto their heads and transported it to the holds of rusting freighters.

In the village post office the girl behind the steel-barred counter had surreptitiously separated the letter from the mail that had arrived on the afternoon Sun-jet service. A black girl of prodigious grace, she considered herself on a higher social rung than most. Her own mother, though, still haloed her head with a *colta*, a banana-fiber ring on which the bent old woman carried tourists' laundry to her washtub at home.

The girl felt superior because she could read. She was the first of her family who could.

The barren building—with its counter and two dozen unlocked, haphazardly numbered boxes, a nonfunctioning electric fan dangling from the ceiling, and one worn wicker chair—was her realm. There she reigned over the twitching, dark-skinned Frenchman who came to the office minutes after each day's delivery and laid with her on the floor whenever the mood moved her.

She tolerated him because he came from beyond the village that bored her, because he smiled a lot, and because he moved his body constantly to the rhythm from the transistor radio strapped to an empty belt loop on faded cutoff shorts.

The shorts, the only clothing he wore, bespoke his poverty, and she treated him as inferior except when she lost control close to a sexual climax.

Like warm sun and rain, he brought life to the post office with its bare wood floor and the smell of dead leaves from the thatch-covered roof.

Today he offended her by picking up the envelope from the counter before she granted permission.

"Ah!" the squirming French islander exclaimed. "*Monsieur* Michael Hawk. *Mon ami.*"

He kissed the envelope and pirouetted in anticipation, holding the prize like a golden chalice.

"Here, you Creole crazy," she cried in English. "Give me dat."

"Eh? Big tip. You want too, *vrai*?"

"*Faux.*"

She stretched to grab the letter.

He laughed and switched to the patois of St. Lucia. "Eh! *Kuté fam-la.*"

She had been told to expect the envelope. Dutch guilders had been offered. Violence was the implied reward for failure.

Fear tightened her throat when she failed to retrieve the envelope. The men who had approached her were the cruel, sadistic type, who for pleasure would pin a bug to a table top with the point of a knife.

"Ah, *padoñ*, mah sweet." Flibustier tucked the prize behind his buttocks and danced away.

Near thirty—he lost count of the years—he read little English, a smattering of French, a dash of Caribbean-convoluted Dutch, and a meager vocabulary of Spanish. He had escaped the literacy being imposed insidiously on the scattered specks of land in the warm, somnolent sea.

So the entreaty for haste on the envelope meant nothing to him. The addressee's name, though, was familiar.

"Michael Hawk."

It was a clandestine title to him, as mystifying as a magician's wand. It represented sequestered wealth, a pirate's loot buried, buried deep. It conjured images in the slender, anoretic Creole's mind: of generous tips; pleasantly brief periods of casual employment; the mellow oblivion that francs, pounds, pesos, and crisp new dollars could buy; liters of orange-peel rum or a case of strong wine.

Usually a woman less haughty than the educated postmistress was a part of Michael Hawk's strange generosity.

There was more. There was the inexplicable camaraderie between the two very different men. The adhesive joining them seemed to be the fantasylands in which they lived.

Flibustier's mental Disneyland was a product of his own brain—the escape of a brilliant but untrained mind from the doldrums of poverty and the void of illiteracy.

He had no idea whether Hawk's world was real or only an extended joke played with play money from a child's game.

The Creole didn't care. The mysterious Hawk was as uninhibited as the sinewy man from St. Martin himself.

Hawk meant fun, friendship, and escape.

The envelope was a ticket to intrude on the generous white man.

Italian stamps pasted over the original American postage meant nothing to Flibustier. His world didn't stretch that far. Nor had he expected the postmistress's violent reaction to his possession of the letter.

She cursed him in the patois of the former British colony and called him "bloody this" and "bloody that" when he escaped into the baking noonday sun. She was still swearing when he swung along the dirt street between the village stores. There was a monotonous sameness about their corrugated roofs, shuttered windows, and unpainted second stories jutting out to provide shade for the broken concrete sidewalks.

"*Au revoir, petite amie,*" Flibustier called loud enough to be heard behind the louvered shutters of the silent village.

He was from St. Martin. Divided between France and Holland, it lay far to the north along the crescent-shaped archipelago stretching from Florida to the Venezuelan shores. Since he liked everyone to know he was from somewhere else, he spoke mostly Gallic French, although St. Lucia had a split Anglo-Gallic personality. There, British bric-a-brac stood among French colonial frame structures, the offspring of incestuous mating between the island's historically alternating rulers.

English was St. Lucia's official language. The people spoke their own blend of Carib (French and African) at home, a dialect the Creole from St. Martin could speak when he wanted.

So he shouted "Farewell, my love" again in Carib.

If anyone heard, no one opened a window.

Sand flies buzzing about his head were the only interruption of the quiet.

Flibustier did not understand the girl's unexpected anger at all. He flitted about regularly, making ourtageously sensual suggestions whenever her friends entered the post office. He provided white tourists special-delivery service for tips he and the girl had shared. The courier service was the latest and least illegal of his petty enterprises.

Why she objected today did not worry him.

"*Faire l'amour*," he cried.

He was growing bored with the business anyway. It tarnished his flamboyant image of himself.

In his mind he was exactly what he called himself, a *flibustier*, a *vrijbuiter* in Dutch, in English a freebooter. Pirate blood streamed hot and fast in his veins. He was a descendant of the infamous female pirate Anny Bonny, he bragged. His ancestors were sired by "Calico Jack" Rackham, Anny's cutthroat shipmate who died on the gallows.

So his mother told him.

"Ah!" he would say. The black strain came through the unique alchemy of pigmentation that created the beautiful *Martiniquaises* of the French Caribbean. Only he explained it in a garbled dialect influenced by his wanderings over a sea salted with islands where new languages were still emerging and brewing in a bouillabaisse of words, slang, and distorted pronunciations.

His Creole mother had been born in Les Trois Ilets on St. Martin near the partially restored home of Napoleon's Josephine, the nineteenth-century empress of all France.

And it was not by error that his last name was the same as that of Bonaparte's wife.

He was Flibustier de Beauharnais, he claimed. True or not he was proud of his prostitute mother's audacity at linking him to Europe's long-deposed royalty. If anyone derisively doubted his lineal claims, he disregarded their cynicism as irreverent envy.

He considered himself doubly endowed. Besides the name, he was the reincarnation of a fearless pirate. His ancestors had pillaged galleons until European rulers discovered more loot in plantations worked by the darker gold of imported slaves.

And Michael Hawk.

Ah, there was a wise man. He would sit by the hour on a luxurious fishing boat listening and believing Flibustier's yarns.

"Flibustier, he comes up the sea on dis yacht *magnifique*," the Creole had related in mangled English last time they met. "West, southwest Nasse-Terre. Me, diesel, she chuggin'. Flibustier, him at dey helm. Yacht she becalmed. Dey man, dey woman on deck. American, ah thinks. Dey woman, she sunnin', body near naked. Dey wavin', ah come alongside. Dey Capt'n—dat me—he board wid nothin' but dey four-barrel derringer. Dey cringe like naughty children. Dey capt'n he puts dem adrift in dah skiff, wid eats for a month. He good mon, dat freebooter. But he takes dey yacht. Ah, she's *beauté*. Like woman of Martinique durin' *Vaval* before dey Lent. Ah tows her north by east. Mah diesel, she chuggin' good, knowins we rich, mah boat and me."

"And where is this yacht and your boat now?" Hawk asked politely.

Flibustier spread his cinnamon-colored arms and made a sad sigh.

"Lost. Dey devil currents in dey Guadloupe Passage, he gets 'em. Ah! Dey fates of a pirate. But 'morrow. Dey capt'n—dat's me—he gets 'nother yacht. Bigger. Prettier'n breasts of dey woman. You see."

The American nodded and made marks on paper that he always seemed to carry, except when he dived in the water and perhaps when he went to bed with one of the many women Flibustier had seen him with during the dozen or so times the two had met.

Hawk was a writer or had been once, the Creole knew that, but the American had reappeared on St. Lucia this last time without his typewriter in tow. He was different too, this wise, friendly man who disappeared and reappeared on the islands like occasional breezes on a still, hot day.

In the earlier years Hawk had been impressed by the modern shops with glass and aluminum exteriors in Castries, the island's main city. The town had been cauterized by fire twice within a couple of years, but Hawk didn't mention the squalor reinfecting the fringes. He also ignored the contrasting white mansions on the hillsides and the million-dollar sailboats in the harbor.

Hawk had been one with the people.

But this trip he had changed. He employed Flibustier to ward off boys nagging him to toss quarters into the murky water of the bay. Hawk gave handfuls of dollars for his friend to disperse without making the boys dive into the pollution.

Yet he didn't stay to talk and joke with the kids who had trailed him in the days when he didn't have a dime to share.

The writer was different in other ways too. He received no mail. The letter today was only the second for him this trip.

Hawk seemed aloof to his old haunts. He no longer visited women he had known in houses where laundry hung from the windows; he kicked at the pigeons picking at the cracks in the potholed streets; and he grew irritable when he stumbled on sidewalks with unexpected dips and rises.

He had come to St. Lucia several months before, but Flibustier still had to bring him bottled water. He didn't walk or hitch rides anymore. Now the Creole had to haggle with quarrelsome cabdrivers to take them from the major resorts to the village near the foot of the twin Pitons, which thrust green mounds at the blue and white sky.

Flibustier had chosen the Cloud's Head Resort of Bieu Fort near the southern tip of the island for his friend, although it was far from the fun places they had once shared. The hotel itself was a dozen rooms in a wooden building with partitions serving as walls. But Hawk chose the more expensive cottages at nearby Beane Field Beach.

"Dis place, she too quiet," Flibustier had commented. "You ears go deaf, how you tell?"

"It's fine," Hawk had said.

In earlier times the writer had had no interest in seclusion.

The two had met on Martinique during Carnival right after the New Year hangover. Hawk had mixed like a native in the masquerades, the singing, the dancing in the streets. On Ash Wednesday he had masked himself grotesquely like everyone else. Then he joined the final ballet of the extended Mardi Gras funeral cortege that paraded behind clarinets and trumpets to the yellow and red pyre of flickering flames and dancing shadows.

Michael Hawk and the self-proclaimed descendant of a pirate wench had wakened to Lent in the same littered doorway. They had been friends ever since, whenever their paths could be made to cross.

But the American had changed. He was richer. He was different.

Flibustier danced up the rise in the dusty road with the letter in his teeth. It was his dagger; a stick was his sword.

There was a bounce of anticipation in his step although he

followed the narrow road graded up one side of the steep hill and down the other. The cliff fell away into the sea, and the sun would glare at him all the way; still he grinned at the prospect of seeing his white friend again.

"Ship ahoy, man dah mains'l." He fenced with imaginary merchant seamen as he walked, remembering snippets of dialogue from a film he had once seen.

So he didn't hear the motorcycle's *varoom* until it was almost upon him. When he did hear, the sound was the rumble of a cannon to his imaginative brain.

He whirled, stick at the ready, to see the chrome and red enamel Kawasaki with long stroke front suspension aimed directly at him. The driver was hunched behind the windscreen. The helmeted head and visored face were hidden from view. Gloves concealed the hands.

Flibustier assumed the rider was black. He must be a slave pressed into the service of the enemy. Attacking.

In the tenuous world where the Creole stole and connived for a living, battles with fists and knives were as common and vicious as in the packs of any predatory animal. His first reaction was fear. That was nature's signal to prepare every nerve, bone, and muscle for survival.

Stumbling sideways, Flibustier headed for the top of the incline. To his left the hillside had been shaved nearly to a perpendicular drop when the road was graded by the British. A mat of bougainvillea fell in a cascade of red down the embankment to the road, its gnarled mass of thorny vines offering sanctuary to the unofficial courier. He thrust his hands into the redness and clawed his way upward. Surprisingly the slender withes supported his weight; it was the earth that failed him.

A great wreath pulled away from the moist soil, letting him topple backward to the pebble-covered road. The motorcycle surged through six gears as it obtained the speed needed for a thirteen-second quarter mile.

"Eh!" he yelled.

He was confused between the reality of a weighty, powerful machine driving at him hard and his imaginary battle of the Spanish main.

He rolled.

The cycle narrowly missed his head and torso, running

over his hand. It left gray, clawlike tread marks across his skin.

He could almost ignore the pain in the exultation of survival. He swung the stick as if it were truly a sword. The attack, he thought, was some friend's joke. Or revenge by a man whose woman he had taken. Freebooters made enemies.

The bike skidded in a shrieking U-turn less than twenty yards up the road. Trailing a bridal train of vines, it shot toward him again with a blip of the throttle.

The Creole from St. Martin remembered who he was, a descendant of pirates and the empress of France. In his mind the motorcycle rider became a British privateer swinging aboard his ancestor's galleon.

Flibustier, knife of paper still in his mouth, reveled in the game. He swayed side to side, forcing the cyclist to choose which way the target would jump.

At the last second the agile Frenchman chose the left. He leaped, extended his uninjured hand with its willowy sword, and attempted to cut his assailant across the throat.

The bike, though, whisked past, made another U-turn and a third adroit drive at the weaving target.

"*Libertatia!*" Flibustier shouted another word he had discovered during his unstructured research into the time of skull and crossbones.

His bravado wavered when he spotted a second cycle churning up the hill. His sweeping gaze assessed the situation.

*L'embouteillage,* he thought. There was a bottleneck now, and he was caught in the throat.

Returning to the village would be impossible. The second cyclist blocked the route. Continuing up the road to Michael Hawk's hotel was impractical too. The grade was steep and Flibustier was in no condition to outrun a powerful machine. The bougainvillea-covered hillside would not hold his weight. This left only one direction in which to flee: down the cliff toward the sea. There was a footpath, Flibustier recalled. But the foliage between it and the road was thick with creepers and scrub trees that might tangle a man in a net of growth. He must bull his way through the vegetation, being careful not to miss the path and plunge to the bottom where the sea washed the island. There giant boulders absorbed the untiring onslaught of fierce, foaming surf.

Yet if he plunged off the edge of the road now, and if the cyclist were armed with a flintlock pistol, the foliage would still imprison the modern-day freebooter when his assailant had braked to a stop.

Besides, the alternative appealed to Flibustier. In the face of the totally unexpected, completely incomprehensible attack, he had a buccaneer's derring-do, a devil-may-care fascination with violence and death. He grinned while the bike sped closer.

The Flibustier played his game.

He pretended panic. He staggered, fell, rose on his hands and knees, and floundered at the very edge of the precipice. A nudge would send him hurtling off the cliff. At best he could hope to be caught in the green fingers of the jungle branches instead of splattering against the rocks.

He pulled the envelope from his mouth and screamed, "No, please, suh, don't." He repeated it in the local dialect. *"Non, mèsi, su plè."*

The bike plowed toward him.

Using body English, he spun. He slid. He caught the handlebar that barely missed him.

The crucial swerve that the cyclist intended to make never happened. Flibustier's grasp was enough to keep the front wheel straight a split second too long.

The scion of pirates and royalty was too busy keeping himself from plunging straight down the cliff to see the expensive bike launch itself from the road. But he saw it in midair. It was a slender-winged bird. It sailed, colorful as a flamingo from the Dutch island of Bonaire, over the foliage and arched slowly, gracefully downward. Partway, rider and bike parted company.

The gloved hands clawed the air before machine and man smashed the rocks below. One crackled and exploded. One splattered like a ripe melon dropped by boys running from a forbidden patch.

Flibustier had no feeling for his squashed assailant, although questions swarmed in on him as he withdrew from his world of make-believe adventure.

Necessity pushed the questions from his mind. The second bike was rapidly approaching.

Afraid again, he threw his body against the thick tangle of oleander, roses, lilies, and blooming shrubs clinging to the cliff. Pampas grass sliced his body like long razor blades; thorns ripped and chunked his skin. Leaves cut at his eyes and caught in his mouth. Branches embraced him. Grimly determined, he fought to the narrow path that ran along the cliffside.

He slipped, slid off the path, and caught a limb before he made the final plunge. He dragged himself up when he heard the second bike on the road above him.

The engine stopped.

The rider must be listening, Flibustier decided. He again considered returning to the village, but the enemy could be someone in authority.

Find Hawk, the cinnamon-colored Creole told himself.

The American would know what to do. He would help. The former writer avoided authorities too and evaded questions.

If anyone would help, it would be Hawk.

Besides Flibustier still had the letter that he had taken from the post office for delivery.

# 2

Michael Hawk drowsed on the hot white sand while the surf approached in soporific cadence. The rising tide would reach his feet soon, and he would have to move.

He would welcome an excuse for action, any action.

As ambivalent as he was restive, Hawk alternately sought and respected the adrenaline-pumping action that played bedfellow to society's turbulence. His life had been a series of challenges, some of the work of an amoral lady luck and others of his own making. In recent years, whatever the crisis or its denouement, he would flee to his fluid Caribbean headquarters when the action was over. This time he chose the peaceful backwater of St. Lucia.

But in Castries, the capital, there was evidence of infectious turmoil. The city was plastered with torn signs posted to boarded-up windows; belligerent graffiti spread like disfiguring acne on walls and fences.

"Stop the violence!" "Down with bombings!" "Kill the terrorists!"

Political protest scarred the quiet utopia that independence was supposed to bring the former British colony.

So he had retreated deeper, away from the city's squalor to Cloud's Nest Resort. He had fed himself on bucolic placidity; it had succored his need. Now the sour taste of boredom rose like bile inside him. He was bored, fed up with relaxation. It was peaceful here—and he'd had a bellyful of it.

It had been like this even when he was a kid. Some

insightful sage had written a quote from Sir Walter Scott under Hawk's picture in the high-school annual:

"One hour of life crowded to the full with glorious action, and filled with noble risks is worth whole years of those mean observances of paltry decorum."

How true, he thought to himself. He was as bored as an alcoholic at a temperance meeting. Tall and fit, Hawk was finding it difficult to cross the hump of his mid-thirties although the usual prerogatives of age had not slowed his physical responses. Occasionally an old wound would nudge him when he overextended himself; otherwise he felt great—physically.

His body adapted well to the island. His usually chestnut-brown hair was lightened in the tropical sun. The hazel eyes had grown accustomed to the glare off the turquoise sea so he rarely wore sunglasses. Having dressed in shorts or swimsuit only, his body was tanned to the shade of lighter-colored blacks.

Yet he looked his age.

The mound he had made from sand raised him to a half-sitting position, and his right arm rested across the shoulder of a girl in a bathing suit, one of those cut-in, cut-out one-piece wonders that managed more nudity than a bikini. A stewardess with British West Indies Airways, Celeste was twenty-two and not particularly good company. She had stopped on the deserted beach one day to shake the lethargic Michael Hawk awake.

She might have gotten her artfully exposed body punctured with 9 mm holes in the most unseemly places had he come armed, but she could not have guessed that. Outwardly he did not look like a tense mass of nerves, muscles, and reflexes.

Surprising Michael Hawk was as imprudent as the early Spaniards had been when they waded ashore to pillage the unspoiled Caribbean islands. The gold-lusting explorers had been greeted by Carib Indians with arrows dipped in the deadly manchineel sap from the Virgin Islands. And the Spaniards had had less to hide than the tall American.

"You a Yank?" Celeste had asked.

He appreciated the fine lines of her body. She was not exactly beautiful. Her hair was a dark blond; her skin was too white for his taste; but she was direct. And he had grown bored with the usual mating games.

"You have your own digs?" she wanted to know early into the conversation.

She had spent that first night with him and many others when she laid over on St. Lucia. She didn't ask questions. She wasn't curious about a sophisticated American who stayed in a cottage on a beach where fishermen hauled nets into dugout canoes just as they had for centuries.

She was unconcerned with Hawk's morbid fascination with the fishermen. Most mornings before dawn they motored to their favorite grounds and played out long nets with weights on the bottom and floats on the surface.

The nets pulsated with life when drawn into a slowly decreasing circumference.

Hawk's interest peaked when all hands pulled together. They heaved a splashing confusion of trapped fish on board to die. Hundreds of gills rose and fell pathetically in the hostile environment.

Each time he watched the operation, he waited for that moment when a fish or two would escape the net or flop off the longboats and dive for safety.

He too was a fish. How often he had been surrounded by cleverly designed nets? But so far he had always flopped free. One day he would get caught; he would gasp his last in some predator's snare.

The girl knew nothing of that either. She saw no contradictions in a man who read Nietzsche and listened to stereophonic Bach while naked kids splashed in the shallows, and pigs, goats, and sheep roamed in fenceless freedom.

It didn't interest her that he kept a pair of Smith and Wesson auto pistols in his cottage. She saw no artistry in the angry, spread-winged eagles engraved on the white grips and the slogan, "Quality Has No Equal," imprinted on a banner draped above the ominous birds.

One pistol accompanied him in the plastic bag he carried to the beach, to the village's sole tourist restaurant, and to the john.

She watched with indifferent curiosity when a spice-colored islander came stumbling and panting toward them across the sand. His body was torn and bleeding, his skin flecked with crystals of perspiration. The nostrils of his broad, flat nose flared like an angry bull's, yet he was half smiling, and the transistor radio flopping at his waist blared the static-filled beat of a steel-drum band.

"Eh, Mike, eh der," the Creole was calling.

Hawk sat upright, instinctively edging the heavy bag closer to his hand. The zipper was open.

"Flibustier!" Mike grinned with pleasure.

Hawk was a man of no pretenses. He knew his friend wasn't quite normal. The man moved between reality and fantasy without differentiating. But Flibustier had bridged any color barrier with ease and introduced Hawk to blacks all up and down the Antillean archipelago. Being part of the local culture had been important when the American was a freelance journalist. Now it was a source of pleasure, besides being a valuable asset. In the islanders' loosely regulated society Hawk's black friends could provide warrens of safety with their incorruptible loyalties to anyone they considered their own.

"What the hell happened to you?" Hawk asked his bleeding friend.

The Creole's eyes widened.

"Flibustier attacked by corsair. Come full sail at him, cannon boomin'."

"No, old buddy, really. What happened?"

"Capt'n—dat's me—kill 'em fast." He sliced the envelope across his own neck.

"What's he talking about?" Celeste asked.

"Never mind." Hawk disliked her denigrating tone. Flibustier had qualities that well compensated for his mental wanderings.

"It's true. Big motorcycle charge . . ."

"Motorcycle?"

Flibustier scowled. The motorcycle didn't fit in his concept of the recent battle either.

He let the problem pass. "Eh, Mike," he started over. "Brings you mail. Corsairs no stop dey capt'n. No, suh. Kill 'em, Ah did. One anyway."

The American took the proffered envelope.

He was puzzled. Usually a filament of truth ran through the airy fabric of his friend's imagination. The Creole had probably just had a run-in of some kind with a local biker. Right now it was the envelope that interested Hawk.

He didn't receive much mail. His whereabouts were best kept secret, and he had told only one man that he would be staying on St. Lucia. The breach in his security had been necessitated by an equally important need to avoid suspicion.

Since he was forced to earn legitimate income to keep the avaricious IRS off his tail, he had worked briefly for an editor in Italy. The story had turned bloody and incomprehensible for the average news reader, but Hawk at least had earned his minimum and expenses. He had been forced, though, to tell the editor of his future whereabouts. That check had come weeks ago.

The new letter had not originated with the editor in Venice, he noticed.

" 'Urgent!' " Celeste read over his shoulder. "Someone want your stud service in a hurry?" she said. "Is that what you do? Hire out for fucking?"

It was as close as she had come to probing him with questions.

"Don't say 'fuck,' " Hawk told her.

"Why? We do it everytime I come here."

"I don't like women who curse."

"Fuck," she said and closed her eyes.

He felt an odd sense of loss. What he had said wasn't true. He didn't care if women cursed or made blatant advances. It was just that Lisa never had.

His wife—she had been dead for years—rarely swore. She wasn't prissy. She just didn't swear.

Vulgarities from other women meant nothing, except that he had not yet replaced his Lisa. Often he had come close. A man with money and a sensual, laid-back approach to life attracted women, enough so that he occasionally found one who could almost be a Lisa.

Or her surrogate.

He had fallen in love several times since he lost his wife. But most of them were too much like her. Like her, they had a way of dying.

Some he had to leave behind. A man with his kind of money really had only two modes of life: on the run, or holed up somewhere warm and remote. And he had to travel alone.

So he stared at the letter, the way people did in movies, as if the envelope were a rare intrusion.

In his case, it was true. He didn't even get junk mail.

He wondered how the letter had found him. Smeared postmarks showed it had wandered the world: a news bureau in Chicago, another in New York, a third in Venice, Italy. That explained it. His last editor had forwarded his mail to St. Lucia.

Hawk liked the Caribbean. It had a hundred islands filled with villages, coves, beaches, and resorts where a man could live the good life and remain anonymous.

Still, if a letter could reach him, so could an enemy.

With both trepidation and anticipation, he opened the envelope. He sensed his leisurely days on St. Lucia were coming to an end.

Surprisingly the first sheet of paper unfolded like a piece of junk mail.

"Whip McComb and his Thrill Circus."

The headline was printed in blood red. Under it a figure in a silver jump suit poised on a Suzuki painted in psychedelic enamel.

"Whip McComb!" Hawk said aloud.

He hadn't thought of the man in years.

Time had eroded the craggy face in the illustration. There were new scars that the retouch artist could not quite obliterate without losing some of the character, and the sparkle in the eyes was phonied up. With his helmet under one arm, McComb looked grayer, too. Streaks of white thrust aging fingers into the carefully combed black hair.

"Must be fifty now," Mike said aloud.

"God!" the girl at his elbow said with disgust.

She was looking at the bed of nails featured in the advertising picture.

They were more than nails. They were twelve-inch chromium steel spikes, forming a deathbed between the lift-off ramp to the right and the landing platform far to the left.

Obviously McComb was still surviving his old tricks, jumping motorcycles through the air over anything dangerous he could place below. And unless Mike's friend had changed, the spikes were real, not painted plastic that would bend under impact. McComb never faked; for him danger was intrinsic to success.

Bewildered, Hawk dug deeper into the envelope. Nobody could be sending him a hand-delivered advertising brochure for a motorcycle thrill show, not even crazy McComb.

He was right. The envelope contained a second sheet, this one expensive stationery. The embossed letterhead bore the same headline as the flier.

"Whip McComb and his Thrill Circus." Below were two addresses: both agents, one was in New York, the other in Los Angeles. McComb had no permanent home except a battle-scarred camper that, like its owner, showed its wear and tear.

The letter wasn't typed. There was nothing businesslike about it.

As indicated by the date on the upper right, the letter had been a full month in transit, this despite the international air mail stamps on the envelope.

The salutation was unusual enough for Celeste to read aloud as she kibitzed over Michael Hawk's shoulder.

"Dear Uncle Mike . . ." Celeste leaned away far enough to direct a surprised look at Mike. "You have a family?"

Hawk ignored her, but yes, he had a family: aunts, uncles, nieces, nephews, and in-laws he never saw. Years ago he had swapped the closeness of family dinners and mandatory visits for the world of a gypsy with a jet for a horse-drawn wagon.

But who would use Whip's letterhead to call him uncle? He glanced at the signature.

The close was not the usual: no "Sincerely yours," "Love," "As ever," or any of the bland notations people wrote thoughtlessly at the end of letters.

"Desperately yours," it read. "Jinx."

Desperately? Jinx? The name was meaningless to Hawk.

Celeste was unabashedly reading aloud: " 'Dear Uncle Mike, There's a man, a reporter who says he worked with you once,' " she read.

"That's what you are? A reporter?" she asked, curious now that another woman, one named Jinx, seemed to have entered the life of her casual paramour.

Again Hawk did not answer her. If he had, he would have said, Yeah. Once I thought it was the most important thing in the world. The truth. I thought I could tell the world about Afghans slaughtered with anthrax, the mad genocides in Chad and Cambodia, and religion that justified murder. I thought people who read my stuff would rise up in indignation and put the world straight. It had taken only a few years for him to realize that his audience read his material hungrily, like curious voyeurs, and then went back to their game shows and sit-coms. What else could they do?

"He thinks a letter will get forwarded to you eventually," he read on. "Soon, I hope. It's Dad. He's killing himself or somebody's trying to kill him. I don't know which. I begged him to let me take his place. I can, but he won't listen. You're my last hope. Whip used to listen to you. Remember how you made him wear the face mask when he drove through the pool of burning oil? He wouldn't wear the asbestos suit, but he did wear the mask. Please, Mike. Make him stop. He doesn't have to ride any longer. Please, Uncle Mike. Make him stop."

" 'Desperately yours, Jinx,' " Celeste concluded the letter aloud. "That is a girl's name, isn't it? Not a cat's."

Mike laughed. He hadn't laughed much lately. Not for a long time. Money didn't buy laughs.

"I just remembered," he said. "Jinx. She was a kid the last time I saw her. Thirteen, fourteen. Maybe older."

"You fucked a fourteen-year-old?" Celeste asked.

Mike ignored the remark.

Jinx. The nickname must have stuck. Everybody in the show had a nickname.

She'd be in her twenties now, he guessed. Since he no longer worked, time fused into a straight line, like an electrocardiogram when the heart stops.

"What does she want you to do?" Celeste asked.

"Save her father," he said. "From himself."

"Oh." If the subject didn't involve sex, Celeste deemed it unworthy of conversation.

Mike switched back to the advertising piece. Jinx McComb had not taken time to explain its significance.

At the bottom was printed the show's itinerary. Dates, cities, locations. A quick run of a finger down the list found the first show Mike could hope to attend.

New Orleans.

Whip and his entourage of daredevils were arriving there tomorrow for a three-night stand.

He returned the papers to the envelope.

"You going?" Celeste asked.

He had never considered doing otherwise. A man would need a pretty serious excuse to let down a friend, no matter how many years had passed since they had last met.

"Yes," he answered.

"Then it's good-bye."

He said, "Keep the cottage. I rented it for six months."

"What good's a cottage?" Celeste asked. "I can't screw a cottage."

Mike picked up his dopp bag.

"You taking the guns?" the stewardess asked.

The question jarred him. Maybe there was more to Jinx McComb's letter than he suspected. Somebody could be using the mails to track him down.

Perhaps he was being lured into a trap by the sentimental memory of a fourteen-year-old girl who fussed over her father, cooking for him, bandaging his minor wounds, and bringing the beer when he got drunk with his friends.

Mike gazed silently at the battered envelope. What was it this time, he wondered. Just a friend and his kid with a problem or a coup designed to destroy him? Was he being melodramatic? When you had nobody you could talk with, nobody to help you maintain perspective, a secret like his could make you paranoid.

Irritated with himself, the rangy American thrust the thought away. No, by God. What I've got isn't mental problems, it's enemies. His lips twitched, the beginning of a stillborn smile. Too often, when he left a place, there were still more predators on his trail.

"Know something, Celeste?" he asked ruefully. "I could use a Dale Carnegie course."

"Why?" the girl scowled. "What's your long-hair music have to do with this Jinx?"

Mike smiled at the girl, his expression uncharacteristically benign. If he remembered her at all, it would be for her limitless ignorance.

He tucked the bag under his arm. Yes, he'd be taking the guns with him. There were too many hunters, too many guns out there who wanted him, or what he had: more millions than he could count, none of which belonged to him legally.

"Ship ahoy," Flibustier called suddenly.

He pointed along the beach, through the palms, to the road that wound down to Cloud's Nest Resort.

A figure poised on a motorcycle paused there under an overhanging mango tree.

The face was covered with a shielded helmet, the hands

hidden in gloves. As usual Flibustier's imagined sea battle had some foundation in truth.

The cyclist twisted in his seat. Mike assumed it was a man. He had his left arm pulled around and crooked in front of his face like Count Dracula held his cloak in late-night TV flicks. His right hand also was raised.

Before Hawk could grasp the significance, Celeste had risen and was brushing the sand from her white skin.

Then she flung herself against Mike's left arm with a force that staggered him.

Her body arched; her head jerked hard enough to give her whiplash.

Blood spurted from her back and coursed in crimson tributaries over her white skin.

# 3

He thrust the girl away from his chest, holding her shoulder. Her head snapped back. Glazed with pain or shock, her eyes were wide, quizzical. She might have been a child keeping herself rigid in a contest to see how long she could hold her breath. Strangely, she made no sound.

Although Hawk's hand came away bloody, there was no mark on the front of her torso. The bullet had lodged inside her.

Stunned as he was, his first action was sheer reflex. Then reason—and a will to survive honed by years of crises—joined instinct; and in the instant before she exhaled and collapsed like a discarded puppet, he choreographed his movements to hers, using the toppling body as a shield. He stooped in one supple, continuous motion, snatched the Smith and Wesson from the kit, then sprinted toward the partial protection of the coconut palms.

The second and third bullets, gushing small sand geysers between his feet, resolved the unspoken question.

He was the target, not Flibustier. Before he reached cover, he found the trigger and fired two wild shots in the direction of the Yamaha. An apparent amateur, the rider toppled off his bike, although the slugs ripped through fronds off to his right. He crouched behind his cycle.

Taking advantage of the opportunity, Hawk dashed across the open space, up the wooden steps, and onto the covered porch. He paused there long enough to yell at his friend.

"Flibustier, for God's sake, let's go!"

He didn't wait to see if the Creole moved. He flung open the door, bolted across the living room, and grabbed the small suitcase that was never unpacked. Throwing the bag out first, he dived out the open window at the rear. He could hear Flibustier's bare feet around the far side of the cottage.

The Creole might be a little flaky, but he remembered Hawk's standard escape plan.

They had been in scrapes together before. In bar fights, in heated differences of opinion with authorities, in misunderstandings with cuckolded husbands. Hawk's usual reaction to unexpected attack, regardless of its cause, was retreat.

Once he had sufficient distance between him and his opponent, he could reassess the situation. If it made sense to return and do battle, go for it; if not, run for it. And just in case, he made a practice of parking his vehicle at the rear of buildings which he entered for any length of time.

Because of their previous encounters, the Creole would know where to run—straight to the back of the cottage.

The two men met at the topless Land-Rover Hawk had bought his first day on the island. Hawk tossed the bag into the rear seat and slid behind the wheel. Flibustier took the passenger side and bent over to get the second Smith and Wesson.

"Man-o'-war off port bow," the Creole cried.

Mike jammed the keys into the ignition. The engine kicked over on the first try, a requisite for any vehicle he bought. Slammed into gear, the Land-Rover spread twin fins of pebbles and dust from its burning rear tires as it leaped forward.

"What in God's name was all that about?" Hawk demanded. "Did someone know you were bringing that letter to me?"

The startled Flibustier hung on, stiff and silent. He was trying to sort the real from the unreal.

The Land-Rover roared past the main part of the hotel where the kitchen help and the manager were pouring out the seaside door, running to the beach.

They would see if the girl was still alive. They'd get her help if it was necessary. They could do more for her than he could, Hawk thought. At least the hope eased his conscience.

One thing was sure: she was better off without him.

By the time he reached the road that led to the village, the motorcycle was behind him. The quick crescendo of its engine left no doubt about its direction.

"Shit!" he said. "So much for peace and quiet."

What had triggered the attack? he wondered.

The letter, of course.

But it was more complicated than that. The cyclist couldn't have been using Flibustier as a lead to Hawk. The dark Frenchman had been accosted before he had arrived at the hotel, if Mike had correctly interpreted his friend's hallucinatory tale.

It had to be the letter the cyclist wanted.

Or rather, it was the letter the cyclist didn't want Hawk to read. And having read it, Hawk had become a target for assassination. Obviously someone was determined to keep him from going to the aid of his old friend Whip McComb, the superstar stunt rider.

"Well, fuck you," Hawk said aloud to the bike coming up behind him. The Rover reached the road and started through the village. If it was that important to somebody that he not contact McComb, then the contact was worth the effort. Besides there was the peripheral benefit of seeing an old buddy again, and maybe helping him. Lisa had told Hawk once that he might avoid a lot of trouble if he could learn to push the "no" button when his motley friends sought help, but that was not his way.

First he had to get off the island before the authorities involved him in the girl's shooting. In his nebulous world-within-a-world, authorities of any kind—honest or dishonest—were as dangerous as deranged killers.

Racing through the village, where chickens, goats, and pigs scrambled for cover, he saw the cyclist had cut off the main road to the harbor. Twelve air miles from Castries, the regular road traversed twenty miles of the Cul-de-Sac and Rosseau valleys.

Unless he wanted to make a U and confront his stalker head on, he would have to take the East Coast Road, which wound up, across, and down Mount Soufriere, the world's only active, drive-in volcano. For a tourist it was magnificent; for a man numbed by instantaneous transition from tranquility to combat, it was a nightmare. The road required concentration; he couldn't mull over what the hell was happening, or why.

Until he knew more, he would not confront his assailant. Like a lion caught off guard at the watering hole, first he would seek the protection of the bush; he would stalk the hunter only if it proved necessary.

To Hawk, heading into the bush meant escaping from the island before today's events brought him under official scrutiny. Notoriety was his nemesis, his only real fear.

When Flibustier saw where they were headed, he grimaced, tucked the pistol between his legs, and strapped himself in. They had hours of horrendous road ahead.

Steep, narrow, and full of curves that twisted like a darting snake, it became an endurance test. Hawk rammed the Rover into high gear and sped through a dark, mildewed forest of towering bamboo and giant ferns. Sometimes they raced above a gold-green sea of banana trees ruffled by a breeze off the Atlantic. Later their path hugged the cliff with the ocean wearing away the rocks below. Then they coursed down, past sprawling plantations and up rock-strewn rises.

The cyclist stayed with them, rarely more than a hundred yards behind. When the rider was beneath them on the lower level of a hairpin curve, Flibustier tried to get off a shot, but the Rover bucked before the hammer fell against the primer. He swore in varying languages and gritted his teeth against the pain in his bruised buttocks.

Abruptly they entered a stark, blighted area, barren as a moonscape, where black volcanic ash had buried the underlying growth in grotesque formations. Pebbled cinders covered the zigzag route through the charred, jutting rock. The slippery, bulldozed path made a skittish, bucking mare of the Rover; the vehicle fishtailed inches from disaster. Hawk's racing experience served him well at every curve.

An athletic dabbler, he had tried many sports—scuba diving, delayed parachute jumps, bullfighting, and occasional stunt riding in Whip McComb's motorcycle circus. From long experience he trusted his reflexes, but the mist pungent with the rotten-egg smell of sulfur was making his eyes weep enough to obscure his vision.

With his sight impaired, he let his front tire carom off a jagged bolder, thrusting the rear of the vehicle toward a three-hundred-foot drop into eternity. While Hawk fought the stubborn steering wheel, Flibustier sucked in his breath and with both feet applied nonexistent brake pedals.

"Watch you starboard dere, Capt'n, or you go ta dump dey mate," he yelled. He had slung the gun between his knees to hang on with both hands.

For a heart-stopping second the jeep's rear tire left the roadway. Then with a balky jerk, the vehicle righted itself, careened across the road to the left, and stopped dead in the pumice and sand.

Pits of black water bubbled around them. Nearby hot springs, which had served French soldiers as curative baths hundreds of years before, threw up steam that encased them in a warm, wet fog.

Farther on, a cavernous hole belched foul breaths that stank of sulfur. They could hear the eerie "plop, plop, plop" that steeped ominously within the swelling mountain.

The motorcycle in pursuit swung off the road, its single wheels carrying the assailant into the protective cover of the steam.

Hawk and Flibustier crouched behind the vehicle, then realized they couldn't tell where the next attack would come from.

"Stay with the vehicle," Hawk yelled. "Shoot the sonofabitch if you see him."

"Yeah, mon," Flibustier agreed.

Taking a pair of shoes from his bag and putting them on, Hawk ran into the mist among the outcroppings and steaming pools. Black liquid splashed rhythmically two feet above a pond to his left where unseen pressures sought relief. The kettlelike basin reeked with corrosive smoke emanating from the bowels of the planet. The place was hell and he was a sinner whose quest was no less impossible than that of Sisyphus in his inferno. Hawk kept scrubbing his eyes with his hands, but he could barely see.

His ears picked up the sound of the bike, approaching, then receding, but with the noise coming from the earth, he could not pinpoint the direction.

He staggered on until he stood at a pit of churning, yellow mud, barely visible through the swirling clouds of smelly steam.

The heat was unbearable.

Carefully he moved to the far side of the fumarole; he ran around rocks coated with greenish-yellow crusts and waited.

Suddenly the motorcycle loomed dead ahead of him.

It plunged straight toward him.

The rider ducked his head, trying to see over the top of his visor. One hand was inside the helmet attempting to clear his eyes.

Hawk feigted to the left; the bike followed.

The American stopped. He lifted the gun, holding it with both hands, and aimed directly at the oncoming forehead.

He fired.

He missed, hitting the windscreen instead. Cracks knifed across it like veins in a bloodshot eye. Blinded, the driver again swiped his fist across his eyes.

Hawk stepped aside.

The bike whipped past, ran into a puff of mist, and dropped its mag wheels into the hellish yellow churn.

Mike heard a scream. He shielded his face and stepped closer, stretching a hand toward the cauldron.

He saw glove-covered fingers attempting to clasp his. They touched but the rider was sinking as if sucked down by quicksand.

Mike strained to get closer.

The glove inched downward.

Then Hawk was forced back by the heat. Face scorched, he stepped away: he yelled, reaching toward the sinking rider.

"Try! Damn you! Reach out! Farther!"

The gloved hand shortened.

Then only the fingertips were visible in the mist.

Then nothing.

# 4

Flibustier and Hawk, standing elbow to elbow near the yellow-hot crater, stared at the point where the motorcyclist had disappeared. Before them, the bike's fuel tank exploded like a giant candle lit by mourners.

The agonizing way the man had died sickened the two at his grave.

Neither could write his epitaph. Neither understood. Who had he been? Why had he come after them? There were no answers.

They knew only that they had to flee. Through the approaching darkness, the sputtering hot mud, and the plopping sounds beneath the surface, they retreated to the Land-Rover. Flibustier dug out two shovels from behind the front seat and handed one to Hawk. Still sobered by what they had seen, they dug quietly. Two minutes later the wheels were freed.

Hawk looked back down the road they had ascended.

"Shorter dat way, Capt'n," Flibustier offered. "By five miles at least. And better road."

Hawk nodded. With their adversary gone, there was no reason to continue on the alternate route.

They retraced some of the road and then climbed spurs of land jutting from the central mountain range running across the pear-shaped island. When they came to Micoud, a village huddled on a semiprotected cove, Hawk reached into his suitcase and passed a handful of money to his friend.

"Get us a boat," he instructed. "Rent, buy, whatever you have to do. Find us a way off this goddamned island."

"Yeah, mon. We go to Martinique? Eh?"

The thought of two, possibly three, dead bodies weighted Hawk's mind like an anchor, slowing his mental processes. He kept seeing the gloved hand disappearing into the fiery earth.

Would the violence never end?

"Eh?" Flibustier prodded him. "Martinique. Okay?"

"Yeah," he said.

Martinique was okay. Anyplace where he could charter a plane. He did not look up as the Frenchman went in search of a boat.

Damn, Mike thought, he was on the run again. Ocean hopping was a big part of his nomadic existence. This time he was running from one danger toward another. To New Orleans.

Was he crazy? New Orleans? The States were always dangerous for him, even more so now. Someone had been willing to kill in order to keep him from making the trip.

Use your head, Hawk. For once, use your head. Find a new paradise and hide in comfort with good food, better women, a warm sun, and quiet.

"Idiot!" he said aloud. He knew he couldn't resist. A friend needed him.

When Flibustier appeared again, Hawk was watching the moonlit surf creaming to the doorsteps of the village shacks.

He climbed into the dinghy and held his suitcase on his lap above the leaking bottom of the rotting boat while his friend rowed to an old forty-foot yawl anchored in the harbor.

The Land-Rover remained behind.

Many of the things Michael Hawk bought with his wealth were left behind. Many of the friends and lovers he knew had to be abandoned too. It was a fact of his strange, haunted life.

Within minutes the two had the yawl moving from the cove under a moon that ducked behind the first of many clouds. The dark puffballs marched across the sky like a parade of balloons on the wind.

They hoisted the mainsails before they passed the last landfall and began the rough ride between St. Lucia and Martinique to the north.

In the cabin they found oilskins and used them. Although

the air had been warm on the island, each patch of cloud was loaded with its own blast of wind that added a countering factor to the strong trades buffeting the open stretch.

Hawk took the wheel, leaving Flibustier to the main halyard.

Neither suggested shortening the sails in the rolling sea. Flibustier could have cranked in a reef, but he didn't. They were on the edge of trouble. In the lulls they needed the power from all the sails to drive them through the angry waters. Without all her canvas working, she might plunge and falter in the following crest.

Across twenty-seven miles punctuated by brief squalls, the aging vessel dipped and wallowed and lumbered. The deck leeward was a whirlpool of spume. Even the stanchions on the life rail vanished.

Michael Hawk reveled in the crossing. Flibustier rode with that unemotional acceptance typical of those to whom nature is both companion and challenge.

Mike liked the danger because it was visible. He could see the waves churning around him. He could smell the salt in the air and feel the spray stinging on his face. The slap of bow meeting surface and the sails flapping wildly when he took a new tack were as soul soothing as a lullaby.

He felt safe on the sea with his one friend. Here, briefly, there was peace without boredom.

It was possible, even probable, that more problems lay ahead. He assumed if any other biker were tracking him or if the police were hunting him, they would be waiting at the St. Lucia airport, a fugitive's natural escape route. Or they would stake out harbors more important than Micoud's cove.

The yawl was slamming past the famous Diamond Rock. There the sea boiled into a fountain where it hit the vertical cliffs of the great conical stone.

In spite of the sheer cliffs Diamond Rock had been a fort. Literally it was a commissioned ship of war. The British had carried her on their Admiralty records in memory of a battle fought from her peak during Britain's reign over the seas.

Just beyond was Fort-de-France, a city of hills around a bay of calm water where cruise ships deposited tourists who deposited money.

Flibustier did not bother to hoist the proscribed yellow quarantine flag, and no French officials appeared to remind them that they were entering the waters of another nation. They continued unchallenged to the yacht club. There they warped the stern into the quay and made fast until morning. Then Hawk, dressed in street clothes, rowed them to shore.

"You come back, mon," the modern freebooter said while Mike lifted his suitcase onto the concrete. "Dey boat, she yours."

Hawk looked into the dark libidinal eyes and grinned. Damn, he hated to leave the guy. The alchemy between the poor dreamer and the rich pragmatist, the wise and the educated, had fermented into raucous drinking sprees, wild nights with wild women, and more recently, brushes with death.

They were friends. They never said it; they had never so much as shaken hands.

Now they would not see each other again.

Flibustier knew it. He laid aside the cloak of fantasy and faced reality.

Mike extended his hand. His friend took it.

"The boat's yours," Mike said. "Capture us a corsair."

"Naw." Flibustier was embarrassed. The dreams were gone.

Mike couldn't let it happen. "You damn well better," he insisted. "If I come back and we aren't rich, I'll take that little piece you got at the post office and show her what a real man's got between his legs."

Flibustier grinned. "Eh, how you know?"

"I know," Mike replied. "I know more than you think." He turned and walked toward the city.

"Eh, Hawk, you take care. You killed, I go Haiti, get voodoo. Brings you back. Big white zombie, nothin' 'tween your legs. Dey Capt'n Flibustier, he say."

"I'll be back," the American lied. "Capt'n."

He seldom doubled back. It wasn't safe. That's why he preferred the Caribbean as a home base. It was a vast expanse of water sprinkled with coves and havens where a man could rest.

In a way maybe he was a modern-day buccaneer himself. No, he corrected himself. He was a pirate. Buccaneers in the day of tall ships had their home-country sanction to harrass vessels of other nations. Michael Hawk was a pirate, loyal only to his shipmates. He had the sanction of no nation for the loot he lived on so lavishly.

Yet, as he rode a taxi past nude sunbathers whose white bottoms and pale breasts announced their tourist status, he accepted that he was looking forward to seeing the States again. It was more than the letter that enticed him to New Orleans.

It was a form of homesickness. Wealth made him a man without a nation, regardless of the perfectly valid U.S. passport he carried.

At the airport he placed one of the telephone calls that set him apart. The calls were the crux of his bizarre, violent life. They blessed him with the wealth of an Arab sheik and cursed him with the loneliness of a trapper trudging through snow with nothing except what he carried on his back.

The calls bought him protection while conversely endangering his life.

He called Liechtenstein. The principality of less than thirty thousand citizens is tucked away in the mountains between Switzerland and Austria. Travelers pass it up by oversight, but a class of the world's rich know it intimately.

His call went straight through to his *Anstalt*, one of the thousands of paper corporations operating in the country for men like him.

He recognized Jennifer's voice. He had met the Austrian girl, who composed his entire multinational corporation's world headquarters, only once. The less he saw of her, the longer they both might live.

"You know my voice?" he asked.

She said, "Ya." It was the code they used between them.

"Our Hong Kong Traders, Limited, has an active account in the second largest bank in New Orleans, Louisiana. Right?"

"Ya, I think so."

"Good. Tell Traders they have a new American representative named . . ." He needed a phony name. He grinned when one came to mind. ". . . named G. G. Pollock, who unfortunately lost all his ID."

"ID?"

"Identification. Lost all his ready cash too. Have them allow Pollock to withdraw up to two hundred and fifty thousand without ID as long as each withdrawal ends in fifty cents. That will give them some assurance the money is going to the right man. Got all that?"

"Ya."

"Good. You'll be hearing from me."

He hung up the phone.

He liked Hong Kong Traders, Limited. Those who ran it for him were a bunch of crooks, but they weren't greedy. They made a reasonable but steady profit, skimming only the top. They would follow the orders that reached them in a roundabout route from Liechtenstein. The fifty-cent withdrawal code gave them a chance to say they had been careful to make certain the money had not gone to an unauthorized person. Of the two hundred fifty thousand, they would rake off no more than ten percent. And as intelligent embezzlers, they never asked questions.

He used them infrequently, of course. The managers could be allowed only occasional opportunities to trace ultimate ownership to the *Anstalt* in Vaduz. A half-dozen numbered accounts in countries with banking-secrecy laws stood between Hong Kong Traders and Hawk's nebulous Crusaders International, Inc., in Liechtenstein, but a clever man would find the connection if operations were sufficiently familiar to him.

The management would be in shock if they ever learned they were employed indirectly by a company that existed almost entirely on paper at a one-room office in the small country's capital. It had one part-time employee—Jennifer—and one bank account that seldom held as much as a million dollars.

And it had one major stockholder, Michael Hawk.

But in safety-deposit boxes and in stockbroker names around the world, Crusaders International held shares in other paper corporations which in turn were holding companies with indirect interests and/or control of a plethora of other firms. Oil in the States, Indonesia, the North Sea. Coal in Australia and North Dakota. Geothermal land rights in New Mexico. A championship cricket club in Britain. A baseball team in Japan. Fifty syndicated horses turned out to stud, a polo team in Hong Kong. *Objets d'art* dating back to the Byzantine Empire, including an entire private museum in Greece built around Hellenistic bronze dancing girls, circa 500 B.C. A fly-in fishing lodge at Great Bear Lake in Canada, plus an entire bush-pilot airline serving the vast land of lakes and timber. Pine forests in Florida. Rubber plantations in Malaysia. Casinos in Las Vegas. Parking lots in Anchorage.

The list was impossible to catalog. The financial empire's serpentine network of divisions, subsidiaries, and concealed control tangled and wove back upon itself. But few threads led to the *Anstalt* in Liechtenstein.

Through Crusaders International, Hawk controlled it all.

He was rich—how rich, he didn't know. One day he had been a wandering journalist with hardly enough money to pay his hotel bill. The next he had more wealth than a man could hope to spend in a gross of lifetimes.

But none of it was his . . . legally. The mountains of stocks, money, and the resulting potential for power belonged to a dead man.

Originally the wealth had been sucked like blood from peasants ruled by a Latin American dictator. Known as *El Sargento*, he was one of many strong men who escaped overthrow alive, with their stash safely out of the country.

Then *El Sargento* died, leaving it all to his daughter.

The girl had dedicated a short lifetime to keeping the money from the victors, the Communist revolutionaries who sought the power for their own nefarious causes. She had lived in seclusion, until Hawk, the reporter, had searched her out and exposed her. Too late he realized his story could cost her her life.

He had tried to save her, tried to find another sanctuary for her. But the Communists found her.

She died in Mike's arms, cursing him with the account number and the signature card he needed to control the secret widespread financial empire.

Since then he had lived like an exiled monarch, a king on the run. Occasionally, like today, he came out of his luxurious retreats to help a friend in trouble or to escape a pursuer—a KGB man, an IRS agent, or any other modern buccaneer who would divest Hawk of the money and put it to questionable, even dangerous use.

Michael Hawk was rich, richer than many governments.

But the giant cache was a tempting bait. Any jackal who discovered his holdings had to die. It was Hawk or the wild dogs who chased him.

He enjoyed what he could, gave away what he dared, and secretly spent vast sums to crusade for a friend or a cause, or to save his own life. He couldn't even die in peace. When he died, the money might be discovered and its power used to further oppress the people from whom *El Sargento* had stolen it in the first place.

It was the money that kept Hawk in hiding. He emerged only long enough to right a wrong and briefly enough that no one could link the former free-lance writer with control of a concealed estate so large even he couldn't estimate it.

Today the money might help a friend.

He spent it lavishly, using cash and assumed names.

He chartered a plane to Miami, feeling naked without the matched pair of pistols in his suitcase. He had left the expensive guns aboard the yawl for Flibustier to find. That was preferable to chancing their discovery when he cleared customs in the States. The stacks of bills in the leather case would cause enough questions if the officials happened to open his luggage.

Even so, once aboard the plane, he relaxed. He ignored the rain-forest plantation below where waxy anthuriums exhibited brilliant blooms with the thin penis-shaped seed poking from each of the brilliant blossoms.

In Miami he caught a commercial flight to Chicago, rented a car, drove around the outskirts of the city for an hour, returned to O'Hare field, and caught the next plane to Baton Rouge.

From a streetwise kid, for three times the going price, he bought a nickel-plated Undercover .38 Special with a two-inch barrel. He loaded it with shells from a sporting-goods store and went hunting for a motorcycle shop.

He bought a Yamaha XS Eleven Special, had a carrier attached, pulled on a new all-weather suit, and streaked off for New Orleans in the pouring rain.

It felt great to be back on a cycle again. Several years back he had been good with the power machines. He had ridden in Whip McComb's motorcycle show while he dug up facts for a feature story. He did stunts and learned from McComb. A natural athlete, Mike was soon taking jumps that only Whip, the superstar, would attempt.

The story had been great. It made money, and Hawk had made friends with McComb.

Although he was anxious to see his old buddy again, the ex-newsman observed the speed limit. Not even the rain pelting the eyepiece pulled down from the top of his white Bell helmet dampened his enjoyment. The weather was even a protective factor. In the rain gear and helmet he was adequately disguised, in case anybody was trying to trail him. From the outskirts of New Orleans he rode directly to the Poydras Plaza with its mammoth Hyatt Regency and from there to the Superdome, the city's giant indoor stadium.

The parking lot was almost filled with cars and motorcycles.

Still in his bike outfit and carrying his helmet, Mike bought a ticket and went inside. The crowd noises told him the thrill circus was in progress. He could tell from the laughter who was performing.

It had to be Yankee Horn, the dwarf comedian, promoter and business manager Whip McComb had been planning to add to the show when Mike moved on to another story and the financial empire he never dreamed he would control.

The soaring laughter did nothing to substantiate the urgent request for Mike's help.

He avoided the performer's entrance. Preferring the cover of anonymity for starters, he went straight to the seat down front. There he was lost in the enthusiasm of the crowd.

Things had changed since he had traveled with the show. And for the better it seemed. Yet he sensed something was wrong. He didn't know what.

# 5

Snug and secure with their Thermoses of martinis or coffee and their Styrofoam-covered sixpacks, the spectators at Whip McComb's Thrill Circus accepted Hawk's late entrance with good grace. Men glanced speculatively at the rangy, taut-bellied cyclist; women gave him a different kind of appraisal, their approval registered in open appreciation of the bronzed skin and sun-blonded hair or in surreptitious second glances at the wide shoulders and trim torso. None protested as he grinned apologetically and brushed past their turned knees on the way to his seat.

Once there, he stripped off his touring suit, shoved it under the seat with his helmet, and relaxed while a parade of bikes began their loop around the hard surface that rimmed the artificial turf.

The show had changed. Whip McComb had elevated the art of cycle jumping beyond the realm of a single act staged in conjunction with a race or other sporting event. He had created an entire evening's entertainment around motorcycles. There were clowns, and animals trained to ride with their masters, and hurdle races performed on bikes. There were unicycles, human pyramids built on the move, a witty master of ceremonies, live music, and girls—lots of girls, the roller-skating equivalent of water skiers towed by the two-wheelers. But the ultimate thrill was watching daredevils risk their lives, not unlike gladiators had risked theirs centuries before.

There was a difference, of course: the roar of the crowd remained the same, but the ring of the cash register was new. There was big money available in Whip McComb's craft, Hawk knew.

These days bikes were no longer brightly painted wrecks. Most of them were new Suzukis and Honda customs. The riders wore gaudy, fluorescent-striped suits and helmets that glowed in the dark when the house lights dimmed during some of the acts. Yellow streamers wafted from the tops of the head protectors.

A stunning black-haired Oriental girl led the opening procession on a customized chopper. The sequined purple and black tights hugging her creamy skin heightened the crowd's excitement.

The fans knew her. They chanted their approval.

"Pu Noon, Pu Noon, Pu Noon."

It was an idolizing chant saved for rulers and royalty, and the girl on the chopper maintained a regal aloofness. She made the rest of the parade her royal court.

The star, Whip McComb, rode farther back between two platoons of performers. The crowd roared their adulation of him too. He returned their salute with a cool, casual wave that was part of his legend: the man without fear; the matador of the bike set.

Still later came a rider in a Texas hat and a sheepskin coat, his pants caught loosely in fancy western boots with golden spurs. A hulk of a man, he too was a crowd pleaser. Although Hawk couldn't name him, he had been around for years.

There was another girl who stood apart from the lesser performers. She rode a bike identical to McComb's.

She was as pretty as the brace of girls in bikinis who rode with their knees on their motorcycle seats, their blond manes flowing in the wind.

Running alongside the riders was a corps of local cheerleaders who brought the crowd to its collective feet by gyrating their satin backsides and gently confined bosoms to the rock-style parade music.

The arena in the infield was filled with hoops, brick walls, tunnels with gas jets for rides through roaring flames, and a series of loop-the-loop devices that looked like scaled-down amusement-park rides.

Farther back were two expensive motor homes, several campers, a van, and a truck—all brilliantly painted in the show's colors: purple, yellow, and black. These were part of the caravan that transported the circus around the country. Around the world, Mike remembered. His story had helped McComb go international—to Europe, Asia, and South America.

The entire effect was prosperity.

The bike circus had grown into big business since embracing the showmanship once restricted to Hollywood.

A delighted surge of laughter burst from the crowd when a miniature bike began weaving in and out of the parade lineup. It was the dwarf, Yankee Horn, in a gaudy red and green outfit, riding wildly in the saddle.

Horn spent his life looking up to people. Perhaps it was partially that fact which had permanently deformed his neck, but he had the crowd laughing while he cavorted and popped wheelies. He pulled back too far once and slipped off the seat on his rear. He was up instantly, pretending to stagger in search of his bike, then mounting it and heading at full speed toward a low wall of bricks. He slammed head on into it; the supple plastic of the phony bricks bounced the bike backward and let the dwarf sail over the top. He spread his arms and yelled "Superman!" his body mike amplifying the cry so that everyone in the giant stadium could hear before he belly flopped on the artificial turf. He lay there, while his fans howled and applauded, and then flailed his arms in a pretense of swimming.

Mike settled in his chair and looked around him. He found a man with a pair of binoculars and offered him twice what they were worth. He peeled off the money for the surprised spectator and used the glasses to study the area around the motor homes.

He recognized names on the campers. It was a bibliography of motorcycling, A repeated winner in the Ascot half mile. An aging claimant of the Winston Pro Series bonus. And a former AMA Grand National champion. The vehicles were owned by top bikers who considered it a privilege to appear with the granddaddy of them all, Whip McComb.

Mike watched the rest of the show, rising when the people ahead of him sprang to their feet during particularly entertaining events.

Toward the end he saw again what he wanted. Whip McComb.

The lone figure was walking across the manufactured green field of the giant arena.

After the parade he had retreated to a long, picture-windowed motor home with his name emblazoned across the side in huge yellow letters against a black background.

Magnified for Michael Hawk's vision, Whip McComb looked his fifty years of age. There was gray sprinkled through the heavy black hair that covered his ears and rose in a small peaked wave in front. His brows, dark as ever, dominated his face and gave a haunted look to the eyes. There were deep crow's feet when he squinted, pulling on stiff red and white gloves. A short beard covered his jowls, his chin, and upper lip, the growth concealing some of the scars Hawk remembered. A stubby, thin cigar protruded from the left side of his mouth. The ash was dead, Hawk would bet. McComb usually forgot to puff often enough to keep the things lit.

Hawk focused in closer. McComb looked upset. His jaw was thrust forward belligerently like that of a man confronting the enemy. He had none of the typical personality stunts of showmanship, yet the crowd was applauding, shouting even before he had approached the bike.

They understood him. He was the maestro, the conquistador, the master of the ring. It was Sunday afternoon and the bulls were about to be released again. His suit of lights was black with yellow and white stripes down the arms and legs. His boots were the reverse, black trim on white.

The closer he limped toward the half of the Superdome reserved for the audience, the angrier he appeared. He looked like a man about to prove something to someone. But what?

Hawk understood. He knew those eyes were gentle and fun loving—until these few moments before he faced whatever challenge he had dealt himself.

He seemed to ignore the customized cycle, although it was like none other. McComb was constantly making improvements, switching mounts like a Portuguese bullfighter who is never satisfied with his horse. Tonight he walked toward a chromium machine with a strange parallelogram for a frame. Mike had never seen one like it. Its front wheel was slung forward almost enough to rank it as a chopper. The shocks were oversized. The wheels were gold cast alloy, and there were triple-drilled disks up front with metallic pads for smooth, fast braking. The leading axle forks were extra large like the fore muscles of a mantis. The rear wheels were complex mechanisms of tough, light metal. The six-into-two exhaust systems looked racy, but Hawk knew enough about Whip McComb to recognize that the pipes offered an extra thrust of increased horsepower. The seat was hard and black, built for a man who had come down on his rump so often his spine was fused in sections.

Rising over the instrument panels and covering the speedometer and the revolution counter was a round-nosed plastic cowling. Unlike many famous thrill riders, Whip McComb relied more upon brains than instinct. He calculated every detail of every stunt in a black notebook that protruded from the pocket sewn into his two-piece show outfit. McComb had been an engineering graduate from MIT, Hawk recalled. It was a fact the rider preferred left out of his publicity.

Years ago a kid died riding one of McComb's designs.

Not only had the incident ended Whip's engineering career, it had put him on a long straight track toward testing the ultimate a motorcycle and rider could endure. McComb had been inching toward that goal for three decades. His body bore the marks that betrayed his motorcycling age like the rings of a tree.

When they heard the cycle, the crowd grew quiet. They knew from reading and rumor that McComb demanded silence before he mounted. He was making one last check of his instruments. He was a man who tended to his homework.

Next he leaned far forward, as though he had difficulty reading.

Apparently satisfied, he straightened.

Then he tossed his cigar to the turf and picked his helmet off the seat. He tugged it into position, covering his head to his shoulders. There were five-inch-long slits down the front for breathing, and a built-in Plexiglas window barely larger than eyeglasses.

Whip McComb had to see nothing except the track, the ramp, and his instruments.

When he mounted the machine, Hawk began to realize how much his friend had changed. The movements, stiff and slow, were those of a man in pain. The famous rider used his hands to position one knee so that he could get his foot on the peg. His assistants moved in to help.

His fans expected, even approved the limp.

McComb had given Hawk a quote once about the battered left knee and the chances he took.

"Every time I sling my leg over a bike for a stunt," he had said coolly, "the odds are even that I'll come away smashed up. That's why the crowd comes to watch, the only reason as far as I know."

"Then why do you continue?" Mike had asked.

"Because I still can."

"Then you won't quit?"

"Not until a bike fails me, no."

Was McComb thinking of that now? Hawk wondered. Was he stretching for a new record tonight, trying a new improvement on the bike, extending the jump an inch or two farther than he had ever made it before?

Was he attempting to break some impossible limit tonight, or had his daughter written out of natural concern for an aging father still risking his body in a young man's game?

As Mike pondered the question, a mechanic kick-started the engine for the star.

McComb carried no unnecessary poundage with him on the big leaps, although he calculated the weight wet—with a full tank of fuel. His own weight was an important factor too. Unlike many men of his age, he kept himself lean, even bony. To him, his body was only another accessory, one that must remain light and sleek in order to enhance the only thing that mattered: the bike's performance.

The rumble of the engine echoed against the cavernous roof of the stadium.

The audience stirred with anticipation.

The big machine began to roll along the circular track, gaining speed gradually as it approached the area in front of the packed stands.

Hawk dropped the glasses to his lap. The bike approached the reinforced ramp that climbed nearly a dozen feet off the floor of the arena. But the machine turned clear of the rising timbers, as Mike knew it would.

Some said McComb's ride before the audience was part of the pageantry; Mike knew better, however. The aging daredevil didn't give a damn for the crowds. He was alone in the Superdome as far as he was concerned. There was only he, the bike, the ramps, and the spikes that lay still covered in canvas.

Whip rode past the steep-sloped takeoff ramp, in front of the open space, and then along the more gradually angled landing platform. He was checking to make certain no one had moved them so much as a fraction of an inch since he last checked them.

The rider's preoccupation with detail, his apprehensiveness, only added to the tension. A hush fell like a blanket over the capacious arena, as if the audience waited with a single in-drawn breath.

The crowd loved the drama. No one murmured while McComb rode in front of them.

Finally the crew appeared from the sidelines. They moved swiftly to the orange tarp slung across the huge gap, yanking the cover aside with a flourish. The spectators gasped.

A field of sharp chromium spikes thrust upward from a black plywood bed on the stadium floor. The bed of nails was more awesome than advertised. Like deadly thorns, the spikes were thick at the bottom and needle sharp at the top. McComb had vowed to leap over more than a hundred feet of them—or die in the attempt.

Like thousands of others in the audience, Hawk felt perspiration forming on his forehead. In the past his friend had jumped barrels, cars, and burning pans of oils. They were obstacles he could roll clear of when he failed. The spikes were new, the macabre design of a medieval mind.

The daredevil was going too far. His desire to provide new thrills, to set new records must have become an obsession.

He was no longer tempting fate; he was offering himself as a blood sacrifice.

Every stunt failed eventually, especially if you continually increased the distance or the danger, as McComb was known to do. It wasn't as if he never failed. As his battered body testified, he had fallen short many times; more than once he'd been burned during tardy escapes from flaming tunnels. He had been hit by falling bricks and hospitalized with concussions. But this was one stunt he couldn't fail and survive.

Why had he gone so far?

Just the thought of hurtling over the foot-deep sea of spears made Mike's skin crawl. He was a compatriot of danger. His work as a journalist had taken him to the battle lines of a half-dozen wars. He had dangled from the bottom of cable cars. In Venice, in storm-lashed Saint Mark's Square, he had survived a shoot-out with a fanatic who might have been a supernatural devil. He had dealt with mad cultists, KGB hit men, and Oriental assassins. But the bed of nails was an inanimate opponent that had only to wait until its challenger made the inevitable mistake.

It was not Hawk's kind of enemy.

From the loudspeakers came a melodramatic roll of drums, but the effect was superfluous. The audience was intent enough.

"And now, ladies and gentlemen . . . ," the announcer intoned tensely. "Whip McComb and his brazen leap across a bed of nails, cycling's most daring stunt by the sport's most daring performer."

The motorcycle was at the far side of the stadium, picking up speed, moving faster in the inner lane of the circular roadway, accelerating steadily.

The crowd came to its feet. Hawk rose and brushed the hair from his forehead. His jaw set; a muscle flicked in his cheek, and his lips tightened into a thin straight line.

He didn't like what he was seeing. He was uneasy and he didn't know why.

Hawk fought an urge to crouch as he imagined himself bent forward from the saddle. His hands folded tighter around the handle grips when he eased the throttle ahead for the final run.

He had made longer jumps himself under his friend's tutelage but never with such a deadly mat below.

Although the bed of nails made the jump no more difficult, the psychological impact was appalling. Mike pictured himself there on the bike, aware of fear but enthralled with the grandeur of the challenge and the place.

His own blood quickened when McComb made the final turn into the straightaway and aimed at the narrow ramp.

Seventy yards, sixty, fifty.

Faster, Mike said under his breath. Faster.

Forty yards left, now thirty, twenty.

"Faster!" Hawk yelled, his voice carrying across the hushed stadium. "Faster."

No one turned, but the ex-newsman felt stupid. Who was

he to tell the great Whip McComb how to ride? The man had made the leap hundreds of times before. Mike saw the white helmet dip slightly during the last few feet before the wheels hit the ramp. McComb was checking his speed. The bike seemed sluggish as it labored up the wooden planks. Still, when it reached the end, it launched itself, shooting gracefully upward on invisible wings; man and machine, Bellerophon and Pegasus, soared toward the heights.

The audience gasped again; they gaped, openmouthed, their eyes wide and unblinking lest they miss an instant of the machine's trajectory.

Mike cried aloud. "No!"

To his amateur's eye the bike was peaking too soon. The front wheel was dipping when it should remain high and proud until the rear tire slammed against the platform a lifetime away from the launching ramp.

The attendants who had pulled the tarp from the ramp were running forward. They too sensed disaster.

Mike shoved his way to the aisle and started for the railing.

The man in the seat was leaning forward, ducking his head, stiffening his arm as though he wanted to leap free of the leather.

So intense was the moment that it might have been a scene filmed in slow-motion.

The crew stood helplessly, like runners poised at the starting line waiting for the gun to go off.

The spectators understood. The trajectory was falling short. The bike wouldn't make it. Time seemed to hesitate.

"Ah-h-h," they sighed with rising disappointment.

Finally the cycle's front wheel crashed against the leading rim of the landing platform. The man was hurtled from the leather seat.

For an instant there was hope that he might fly free, but his mechanized steed held him and dragged him down. His hands groped the air as if to continue his flight. Or, some would say later, he might have been praying.

Bike and man tumbled onto the chromium spikes.

# 6

Shoving and sidestepping, Mike elbowed a path through the aisle packed with spectators and vendors. The steps were crowded with people struggling against each other for a better view of the drama playing before them on the arena floor.

"Move," Hawk implored. "Let me through."

The onlookers' mood—so cordial earlier when his late arrival had inconvenienced them—had changed, and the women were as resentful as the men.

"Bug off, buddy," said a redhead with a fifteen-dollar hairdo. "Who the hell do you think you are?"

Her male companion remained silent even when Hawk straight-armed her to one side. "Well, Jesus!" Mike heard her howl. He plunged forward to the lowest row of seats. He was throwing his leg over the railing by the time a uniformed employee grabbed his shoulder. The slender young attendant was no match for the determined Hawk.

"Hey, you can't go down there" he protested.

Mike knocked him away. He dropped over the railing and ignored the orders from a rent-a-cop moving in fast to stop the curious who wanted to see the accident.

"Hold it there, buddy," the cop said.

Hawk heard but broke into a run. His gaze was on the growing knot of crewmen gathering around the fallen cyclist. The cop lunged for Hawk, who twisted away and left him a dozen paces behind.

He pried through the barricade of men clustered around the foot of the platform. It was a half man, a belt-high elf who finally managed to stop the adventurer twice his size.

The dwarf whirled and thrust out his palm as though he were directing traffic to halt. The hand was tiny and puffy like a child's, and his arms were stubby. His head was too big for his body.

For the moment, though, his round face was intent with his own importance. None of the clown's good nature remained. He had become tough and authoritarian.

An ambulance siren shrieked at the vehicle entrance.

"I'm Hawk," Mike snapped irritably. "Whip's old friend."

The dwarf, recalling the familiar name, was offering a welcoming hand when a mechanic pushed forward to waylay the intruder.

"Listen, punk," the mechanic growled. "Whip McComb is in there dyin'. At least let him go without you bloodsuckers gawking at him."

Dying! The word was like a splash of ice water.

Was it coincidence, only chance, that McComb had crashed just minutes after Mike's arrival?

No. The crash must be directly linked to the letter that had traveled a gamut of transcontinental postal systems before reaching St. Lucia.

"Let me see him," Mike demanded.

Yankee Horn touched the mechanic's arm.

"Let him go," the dwarf ordered.

The wall of crewmen and performers opened a path to the wreck. Mike hurried through, while memories of the Whip he had known flashed through his mind.

He remembered when McComb had a wife, a beautiful woman who had borne him a daughter. Whip was then riding a thousand miles away. McComb, always a thrill seeker, had been racing before he met her, trying to win enough money to pay his tuition. Hooked by the challenge and excitement, he had stayed in it after he was married, using his engineering skill to squeeze another mph from his custom-built bikes.

Then the boy had died using a McComb design, and Whip had gone overboard. He became reckless at the tracks. Although his winnings multiplied, he took stupid chances and cracked up so often that the events' sponsors worried he would bring the wrath of the regulators down upon them. So he was barred from track after track until the stunt business was the only thing open to him.

His wife had left him.

"I couldn't bear to watch," she had said. "I couldn't sit and wait for him to crash, knowing someday he would miss, knowing he would kill himself."

Ironically she died first, in an auto accident.

She had left the young daughter for the obsessed stunt man to rear. Still Whip persisted, tempting death, living in cheap motels when the show paid enough, or sleeping in his truck when he was broke. The daughter must have survived.

It was she who had written, begging Mike to help.

Hawk looked down at the broken motorcycle, the mag wheels twisted, its gas pouring from the punctured tank. Then he saw the man pinned beneath it.

Mike stooped to help lift the mangled bike away.

His lips moved, forming a word that was never spoken. Accustomed as he was to death, nothing had prepared the ex-newsman for the sight at his feet. A mechanic turned away, retching.

A chromium spike protruded six inches through McComb's chest. He was pinned like a scrap of paper impaled on a spindle. Other spikes pierced the right leg and shoulder.

A man in a business suit who acted like a doctor stepped in and knelt beside McComb. He paused, his down-turned lips wordless but eloquent; then he motioned the stretcher bearers into position. Before they could lift the injured man to the canvas sling, the dwarf whispered in the doctor's ear. He pointed to Hawk.

"You some kind of special friend?" the doctor asked.

Mike nodded.

"Better speak to him now."

Mike bent over his dying friend. "Whip, it's Michael Hawk. Jinx sent for me."

"Mike," the dying man's lips barely moved. The gloved fingers twitched.

The tired, pain-twisted face grew intense. Lifting his eyelids was an effort.

"I didn't . . . ," he said.

"What?" Mike leaned closer.

He was so close he could feel breath on his cheek.

". . . didn't screw up," McComb said, ". . . didn't . . . know. I didn't fuck up."

The breath stopped.

"Whip?" Mike called to him. "What do you mean? Whip?"

He was gone.

The doctor bent over the dead man from the other side. Hands helped Mike to his feet. The doctor sighed and shook his head. "Sorry," he said to no one in particular.

Hawk waited for confirmation as the dwarf knelt and felt for a pulse.

"Oh, God," the squat little man cried. Tears streaked down his cheeks.

Guilt twisted like a knife inside Hawk.

If he had arrived a day earlier, would Whip be hoisting a beer in friendly toast now, instead of staring up at the roof of the amphitheater with dead eyes? Could he have made it to New Orleans, Mike wondered, if he had flown a chartered plane straight from Martinique to New Orleans? Since money meant nothing to him, why hadn't he come the fastest way? Had his caution condemned his friend to death?

But maybe it was an accident. He wanted to believe that. His mind wanted to construct a protective barrier against the guilt. He hoped to God it had been an accident.

"Somebody stop the kid," a crew member called.

A tall, sunny-haired girl in a two-piece show outfit that matched McComb's was running across the turf from the biggest motor home. Mike had seen her in the parade. Her long hair was tied back in a ponytail. She was screaming as she ran.

"Dad! Dad!"

A crewman caught her and Yankee Horn tried to explain. It was over. It was nothing she would want to see.

She broke loose and ran recklessly into the bed of nails.

She screamed, dropping to her knees beside her father. She tried to lift him up, but he was too heavy for her.

Although the solicitous bystanders tried to pull her away, she pushed them off, frantically coaxing her father to cooperate, to help her release him.

"Daddy! Come on! Lift up just a little. Help me . . ."

The spike poking from his lung was intolerable. The spears kept her from bending close enough to embrace him, to cradle the beloved, grizzled head.

Almost guiltily the uncomfortable onlookers witnessed her grief. The crowd stood in muted silence, uneasy with this reminder of their own precarious mortality.

Finally the girl gained control. Touching her father's face one final time, she took the notebook from his jacket pocket, and then she let her friends lead her from the bed of nails.

Hawk touched her arm. "Jinx," he said. "It's Mike."

"Uncle Mike!"

She stopped; at first she seemed glad to see him; then her expression changed as if a light had been turned off.

"Why didn't you come? I said it was urgent. I . . ."

She was fragile—not physically, but emotionally. There was a vulnerability about her, a trusting expression like that of a pet that is used to being loved.

She was stunning—creamy young skin, delicate features, wide dark eyes. Although some of the child he had known came through, her body had blossomed.

She was the type who would be a one-woman man, he thought. She would date cautiously, fall for a guy, and want nothing more from life except him and his children.

"Your letter caught up with me day before yesterday," Mike told her. "I came immediately."

He considered telling her about the attack in St. Lucia and decided against it. It would serve no purpose. Besides, only the person who dispatched them to intercept the letter would know about the attacking bikers. There was a chance he might make use of the information later.

"Oh, Mike, I knew this was going to happen to Dad. I wanted him to quit."

The men had gone to work with quiet efficiency; stretcher bearers lifted the body to the sling. While the girl watched, they covered McComb's face with a sheet.

She collapsed against Mike's chest.

Her depending on him surprised Hawk. These were her father's people—men and women who had known Whip longer than Hawk had. Yet she turned to him, a man she had met irregularly through the years. It said a great deal about McComb's obsession with his career. A man as ambitious as Whip would resent the expenditure of time that friendships required.

Men began to clear the wreckage and wipe away the blood while the audience stood in silence. The PA system assured them that the show would go on. Whip would have wanted it so.

Then people began retaking their seats. The dwarf was waving Mike toward the motor homes. They led the girl across the field to the vehicle with her father's name lettered boldly across the side. For Whip the motor home had represented more permanence than he'd ever wanted.

"He would have let me bear Jinx in a camper outside Daytona if he'd had his way," his wife had told Mike. "He couldn't breathe unless he could smell the oil and hear the rumble of the engines."

Hawk twisted slowly. The spectators were far away, yet he could sense them coming alive again. They'd had their thrill, dutifully given the dead his moment of silence, and now they stirred, impatient for more.

Mike sighed. Whip was gone, and violent as his death was, it was somehow fitting.

Dying skewered on a spike was only the final, the ultimate, in a long series of ironies that had been McComb's life. He had suffered more than his share of fate's slings and arrows; why not the shaft?

## 7

From the step of the motor home Mike glanced toward the staccato rattle which broke the relative silence of the arena. The bike was close to him, and the man who straddled the saddle was looking his way so Mike could see the face clearly.

"Joe Blackwell," Jinx said, reading his mind. "Husky, he calls himself now."

Hawk had heard the name.

Blackwell was an "also ran," a perennial part of Whip McComb's show. His name appeared on the posters and the newspaper ads, but in small type. It was he who rode the bike between the ramp and the landing platform while McComb made the most spectacular, crowd-pleasing leaps. Sometimes flaming torches stretched upward from the handlebars of Husky's bike or occasionally a large wick in the shape of a loop extended above his head. Mike had seen him ride in front of a ramp with the wick in flames while McComb leaped through the moving circle of fire.

Blackwell also played stand-in and held the show together whenever the star was mending in the hospital.

His role had been that of an imitation Whip McComb, riding a similar bike and dressed in an outfit the same color as the star's.

Tonight Husky Blackwell had a personality of his own. Astride a bike with steer horns adorning the handlebars, he was an arresting presence. Incongruously he was dressed in a sheepskin coat, cowboy boots with gold spurs, and jeans cinched by a belt with his own likeness etched in the gold buckle.

On his head he wore a black-crowned "High Range," a classic ten-gallon stetson with the rim rolled in at the sides. Below the hat the Buffalo Bill goatee and moustache were almost predictable. The only thing missing was a Colt .45 strapped to his waist.

The crowd didn't seem to mind the mix and match of cowboy and biker. Blackwell had changed since Mike had last seen him. He was no longer too scrawny with sallow cheeks and deep-set eyes. The haunted look of a man caught in some foolish prank had disappeared. His nose was still hooked from an early fracture, and his brows were bushy and black like the hair showing beneath the broad ribs of his hat.

Blackwell looked prosperous and proud. With a John Wayne nonchalance, he tipped up the brim of the hat with his left thumb. A rawhide cord, looped under his chin, held the hat in place.

Unprotected by helmet or visor, the big-boned rider might have been astride a cutting horse instead of a powerful machine. As Husky rode away from the motor home area, a second cyclist rode out to meet him.

The beautiful Oriental woman who had led the preliminary pageant was mounted on her own bike. She wore no helmet, her black hair flowing behind her. She was young, under thirty, Mike surmised.

She cut across the grass until she was riding side-by-side with Husky Blackwell.

"Who's that?" Mike asked.

"The last empress of China," Yankee Horn answered. "Pu Noon."

"Empress of China?"

"It's a long story. She's Whip's wife. His widow, that is."

McComb married again? That surprised Hawk, but the girl they called Noon would have tempted any heterosexual male.

"What are they doing?" Mike asked.

Jinx didn't answer, nor did the dwarf. Husky and the woman had approached the ramp and were riding slowly past the bed of nails.

The audience rustled with excitement when Blackwell inspected the equipment and judged the distance. Finally the riders began to circle the stadium. They picked up speed and the crowd hollered its approval and encouraged them with applause.

"They're not going to try it, are they?" Jinx asked incredulously. "Not now! Not with Dad just . . . ."

"All the world's a stage," the dwarf quoted dryly.

"Not three of us on the same night," Jinx protested. "Stop them, please!"

The prospect of two others trying her father's stunt terrified her.

"No way, Jinx," the dwarf answered. "One of them has to take your father's place. There's too much at stake."

"But do they have to do it now? Can't they wait till we bury Dad?"

Hawk questioned the psychology of the two riders. Weren't they denigrating the knowledge and precision that went into cycle jumping?

He knew from personal experience that the skill needed had been reduced drastically since Evel Knievel pioneered the field. Since those early days fourteen-year-old kids matched or surpassed the distances that were mind-boggling world records when the champion jumper of all time had survived them, albeit broken in a hundred places.

McComb had made a science of the sport. "Any reasonably good rider can do what I do," he had said once, "if they do as I tell them."

If they don't know fear, he might have added. If they don't care whether they live or die. Or maybe if they feared poverty or boredom more than the hazards of jumping a motorcycle fifty feet in the air over cars, rocks, glass, spikes, or whatever the danger below.

He had proven his statement by teaching Hawk, a long-time cyclist himself, to leap distances the writer had never dreamed possible. In the beginning, of course, Mike had a safety ramp under him in case he fell short, but he had soon dispensed with that. He even came within a few feet of equaling some of his friend and teacher's own show stunts.

Whip had taught others in the circus to perform his feats as a backup in case he was incapacitated, but the stand-ins always used the safety ramps and shortened the distance, thus maintaining top billing for the boss of the outfit.

Probably, though, the show people knew what they were doing.

With their top star dead, the two heading for the ramp apparently feared the extravagant show could lose its following unless a new king, or in this case a new queen, was born.

For whatever reason, the pair had rounded the stadium and was gunning their engines. They raced back, Husky Blackwell's hat trailing like a kite on a short string. Still he held his chin up defiantly. The girl's head was just as high and determined.

"They should be wearing helmets at least," Jinx was saying. No one commented.

The machines revved to their optimum performance. They aimed at the ramp.

Watching them, Mike compared their approach with McComb's. Maybe there was a difference.

Husky and the girl seemed to be traveling faster than Whip McComb had. The difference, if there was one, was slight—perhaps only three or four miles per hour.

The question mushroomed in Hawk's brain: had McComb, the expert, misjudged his speed? If so, why?

Stunt show riders, Mike realized, had to make the trick look tough. If they had too much margin to spare when they landed, the crowd would think the leap didn't test either the man or the machine.

Were Husky and Noon leaving a safety margin or was everything the bikes had to offer necessary for the leap?

Whip had glanced at his speedometer at the last possible second. Then why had he misjudged?

In front of the stands while the pair of bikes was darting up the ramp, again the audience held its breath; but this time the powerful machines rose higher and the front wheels stayed high. It was instantly obvious Blackwell and Noon were going to make it.

Their form, though, Mike thought, was poor. Lacking McComb's fearless self-confidence, Blackwell squeezed down in the seat and narrowed his shoulders against the expected impact. Yet when the rear wheels slammed onto the platform, the audience screamed approval.

Few noticed the wobbling front wheels or the shaky departure from the platform. Instead they saw only new heroes being born.

"The king is dead," the dwarf said. "Long live the king." And as an afterthought he added, "And the empress."

Jinx stood on the step, her hand clutching Hawk's.

The riders zoomed a short distance along the dirt track and braked into a skid that left them directly before the TV cameras, where they came to a complete halt.

The crowd cheered, then was silent again.

Husky had removed his hat. A man in a bright sports jacket rushed to him with a microphone.

Blackwell spoke in a low voice, each word labored. It was difficult to tell whether he was exhausted by the ride and its tension, or whether he was overcome with grief for his dead friend.

"We done it for Whip," his voice boomed from the speakers around the Superdome. "That's the way he would have wanted it . . . for his old sidekick and his wife to finish what he started." The audience rose in unison, applauding with respect and admiration.

The empress part was pure showmanship crap, Mike thought until he remembered having read an article in the *Wall Street Journal*. He didn't recall the details, but at the time of the article there had been a man still living in Communist China with a rightful claim to the supreme title of the long-deposed Manchu dynasty. The surname was Pu.

Whether Pu Noon had any remote legal claim to the title or not, she at least had some credibility. In the strange ways of the East, a few members of former royalty, even a few millionaires, still lived in secluded luxury in the equalitarian regime of the Chinese Reds.

Blackwell waited until the din died away. Only when he had rapt attention did he speak again. Once more his voice was almost reverent. "You watch, folks. The show ain't dead. The empress and me will be back soon with more and better stunts that Whip and I were working on before . . . before . . . Anyway, like Al Jolson said, 'You ain't seen nothin' yet.' "

The roar of approval drowned the triumphant music while he and the woman rode to an exit, his stetson on his head again, his sheepskin coat flapping away from an embroidered shirt.

Jinx fumed. "The leeches! They used my father's stunt and took the glory."

"Easy, kid," the dwarf warned. "Your father made a mistake. That's all."

"He couldn't have. He was too careful. He rode by the book."

The dwarf nodded. "Maybe that was his mistake. He wouldn't ride by feel like the other guys. Figured everything out in advance . . . speed, angle, tach reading. He increased the distance by inches during the tryouts until he knew exactly what the machine would do. Wrote everything down in his book. Watched his speedometer like it was the Bible. 'Believe your instruments,' he used to tell me. 'Not your instincts.' But look what it brought him. A one-way ride to the cemetery."

"You knew him as well as anyone, I guess," Mike said.

"Too well," came the cryptic response.

"Then why didn't Whip warm up the crowd? You know, race for the ramp a few times and abort at the last second?"

"Whip hasn't done much of that lately," Horn replied.

"I don't think he even made a moving check of his instruments—his speed and his tachometer."

Yankee spoke defensively. "Everything was checked before the boss mounted up."

"By whom?" Mike asked.

He never got an answer.

Jinx had gone inside and several of the girls from the show went with her.

A crewman drove up with Whip's bike on a pickup truck. The custom-made machine was pathetic; its chrome was dented and scratched, the leather seat was punctured. The bars were twisted and the front wheel bent.

Mike climbed up and lifted the wreckage to an upright position. The glass of the tachometer was broken. The speedometer was in worse shape. The glass had popped out, and blood smeared the dial. It showed eighty-five miles per hour, although Mike knew that was not necessarily the bike's true speed at impact. It was not like the proverbial broken wristwatch on a dead man's arm.

Still it warranted a question. "How fast would Whip have been going when he made that jump?"

The dwarf cocked his head. "Eighty-five," he said.

The bike could have gone faster than that?"

"Hell, yes, but eighty-five made it look good to the audi-

57

ence. Whip cut it close and liked to make the leap last every fraction of a second possible. Besides, he had to have stopping space after he came off the landing platform. If he went much faster he would have crashed."

Mike nodded. He found the cable leading up from the hub of the front wheel. He saw the simple mechanism that translated the rotation of the wheel into the speed shown on the meter between the handle bars.

His suspicious mind was looking for a new gear or rotation plate; he found none. The parts all showed approximately the same wear.

There could have been a defective instrument, a faulty cable or a wrong-sized part somewhere in the mechanism. If any part of the speedometer failed, it would give an incorrect reading on the dial. McComb could have thought he was going faster than he really was.

What the dwarf said had diverted Hawk's brain to a new approach. Whip McComb believed in his instruments, not his instincts.

"Looking for something in particular, Mr. Hawk?" Horn asked.

Mike stood. "No, no. Just wondering why Whip was going so slowly."

"Slow?"

"I got the feeling he needed more speed."

"Did he now?"

A mechanic nearby nodded. "Had the same feeling myself."

"The speedometer still reads eighty-five. The needle must have been smashed down against the dial by the impact."

His response satisfied everyone except himself. He left the wreck with a gnawing sense of doubt. It was that skepticism that had guided him into more than one good story during the days when he had made his living as a reporter.

# 8

The empty stadium was a vast cavern. Walls and ceiling disappeared into distant shadows in the remaining light. In the stands, where echoes multiplied the tiny clacks of push brooms against seat legs, an army of sweepers shoved popcorn boxes and beer cans and candy-bar wrappers into heaps of debris on the aisles.

Would they have swept up Whip McComb with the rest of the junk if he had died in the stands instead of on the playing field? Hawk wondered. With capacity for seventy thousand spectators, a stadium could dehumanize all but the performers.

In the center of the artificial turf the remaining crewmen and stunt riders formed a circle around the end of the pickup truck where the battered bike lay. Near the bike the elder of two plainclothes detectives scribbled voluminously on a yellow notepad. When he closed and put it away, he sighed. The investigation was complete.

A sense of relief settled over the group. The consensus accepted the accident theory. No one argued.

Yankee Horn had called the police. Routine, he said. And a scar-faced mechanic, along with Hawk, had poked around the wreckage before the authorities had arrived.

Finally Husky Blackwell and Pu Noon had ridden into the center of the field and skidded to a stop.

Pu Noon—Hawk had difficulty with her married name, Noon McComb—dismounted, brushed aside words of condolence, and rushed into the motor home, apparently to console her stepdaughter, Jinx. When she passed close to him, Mike realized what a striking woman she was.

In her late twenties with fake eyelashes and artificially long, red-lacquered nails, she was beautiful enough for Las Vegas.

Even without makeup the flawless ivory skin was the perfect setting for her arresting black eyes. They flicked over Mike, obviously prepared to dismiss him as just another male on the make. With her beauty and the tiny waist accenting the swell of bust and hips, she would be used to that.

But then, as her gaze locked into his, her expression changed. Mike was aware of the difference. He had felt it before. For whatever reason—the tall, finely tuned body, or the shock of light brown hair that fell boyishly over his forehead, or the slow lopsided grin—many women, they told him, found him attractive. Although he wasn't particularly concerned about the fact, he enjoyed it and occasionally had even used it to his advantage on a story—or sometimes just for the hell of it.

He tried to keep his own expression noncommittal. She was a knockout, all right. Surprisingly tall, she must be partly Occidental. There was an undeniable sensuousness about her; no wonder Whip had married her. Conversely, why had she married Whip? He was twenty years older, scarred by repeated spills, and engrossed in his work. He couldn't have been all that a beautiful girl could attract.

Hawk's curiosity might have pursued the question had not Husky Blackwell intervened.

Behind him came a scrawny kid with a waxen face. The others called him Billy. Apparently a general flunky around the show, the kid was of indefinable age. He walked about with flapping arms and a foolish, happy grin, an adoring shadow of the man sweating inside the sheepskin coat. He wore blue jeans, a cheap imitation of Husky Blackwell's coat, and a cast-off western hat.

"You see that, Yankee?" Blackwell asked as he ruffled the dwarf's hair. "Your old buddy signin' autographs after the show."

"Hundreds of 'em," Billy bubbled. "Thousands of 'em. All wantin' Mr. Blackwell's signature. Girls too."

The dwarf leaned close to Mike and spoke in a conspirato-

60

rial tone, "That's Billy. Noon took him along when we found him wandering the streets of San Antonio."

"He's slow?" Mike observed.

"He's different anyway. He's anyone else. Walk and he walks with you. Take a pogo stick down Bourbon Street and he's bouncing right beside you. Later he doesn't even remember. 'Each frail fibre of his brain sets forth thoughts all wide and wild,' " Yankee ended with a quote.

Husky thrust out his chest and slapped himself with an open palm. "She-it. I had to fight off fans like a Texas longhorn bucking a rodeo rider."

"I'm Michael Hawk," the ex-journalist introduced himself.

The stunt man frowned.

"We've met several times," Mike added. "A few years back." He wondered if the boastful Husky remembered. They had met when the new king of the stunt riders had been plain Joe Blackwell. Hawk had beaten him in a game of chicken on a matched pair of Suzukis, with some tutoring from Whip McComb and more luck than sense.

Blackwell apparently had forgotten. "You a friend of Whip's too?"

"Yeah."

"Old Whip and me were like brothers. Been busting our asses in this business more years than I care to remember." Losing interest in Hawk, he confronted the police. "Find anything?"

"Like what?"

"Like why the hell my partner is dead, for Christ's sake!"

"Cause of death is the coroner's province," the officer commented.

"You mean there'll be an autopsy?"

The cop nodded. "Routine."

"She-it! That'll hold up the funeral."

"For a day or two."

Husky glanced at the dwarf. "What's that do to the schedule?"

Yankee Horn appeared pained. "We had a three-day layover, remember? The drivers could go on ahead. The rest of us will catch up later."

"Bury Whip here, you mean?" Mike asked.

Horn shrugged his misshapen little shoulders. " 'Bury me

61

where I crack up,' he always said. If it's okay with Jinx. And Noon." He tacked the last on at the end as if he had forgotten the widow. The slight was definitely deliberate.

"Why not?" Husky shrugged off his heavy coat and slung it over his shoulders. Perspiration marks under his armpits made it apparent that the coat was not comfortable in the Superdome.

"Be best if you stayed in New Orleans a day or two anyway." The detective put his notepad in his pocket. "Check with the coroner. He'll tell you when he can release the body. Tell McComb's daughter I said I was sorry Old Whip bought the farm. I was a motorcycle cop in the beginning. Never missed his show when McComb got within a hundred miles of town."

The officers turned.

"Officer," Michael Hawk stopped them.

He glanced about, hoping to catch a worried expression on one of the showmen's faces. He had no intention of telling the detectives of the action in St. Lucia. The police down there surely wanted him for questioning as it was. On the other hand, one of the men around him might be sweating blood, praying that the detectives would leave before Hawk told what he knew.

"Yes?" the older cop said.

"Is it okay if I call the coroner's office—for the family?"

"You a friend?"

Husky grunted. "He's a newspaper ghoul."

So he did remember!

"Local?" the officer asked.

Hawk shook his head. "Free-lance. I'd like to do McComb's obit; he taught me to ride once. He deserves more than a one-column head and a couple of paragraphs."

"Whatever." The officers walked off. The group watched them clear to the gate before they began drifting away, some with hands thrust in their pockets, their eyes on the artificial turf.

They cared, Mike decided. They were men like himself. The loss cut deep but the wounds were all inside.

Mike started for the motor home. He ought to be with Jinx. He wasn't family, but at least she still called him "uncle."

Behind him he heard a snatch of conversation that slowed his pace.

"What about holding the show over till the funeral?" Blackwell was saying.

"Here?" The second voice was Yankee Horn's.

"The Superdome's available. Remember when we were making arrangements last year?"

"Yeah, but why?"

"Why?" Blackwell laughed. "Hell, Shorty, you're supposed to be the business manager of this outfit."

"I don't get it."

"Publicity, man! The locals would pay double to see the show tomorrow."

"You mean cash in on Whip's death?"

"Hell, yes. Noon and Jinx will need the money. I need the money. So does everybody else in the show. Get on the phone tonight. The radio and television will be reporting McComb's death. Get a blurb in that we're holding over until after the funeral. A memorial. Yeah! A memorial to Whip. That's just what he'd want. No flowers, no wreaths or black armbands. Just a show, bigger and better than ever."

"But who . . ."

"Me! You think I'd let Whip's family down now? Hell, no. I'd jump that bed of spikes if I had to leap a mile."

"But the officials . . ."

"Screw 'em. They'll go along. Whip was getting to be a legend. They couldn't cancel this memorial. Get with it, Shorty."

"Yankee," the dwarf corrected him. "Yankee Horn."

"Sure, Shorty, only get on the telephone. Buy us spots on radio. The TV stations might even have time for sale. Hell, they'd make time."

"I don't like it," Yankee Horn said.

Blackwell exploded. "Like it? You little runt. How the hell do you think I liked making that jump tonight? I haven't gone that distance in months. And tomorrow night and the next and the next. I'm risking my life for Whip's kid, and you don't like it!"

"Yeah, you're right."

The midget was agreeing to make the arrangements as Mike Hawk stepped up into the carpeted interior of the motor home.

Jinx McComb sat at the table, her face covered with her hands, her stepmother beside her, several of the girls from the show nearby.

"Kid," Mike said softly. He had called her that when she was a gangly teen-ager. Her hands lowered, revealing a tear-ravaged face.

Pu Noon's concern seemed to be entirely for her stepdaughter. The casual observer would not have guessed that the beautiful, inscrutable face with the dark, deep-set eyes was that of a woman widowed an hour before.

The other girls felt out of place. They slipped away until Hawk was alone with his old friend's family of two.

"I should be out there," Jinx said through her tears. "There must be arrangements to be made. I'll have to stay behind and take care of things. The show has to move on."

"I'll make all the arrangements," Mike told her gently. "And the show's not moving on until after the funeral in any case."

"Oh?" the girl's surprise didn't last. "Of course. We'll make a fortune; we could triple ticket prices and sell out." There seemed to be no bitterness in the statement. "Dad did the same thing the last time one of his riders was killed."

She approved. Hawk didn't know whether to be disgusted or sympathetic. He checked the stepmother's eyes and saw no objection there either. But then stunt people lived with death, profited by its continuing threat.

"Is burial here all right, Jinx dear?" Noon asked.

Jinx said, "Yes."

One place was as good as another. Neither had to say it.

"Oh, Uncle Mike." Jinx scrubbed away the tears with the heel of a palm. "Do you think someone could have . . . you know . . . deliberately . . ."

"Now, Jinx darling, you promised," Noon interrupted.

"Promised what?" Mike asked.

"We all saw this coming," the pretty widow answered. "The way he was driving himself."

"Noon is right," Jinx conceded. "I had no right asking you to come here. I hired private detectives before."

"For what?"

Noon brushed her daughter's hair from her forehead. It was a motherly act that seemed out of place between two women so close in age. "Jinx and I found it hard to accept. Whip was making so many mistakes lately, having so many spills. We even hired detectives to be sure that they were all accidents.

"And?"

"They found nothing, but then they had difficulty keeping the same men on the case; we moved so often."

"You'll stay on, won't you?" Jinx asked. "For the funeral, at least."

"You can stay here with us," Noon offered. "There's more room than you think in one of these things."

"Of course," Mike accepted. "I'll stay here tonight and get a room in town tomorrow."

"Really, Mr. Hawk, that's not necessary. Jinx and I would feel safer with a man around, an old friend of Whip's."

Mike nodded. "I'll have to make some calls."

"There's a phone in here." Jinx said.

He frowned. There was a call he wanted to make in private.

"I'll bring my bike in from the parking lot," he said, rising. "It has my things in the saddlebags."

Noon smiled. "I'll have it brought in."

"It's parked in section B-20. I imagine it's the only one still out there."

Noon stepped outside and Mike glanced at the girl. It was difficult to relate the desirable woman Jinx had become to the egg-breasted kid he'd known earlier. Age improved and age destroyed. She was definitely in the best phase of the aging process.

"I need to make a personal call," he told her.

"In my bedroom," she said. "First room back.

He rose and walked through the kitchen into the first bedroom and found himself surrounded by postcards stapled on the walls. They were from everywhere in the country—Los Angeles, Chicago, Washington—and from other nations too.

Apparently McComb had kept in touch with his daughter while she was in school.

Mike glanced over them. He found several that interested him, one from Rome. Reading the brief message, he saw what he expected. The show had performed in Italy for several months. The cast had visited Venice.

So there was a link. Somebody connected with McComb could have met a couple of goons who might have tried to intercept the letter Jinx had sent him.

There was a Caribbean link too. A stripped-down version of the circus that had played several of the islands and the city of Caracas in Venezuela. Again there would have been a chance to waylay a plea for help from Whip's daughter.

It wasn't evidence, but the potential existed.

Interesting he thought.

Digging a number from the recesses of his mind, he dialed Washington. He'd call the press associations later with the obituary; his old friend had earned a decent sign-off. But the Washington call came first.

Mourners might enjoy epitaphs, but victims of murder would prefer vengeance.

# 9

CIA agent George Pollock kept his face down in the warm clear water. To the observer he might have seemed intent upon the eels and rainbow-colored fish below him, but he raised his head frequently. Like a whale, he spouted water from his snorkel while he peeked through the smeared face mask at the girls sunbathing nude on the tiny picnic island between the coral reef and Mooréa itself.

A lean, business type just past thirty, he was trying to garner the courage to walk ashore, sans swimsuit, and lie on the sand close to the brunette with the nice body and the white rear.

Maybe she spoke English, he thought. Because of their employee travel discounts, stewardesses from the States composed a significant segment of the Tahitian tourist trade. And Club Med was one of their favorite stops. They liked the price and the informality of the thatched-roof huts and the strings of beads guests used for money.

Or the girl with the white bottom could be French.

It didn't matter. He spoke enough of the language to communicate—if he could just find the courage to approach her.

With sudden masterful resolve he started to swim ashore.

Simultaneously he heard an outboard motor approaching from the main island and rolled on his side, startled to see it heading in his direction.

From long habit his hand darted for the shoulder holster

where he normally carried his gun. It struck his own bare chest. He was more than just unarmed: he was practically naked. It had taken a week before he had mustered the gall to go out among people in the skimpy suits worn by the Frenchmen—enough cloth to cover his pubic hair, but not quite enough to conceal the crack in his back. He still walked around on shore with a towel draped over his shoulder so the tip hung over his hips.

"Pollock *tane*" the coarse-voiced Tahitian shouted. "Pollock *tane*."

Pollock knew the brown-skinned boatman. Older than the main force of employees on the tropical island, he ran a fishing boat out past the reef. He wasn't the typical graceful islander. He was built like a gorilla: short in stature with thick bowed legs and long muscular arms.

Captain Bligh, the tourists called him.

On his boat you were his. You took off your shoes and left them ashore. You washed the sand from your feet. He threw your suntan oil overboard; it made the deck slippery, he said. If you got seasick—one or all of the passengers, it made no difference—you didn't go home.

"You fish," he would order. "You fish."

If the fish started hitting at quitting time, you quit. And he bellowed at those who tried to sneak him a tip. He didn't accept them.

"Telephone," he snarled now at Pollock.

George Pollock's hopes rose. It had to be Washington. They needed him at last.

"Wait, I'll climb aboard," he called good-naturedly.

For an answer Captain Bligh shifted the engine, twisted the throttle handle, and made a wide sweeping turn to the main island, his wake douching warm, salty water into Pollock's mouth.

Resigned, George began the easy swim back, ran to his cabin, wrapped a colorful *pareu* around his waist for the sake of modesty and hurried beneath the rustling palm trees to the club office.

A smiling G.O.—the club abbreviation for "*gentil organisateur*—looked up as he entered the office of the *Chef de Village*, the casual headquarters for the resort complex.

"You have a phone call for me?" he said. "George Pollock."

The tanned blonde motioned idly at the phone off its hook at the edge of her desk.

"Oh, is there somewhere I could take the call privately?" he asked.

She shrugged. *"Aita pea pea."* Nothing really matters.

Nervously he accepted. You didn't argue with the French—they flew into rages; and you didn't dispute Tahitians—they simply walked away.

"Yes," Pollock said into the phone.

"Howdy, Georgy Girl, you getting any of that *vahine* stuff, or are you still a virgin?"

The voice came through loud and clear from New Orleans, bounced off a satellite, and echoed down onto this South Pacific paradise to shatter George Pollock's calm.

"Oh, no," he groaned. "How did you find me?"

Michael Hawk's cheerful voice continued. "I keep telling you, you have enemies in high places, Georgy Girl."

"God, what is it this time?"

"Relax, nothing that involves your super sleuths."

Pollock stewed. "Don't say that. Not on an unscrambled line." Immediately he realized the girl at the desk probably understood English. He was blowing his own cover. Even if he was on vacation—involuntary leave actually—he was supposed to keep his work a secret.

"I need info, buddy," Hawk was saying.

"Don't you always?"

"Yeah. But this is strictly a personal matter. An old friend was killed."

How could you have an old friend? Pollock wanted to ask. Everybody around Michael Hawk seemed to die young. George himself had come close to the grave every time he got within pistol range of the former newsman.

"Get hold of someone on St. Lucia island in the Caribbean," Hawk ordered. "Find out what happened to a girl who was shot there day before yesterday. And two guys on motorcycles. One ran off a cliff. The other took his mount boating in a volcano crater."

Pollock squeezed his eyes shut. Two, probably three dead already. It was always that way when Hawk was involved: an undertaker's bonanza.

"And see if you know who was trying to track a letter that

a girl named Jinx McComb wrote me about a month ago. It got as far as St. Lucia, that much I know."

"Hawk, damnit," Pollock pleaded. "This isn't official business. I can't help you."

The voice on the other end of the line ignored him. "I'm in New Orleans with Whip McComb's Thrill Circus."

"For God's sake man, you can't be in the States."

"Get the information and meet me at Le Richelieu tomorrow."

"You maniac, I must be nine hours flying time from New Orleans."

"Charter a jet. Charge it to Hong Kong Traders, Limited. They have an account in New Orleans. It'll honor any withdrawal by a G. G. Pollock, no questions asked. Just remember the amount must always end in fifty cents. And get me fifty thousand while you're at it. You stay near Le Richelieu and get in touch with me."

Charter a jet. Pollock groaned internally. He could never get used to working with a man to whom money meant nothing.

"Have clothes sent to my room. Everything. Include something appropriate for a funeral."

"Yours, I hope."

"You can get my sizes from the shop in California. You remember the routine. Buy yourself whatever you want as long as you don't dig it out of Great Gatsby's trash can like you usually do. Okay, Georgy Girl?"

"No!"

"Good. Be seeing you, tinkle toes."

"The hell you will, Hawk. Hawk?"

The line was dead.

Pollock jammed the phone onto the cradle.

He wouldn't help, he vowed. He was going back to the beach, swim across to the picnic island, drop his skimpy trunks, and lie close to the girl with the pale backside. He was going to pretend he had never heard of anyone called Michael Hawk.

Before he could leave, the girl at the desk pointed at the second button on the phone. Its light was on and flashing.

Pollock closed his eyes again.

He knew who was calling.

"Yes," he said into the phone.

70

The voice made no attempt to identify itself, and from its strange metallic tone Pollock could tell it had been scrambled, treated to defeat any attempt at a voice print, and unscrambled again before it ever struck the satellite. Still Pollock knew who was calling, the one man in Washington he could never refuse. Thanks to that damn fool Hawk, holdovers from the pre-Watergate espionage days had enough on Pollock to hang him.

"You talked to him," the voice said.

It was a statement, not a question, yet Pollock answered anyway.

"Yes, he wants information as usual," he said.

"Get it for him."

"It has nothing to do with us. He's involved in a strictly personal matter this time. It's of no importance to us."

"True," the voice agreed. "Nevertheless he's a walking weapon we might want to use again someday."

"But . . ."

"Do as he asks and join him."

"Not again." Pollock groaned.

"Try not to get yourself killed," the voice continued. "If things look bad, call me. I'll cancel your insurance policy. The company is on a tight budget these days."

Again the phone clicked.

George replaced it more gently, but he was swearing to himself.

His vacation was over. He was going back; and if things went as they usually did when he was with Michael Hawk, he might as well paint a bull's-eye on his forehead. And it wasn't even department business. All his superiors in Washington wanted was to have him keep Hawk alive. Pollock and the small cabal inside CIA were the only ones who knew about the illegal wealth of the man who was once an itinerant newsman. It gave them a distinct advantage when they were promoting a mission that the timid leaders of the agency would never dare fund.

"Shit!" Pollock used one of his mentor's favorite words.

*"Parahi,"* the girl at the desk said sweetly.

"Yeah," George snapped. "Good-bye, and get me a driver. I got to get off the goddamned island."

*"Monsieur?"*

"A taxi, get me a taxi."

He stomped out onto the hot sandy path leading to his thatched hut where the door didn't lock and there was no glass on the windows.

As he walked, a coconut dropped from a tree, swished by his head, and landed with a heavy thud in the sand. It had missed him by inches.

"An omen," he mumbled. "A goddamned omen."

# 10

He lay awake in the motor home, his tall frame cramped in the bed above the driver's seat. Noon McComb was in the more luxurious quarters at the very rear of the vehicle, and he still visualized her slender body in the sheer negiligee she wore over a revealing pink nightgown.

The exquisite furnishings of the vehicle were atypical of Whip McComb. When Mike had known him, the champ was content with a camper large enough for only him and Jinx.

Something McComb was not was acquisitive. His first wife, examining her Spartan home, had once told Whip that the next time she married, her mate would be a bowerbird she had read about in *National Geographic*. Nobody could ever say McComb was one of those. The rustic bower of Australia, the male that is, builds chambers and runways from grass, moss, and twigs, laying bright berries, shells, and flowers at the entrance to entice a female inside. There the colorfully plumed male bows and dances until he has won his mate.

McComb bowed to no one. He took the women who came to him.

Noon must have bought the expensive home on wheels after she married Whip.

How would she and Jinx get along, now that Whip was gone? Hawk wondered. Whip seemed to be about all they had in common. That, and their beauty—seldom a cohesive factor among women. If he had been given a choice between stepmother and daughter, he would have been hard pressed as the mythological Paris, Hawk thought ruefully. That poor devil, albeit a prince, forced to choose the most beautiful of three goddesses, had wound up starting the ancient Greek-Trojan war.

Earlier Jinx had kissed him good night as she had when she was a child, but now in her tailored yellow pajamas she aroused him with the same fervor as did her stepmother. The girl had gone to the smaller bedroom just beyond the kitchen with a reluctant, forlorn step that had made him call her back.

He had held her protectively until she drew away, her eyes pleading. "You'll stay, won't you, Uncle Mike?" she asked.

"Mike," he corrected. "Anybody as pretty as you makes me feel old when they call me 'uncle.'"

She tested it. "Mike? Yes, I could say that." Women usually wanted to call him Michael; Jinx was different. "You will stay though?"

"Yes," he had answered too quickly. How could he tell her he could not stay anywhere, with anyone, for long? He was wanted for questioning in California, the Midwest, Washington, D.C., and in a dozen foreign countries. A nomadic life was his sole chance of survival. There was no way he could remain in one place or on a schedule such as the one that governed the thrill circus. So he hedged. "Yes, I'll stay . . . for a while."

She had kissed him again, leaning against him until he had turned her about by the shoulders and aimed her at the room.

"Get some sleep," he ordered. "You're exhausted."

He had slapped her lightly on the backside the way he had when she was little. It was a mistake.

She was no child.

Lying on top of the bedding in his shorts, he damned himself for even thinking about Whip's kid that way. But she wasn't a kid, he reminded himself again. So what happened to her now?

He was still staring at the ceiling when he heard feet padding through the kitchen. Out of habit he took the gun from his clothes on the rack above the foot of the bed.

The curtain that draped off his bed parted. Fortunately Jinx McComb spoke before he swung the weapon directly at her nose. He put the gun away.

"Mike, I've been thinking."

He couldn't see her. There was no light whatsoever in the

motor home. He guessed she was standing on the removable ladder leading to the bed.

"You should be asleep," he said.

Sensing her closeness, he reached out a hand until he touched her shoulder. Her own smooth palm and fingers cupped over his knuckles, as if to reinforce the link between them. He wanted to slide his hand lower to the erect young breasts.

"You could take Dad's place in the show," she said. "You were good. Dad said you were. He considered asking you to join him a few months ago. He trusted you."

"I already have a job," Mike replied.

"Oh!"

He had dismissed the idea too bluntly. She slipped away down the ladder.

"I'm sorry," she apologized, the hurt evident in her tone. "I shouldn't have asked."

Spreading the curtain and dropping to the floor, he caught her before she crossed the kitchen. In the darkness he brought her close, his hand upon her hair, holding her cheek against his bare chest. She was smaller than he had realized, and so vulnerable. Her tears were wet on his skin.

"How did you get mixed up with the show anyway?" he asked. "I remember your dad saying you were going to get an education."

She said, "I did. Dad sent me to exclusive schools. I joined the show every vacation, weekends when they were close enough. I learned to ride in spite of him."

"How did Noon meet your dad?" he asked out of curiosity.

Her cheek remained against his chest; he had to veto the urge to lower his hand from the small of her back. Something he could not control was the physical response she was causing in him; she must be aware of it.

"I brought her home with me one summer," Jinx explained. "She was my PE teacher, my friend."

"Whip taught her to ride?"

"She already knew. She stayed on with the show. When I came home at Christmas, they were married."

"You approved?"

For answer she pulled away so quickly he knew he had struck a nerve.

She would have returned to her room had he not stepped between her and the door.

"I asked if you approved," he repeated.

"She really didn't *try* to make Dad quit," she said. "She could have. She knew he was killing himself too."

"She knew you wrote me?"

"Yes, of course."

"Anyone else know?"

"Everybody."

There went one possibility of discovering who had tracked him to St. Lucia.

She tried again to step around him into her room. This time he stopped her with his arm across the door.

"Look, kid . . ."

"I'm not a kid."

"All right . . . Jinx. What will you do now?"

"Try to keep the show."

"You think it will fold without Whip?"

"No, Husky, Noon, even I could keep it going. The way Dad died will keep the customers coming long enough for one of us to establish himself as a star. Please, let me go. I'm sorry I asked you."

"Then what do you mean, keep the show? Your Dad left it to you or Noon?"

"To me, temporarily. It's complicated. Now, may I go to bed? You can leave right after the funeral."

He cursed himself. "I'll stay," he said, "afterward, for a while. Then we'll see."

"I knew you would," she exulted, hugging him joyously.

He held her until he became aware of a spot of light reflecting in the side window of the coach. How long had the light been there? He wasn't sure.

Then the cryptlike darkness of the vehicle struck him, and he pushed Jinx to the side.

"What's wrong?"

"Find a light switch," he told her urgently.

"Why?" she laughed. She knew he was wearing only shorts.

"Just do it," he ordered.

Fumbling about on the wall, he found one first. It didn't work; the one-ten power was off.

"Try the twelve volt," he said.

"Doesn't work either. Strange."

By feeling his way along the sink and stove, he reached the side door. Outside he confirmed the direction of the light. It came from the general area of the truck where McComb's wrecked bike lay on the flatbed.

"Mike, what's wrong?" Jinx asked.

In the vash hollow stadium her voice carried; the light at the truck blinked out. "Damn," he said.

He broke into a run across the turf, trying to maintain his bearings in darkness so total it might have been created by the goddess Hecate, so total it could blind a man to danger. Every light in the massive structure was off. "The "exit" signs should be glowing. The main power to the buildings had been switched off, just as the twelve-volt system in the motor home had been disconnected, probably by pulling circuit breakers or wires.

He was blind.

Trying to establish a sense of direction, he ran toward the truck, altering his course at the sound of running feet, sure at first that he had heard two people running. Now he was certain of only one. With his arms extended he tried to block a larger area. expecting the prowler to pass him on the right. The moving body hit him from the left.

He staggered, so did the other person. Disoriented, they thrashed and wallowed in the plutonian depths of the lightless arena. The sensation was that of floating, each step requiring Mike to probe, like walking down steps that might not be there.

Arms out, he groped forward, trying to avoid a collision with one of the show's vehicles or props. He stopped. Silence. Although he heard nothing, something was there, near him; he could sense it. Prickles of tension crawled along his spine. The thing faded before he could locate it.

Now he heard breathing, felt the vibration of foot on turf. He trailed the sound, then stopped to listen again.

"Mike!" It was Jinx calling from the direction of her father's rig.

The sound of feet thumped into a run; the figure in the dark was escaping like some bodiless phantom.

Mike broke into a clumsy lope, unsure of his footing,

hoping Jinx had given him direction with her call. He thought the person from the truck was moving in a wide circle. If he could just reach him, cut him off . . .

A sharp pain knifed through his right foot; he stumbled, lurching sideways before recovering his balance. Something gouged his bare legs, something sharp, like barbed wire.

He stooped. Cold metal pierced his leg, the quick, hard pain pushing an involuntary cry from his throat.

It was a mistake. His quarry had been standing still. Hawk had revealed his own position.

He tried to move quickly to a new location in the black void; he only became more disoriented. Without sight or sound to guide him, he was bewildered, almost dizzy. Again the steel thing poked at him: he knew where he was.

He had stumbled onto the bed of nails that had claimed his friend hours before. The realization was sobering. He had to get his wits together. This game of blindman's buff could be fatal for the loser. His instincts weren't working; time to use the head.

The chromium spikes could be all around him, or he could be standing at the edge of the field. He pictured the place: spikes eight or nine inches apart, spaced randomly, in no rows or systematic order. The daredevil McComb had strewn a deadly mine field.

"Mike!" Jinx yelled again. She seemed closer.

"Get a flashlight," he yelled.

"I can't."

She must have come too far into the opaqueness. She couldn't get back to the motor home either.

He had hoped the intruder might fade away into the anonymity of darkness; instead the light came on and began swinging in an arc that would eventually catch him.

Hawk gambled. "Don't move or I'll shoot," he commanded.

His empty threat drew the light like a magnet. It came at him neck high and made a portrait of his face.

He ducked, stooping so far a spike narrowly missed the tender organs of the groin.

From above the glaring circle of light, a red flame spit at the point where his head had been. The gunshot reverberated in the empty stadium.

And my damned gun is back on the bed, Hawk growled at

himself. The whole thing was like a crazy nightmare.

Feeling for the foot-tall needles, he fought to escape the sea of steel while the gunman was still deafened by the echoing detonation.

He floundered deeper into the spikes. And the light continued its search like a capricious moonbeam among the glistening expanse. There was an eerie beauty about the scene, but it needed music. Instead there was only silence—a dead, ringing nothing. He froze in a stooped position, his heart pounding like a fist at the inside of his rib cage.

The light went out.

He moved. His opponent heard him, and the light came on again. A second bullet cracked at his ear.

Chancing McComb's fate, he tried running through the nails. The enemy was moving steadily closer. Soon there would be no missing, regardless of how poor a shot pursued him.

Hawk cursed. Acres of open space and he had to stumble into the one place that would kill him. He changed directions, heading for the light. When all else failed, according to his credo, you went for the opposition; go for broke.

The light went out again.

"Mike! What's happening?" Jinx was headed in his direction.

"Stay back," he yelled.

The light flicked on up close and found him. It was only a few feet to his right. The gun would be leveling, the barrel lowering to the chest, the biggest target his body offered. He leaped, not at the assailant, but straight ahead.

Hawk went for distance, knowing he would come down like a diver belly flopping into a pool. But if his dive fell short, it would be the jab of sharp chrome-needles, not water, that stung the length of his body.

Hard, flat turf scraped his bare chest and legs. Only his ankles bled. He had cleared the bed of nails.

The light found him once more and he rolled over and over, a bullet digging in close enough to burn his skin.

Rising, he bolted away.

There were more sounds. Those who lived inside the stadium were emerging from their vehicles. A second flashlight came on and the first went out.

There was shouting; the voices were garbled together. More

narrow beams stabbed the velvet blackness. One of them caught him running.

Instantly a shot struck at his feet. Plunging ahead, he stumbled into the wall prop. Its fake mortar disintegrated on impact and buried him in bricks. All the lights focused on him.

"Shut 'em off, damnit!" he bellowed.

Chips of brick sprayed his back. Rolling away, he sprinted for the stands, the lights still on him, but at least he was putting distance between him and the gun.

"Douse the lights!" he yelled again.

Finally the curious samaritans understood. They were illuminating a human target for an assassin.

He was into the stands when the last light went out. Feeling his way with his hands, stooping like a hunchback, he climbed quickly; then he stopped.

Seconds ticked away without a sound. The others had realized his—and their—predicament: they could become targets too.

Nothing happened. Time stopped.

He was immobilized in a vast cocoon of darkness; the blackness continued to bind him in a psychological confinement that was no less restrictive because it lacked physical boundaries. If a man had phobias, an unlit, enclosed arena was no place to be. The inky blackness of a grave, the limitless space, the soaring height of the stands, the eerie echoes, the silence that amplified a man's breath into a raspy hiss, the fear of the next moment and the next step's consequences; this was the terror that enveloped Michael Hawk.

He did not remember having felt more helpless.

He could only wait. Movement would disclose his position. He couldn't yell. A shout might be enough to provide the gunman with an accurate shot if he were close.

So he waited.

Brilliant and blinding as lightning, the lights came on, flooding every corner of the mammoth Superdome. The illumination revealed a scene that might well have been a still from a silent film. The players were frozen in place.

Jinx McComb had stopped short of the bed of nails. Her stepmother was poised near the steps at the rear door of the motor home.

Husky Blackwell and Billy stood close together in the

space between their two living quarters. The dwarf was stooped over. He had his hands out as though he had been sweeping the turf, searching for something in the dark. A gun lay no more than a foot away.

The first movement came from an entrance into the amphitheater itself. A night watchman trotted in. He had his gun drawn. Middle-aged, with a family to think about, he was terrified, yet ready to do his job.

Seeing the show people momentarily paralyzed by the lights, he slowed. He lowered the gun, but he did not return it to his holster.

"I heard shots," he said. In spite of the distance his voice carried.

Yankee Horn moved first. He picked up the gun, a small revolver, opened the cylinder, and shook the cartridges into his palm.

"Just having a little fun with our friend up there," Horn smiled.

"Yeah," Blackwell confirmed. "The runt is right; we was just having fun."

The officer switched his attention to Hawk. He was too far away for Mike to ascertain his reaction to a man in undershorts standing halfway up the rows of seats.

"Fun?" the watchman asked.

Horn held up one of the empty cartridges. "Blanks," he snickered. "You hear that, big shot?" he yelled at Mike. "They were blanks and you ran like a bunny rabbit with his cotton tail on fire."

Billy laughed. Husky joined him. Neither of the women appeared amused.

"You can't be doing that in here." The guard came closer. "What happened to the lights?"

The dwarf stalked straight toward the guard. When he passed Husky, he handed the weapon to Blackwell.

"Yeah," Horn took the offense. "What the hell is wrong with you?" he challenged the guard. "Why'd you turn off all the fucking lights?"

"Me?"

The guard did not know how to react to the accusations of the man half his size. He was almost apologetic by the time Mike came down off the stands.

Jinx ran to Mike.

"Those weren't blanks," she said urgently, her voice low so that only he could hear.

No, Hawk thought. They weren't blanks, but there was no point in confirming the girl's fears.

He said, "One of your friends is a joker."

"I don't believe you."

He led her toward Husky and stopped. Billy came closer. Noon McComb held her position.

"Was that your gun?" he asked Blackwell.

Bare to the waist and wearing only a pair of trousers that he must have pulled on in such a hurry he forgot to zip the fly, Whip McComb's stand-in didn't flinch.

"Looks like it," he admitted.

Billy said, "Yeah, Mr. Blackwell. That was one of yours. I remember reloading shells for you. I . . ."

"One of yours?" Mike snapped.

Blackwell zipped his fly. It seemed more important to him than the recent attempt to kill the newcomer. "That's right," he admitted. "I got an arsenal inside. Reloading equipment. Everything."

"Why?"

"You saying I took those shots at you? I wouldn't have missed, fancy pants."

Mike's left hand darted out, caught Blackwell by the neck, applied enough pressure to gag the stunt man and held on while he smashed his right fist into the phony cowboy's lower belly.

Blackwell's eyes bulged; he gagged on his own vomit. Hawk released him, shoving him away so he could empty his gorge on the turf.

"You bastard, I'll . . ." Husky choked off his own threat. He couldn't get his breath.

"The name's Hawk," Mike snarled. "And the little guy is Yankee Horn. You hear, boy? You call him anything else again in my presence and I'll stuff your spurs up your ass."

"Go to hell," Blackwell squeaked.

Hawk took a step forward and the retching man conceded. "All right, all right." He vomited again. "They're my guns. Everybody uses 'em," he said.

"That true?" Mike asked Jinx.

She nodded.

"We're going to put on a Wild West show," Noon McComb

said, walking closer. "Real bullets. Shooting at each other on the move. Husky is training us all."

"Dad didn't like the idea," Jinx said. "They'd shoot away from the audience, of course, but he was afraid we couldn't get the permits."

"If you think that was me shooting at you, call the police," Blackwell challenged.

"Mike, you'd better call. Those weren't blanks. I know they weren't."

He ignored the girl. He couldn't call the police. Only he knew that.

"They were blanks," Yankee Horn offered from the entrance. He had returned alone, apparently having satisfied the night watchman.

"Like hell they were," Mike contradicted him.

When he was closer, Yankee spread his hand. He showed five spent shells as if to prove what he said.

The gun's cylinder had room for six.

Mike didn't ask about the missing bullet. There was no question it held a deadly slug just like the rest had. The dwarf had probably disposed of it on the way back from his walk with the guard.

"You call the police, Hawk, and the city will close us down," Horn reminded him. "We'll have to go to court and stall as it is to keep the Superdome after what happened to Whip. We promised the management the spikes would be soft plastic."

Now Hawk knew how far the show people were willing to go to keep the circus operating. It was their life, not just their livelihood. They would risk a gunman in their midst to avoid further police interference. Risk was a factor they could live with, the end of the show was not.

The others waited.

It would be easy, Hawk realized. A paraffin test would show who had fired a gun recently, but even that wouldn't be enough evidence to hold anyone for long. It wouldn't prove whether or not McComb had been murdered.

He looked at the pickup truck again. The bike was still in the same position he had seen it in last. Maybe he had come out before someone had a chance to make whatever change he had wanted. That was good enough for Mike. He didn't need detectives to help him avenge the death of a friend.

Equally important, Hawk had no desire to call in the police. He couldn't stand the scrutiny of even a cursory investigation. It wouldn't take much to arouse interest in how a free-lance reporter managed to charter jets and go through cash like it was good bourbon.

"Probably Billy's idea of humor," Husky suggested. "He's a real joker."

The kid grinned his simple smile, pleased at the compliment.

"The next joker who takes a shot at me is going to die laughing." Mike took Jinx by the arm and walked her to the door.

They went inside together. She was still clutching his arm, trying earnestly to convince him that he should call the authorities when he gave in to impulse.

His arm circled her waist, and he lifted her onto her toes. It wasn't an uncle kind of kiss.

She was no longer a child.

## 11

They buried Whip McComb in the rain. The gray skies had wept since dawn. Preceding the limousines and the hearse in the cortege were the cyclists, wearing clear plastic raincoats over their show outfits.

The procession wound through the old section of the graveyard where concrete crypts held the remains of the dead above ground. In the newer part a small rise and an improved drainage system made it possible for the recent dead to be buried beneath the surface. There the gray stones protruded from the wet sod like dry bones thrust up from below. Still the cement angels directing their frozen prayers into the magnolia trees and the tall headstones punctuating the grassy knoll retained the gothic mood of the older area.

Michael Hawk detested cemeteries. To him they were futile delusions of immortality. They were also grim reminders of how thin was the barrier between him and his own eventual burial.

He attended the ceremony only for Jinx and Noon. Whip wouldn't have cared.

The rain made the ceremonial ride even more grim. A striped awning had been stretched above the open grave. From the road the pallbearers carried the casket to the grave where strong web belts extended across a rectangle of stainless-steel tubing.

A blanket of imitation turf covered the dirt that would seal off the stunt rider's grave. Whip's bike lay on the artificial grass with a few flowers covering the most damaged parts. Apparently they were burying it with him.

There was no minister or priest.

Many of the show people plus a collection of fans, newsmen, and the merely curious stood beyond the tarp. Jinx McComb was at the foot of the grave, flanked by Hawk and her stepmother Noon.

By some preordained reasoning, it fell to Yankee Horn to speak the last words.

"I spent the last twenty-four hours thinking about what I would say today," the dwarf said almost too softly to be heard. "And all I could think about is how I came to be called Yankee. Before I met Whip everybody had their own nickname for me. Shorty. Squirt. Half Pint. Runt. A lot worse. Whip called me 'Yankee.' It was a name with stature, he said. 'And a man with stature doesn't need to be tall.' That's what he said. I haven't taken much shit . . . excuse me . . . from anybody since. That was Whip McComb, a great guy, a great bike rider, a great stunt man. And the way I see it, he didn't fail the other night. He just made the biggest jump of all."

Yankee paused, then postscripted with a quotation. "The temple of fame stands upon the grave; the flame upon its altar is kindled from the ashes of the dead." Again he paused. "And I guess Whip McComb will go on lighting the altar in the temple of fame like the other men who never stopped trying to go another step farther, another mile an hour faster. So keep riding, Whip, wherever you are."

The funeral ended with a quiet mutual consent; Jinx and Noon walked with Hawk and Husky Blackwell to the limousine. The women talked with friends while they sat inside; the delay gave Mike a moment to slip back to the grave where some workmen were quietly lowering the casket.

Mike found the person he wanted, a man in a raincoat and a hat. The top of his tie showed above the collar of the raincoat. He looked as if he were in charge.

"Don't bury the bike," Hawk told him.

The man frowned. "But my instructions were to . . ."

Mike said forcefully, "I paid for the funeral, the burial plot. Check with your superiors."

"You aren't the guy who brought out the bike."

"No."

The head groundsman pointed to the old van where Billy was getting into the driver's seat. "That goofy kid did. I came in this morning and there he was. He had the cycle out of the truck and laying on top of the dirt. I think he was trying to fix it so it could run in the hereafter."

"Oh?" Mike's attention picked up.

"Yeah. Then he tells me to bury it with the coffin. I argued, but he got kind of wild, so I said okay. It probably isn't legal." The man's voice was soft and Southern.

"He's retarded," Mike said pleasantly. "Nice boy. We didn't want to discourage him. It was his idea."

"I should have known."

"I'll have someone pick it up tomorrow. Do you have an unlocked shed where you could store it for a while?" Mike asked.

"Well, yes, near the crematorium. There's a padlock on the latch, but it opens without a key. Just keeps the kids away, that's all. They play cowboys and Indians around here. I don't chase them away except when we have a funeral. I figure, what the hell. You know, so few places for a city kid to play? So why not? Cemeteries aren't like they used to be."

Mike said, "Yeah."

"Hawk!" Husky called from the limousine. "You riding with the girls?"

"Sure."

Blackwell placed himself between Hawk and the lead car. With his thumb he pushed up his plastic-covered cowboy hat and looked at the bike being removed from the tarp.

"Snooping again, Hawk?" he asked.

"Maybe."

Blackwell nodded. "You're going to hurt the girl, man. Noon too."

"How?" Mike asked skeptically.

"You're going to find things about Whip they'd rather not know."

"Like who killed him?" Mike said pointedly.

The man in the western outfit made a snorting sound of derision. "Whip McComb killed himself. We all know it. The women just don't want to accept how he did it. You snoop around enough and you'll show them he wasn't the man they thought he was."

He went ahead of Mike to the car.

87

Hawk hesitated only a moment, collecting his thoughts. He felt more certain than ever that his friend had not died accidentally. He could logically guess how it had been done. The bike had been rigged, probably by Billy. Maybe it was he who had been trying to conceal what he had done the night Hawk had been shot at in the stadium. Having been interrupted, he had tried again to cover his tracks when he drove the bike to the cemetery. Once the wrecked cycle was in the ground, the kid could rest easy.

Only Billy couldn't have worked alone. He might sabotage a bike, but he wasn't capable of tracing a letter across the Atlantic and back again. Somebody else was probably using him.

But who?

There was no answer—for now. He needed more facts.

He caught up with Blackwell and slid into the limousine beside Jinx. On the far left her stemother sat and eyed Hawk with a curious expression he could not quite interpret.

The procession, minus the hearse and all the hangers-on, returned to the Superdome. Nobody said it, but the performers were in a hurry to get ready for the evening show. Banners proclaimed Whip McComb's "memorial" for a second night, and fans were lining up for tickets.

At the sight of the banners Jinx slid closer to Hawk. "Take me somewhere else, Uncle Mike," she said. "I don't want to go in there now."

"Are you sure, dear?" Noon said. "I think it would be better if we stayed busy."

"I'm sure, Noon. I'll be all right."

"Okay, darling. Do what you think best. No one expects you to perform until you're ready."

The two exchanged a perfunctory peck on each other's cheek.

Hawk hesitated. He wasn't sure he wanted the girl with him. After all, two attempts had been made on his life, and besides, he had to work fast. Every minute he hung around the States, he jeopardized the anonymity he needed in order to stay alive.

The girl's eyes pleaded.

Weakening, he tapped the driver from the funeral parlor on the shoulder and gave the name of his hotel in the French Quarter.

Once there, he led Jinx to his reserved room, helped her off with her raincoat, and let her fall wearily across his bed. He called room service for a meal and drinks. Before he finished the order, he canceled. Jinx was asleep.

There were things he needed to do. He put through a call to the stadium and had one of the show girls send an overnight bag for McComb's daughter. Then giving the name of the Crossroads Hotel, he asked to have a couple of the crewmen bring his bike and saddlebags.

He met the couriers at the Crossroads and waited until they had gone before he returned to Le Richelieu. At the desk he pleased the manager by asking for a room adjoining the one Pollock had reserved for him.

Alone finally he placed a call to the coroner.

"You again," the coroner said irritably. "You called yesterday."

"Just double-checking," Mike told him. "You're satisfied McComb's death was an accident?"

"Yes, accidental death," the medical man answered in a dry voice. "A man crazy enough to go leaping over a bed of spikes can expect to get his sooner or later."

"Then, you're positive the spikes did kill him?" Hawk quizzed. As a newspaper man, he knew better than to leave a subject with a single question. You rephrased it, twisted the words around, and said it again. Usually you got different answers or more information.

"Hell, yes."

"No liquor, no drugs in the bloodstream, nothing that might impair his judgment?"

The coroner gave a disgusted grunt. "Bloodstream? Your friend's veins were so full of morphine and other pain-killers there was hardly enough blood to carry it all."

"Oh!" Mike's interest gathered momentum. "Then that could have caused McComb to misjudge his speed. Perhaps impair his vision?"

"No more than usual."

"What's that supposed to mean?"

"Your friend was a drug addict, Mr. Hawk. He had needle tracks on his arms, under his fingernails, even his toenails. He'd had acupuncture too, I'd say. The man was a living pin cushion. And his stomach was eaten away with the junk he took by mouth. I suppose you knew that."

"No," Mike said. "I didn't. Heroin, angel dust—was that the sort of thing he was on?"

The coroner grew defensive. "I didn't say that. I didn't find anything you couldn't get with a prescription, but I suppose he had a new doctor in every town. Only one good thing."

"What's that?"

"Your champion bike rider probably didn't feel a thing when those spikes poked through his body."

Mike grimaced and slowly replaced the phone.

He sat on the bed and stared at the baroque wallpaper.

It didn't sound like the McComb he had known. Whip rarely even drank the day before a performance.

"Need my senses for the show," he had said. "Nothing is going to dull my brain before I make a leap or take a chance on the cats." The latter referred to one of his less successful ideas. On his first attempt to ride through a cage of lions, the cats had pounced on him and his machine as if together the pair was no bigger than a field mouse. The trainer had not driven the beasts away until the lions' claws had dug bloody tracks down Whip's back and legs. The stunt never got official clearance, even in the cowpoke towns, and the audience never saw a second attempt.

Later when Mike rolled off the bed and checked on Jinx, she was still sleeping.

He took the .38 Special and holster from his saddlebag and fastened the straps to his ankle, covering the gun with his pant leg before going out into the street.

The rain had abated, and some tourists were emerging. They were ready for an evening on Bourbon Street, even though the distant thunder suggested the lull in the weather was only temporary.

He rode the cycle through the twilight to the cemetery. Leaving the machine at the gate, he wandered about until he found the mausoleum.

The thunder was closer now and fingers of lightning snaked through the trees. It was no longer a gentle rain. The sky was angry, threatening the trespasser in the land of the dead. Hawk felt unwelcome. Let the dead keep their secrets, they had nothing else, the storm seemed to be saying.

Inside the shed he pulled the light cord dangling from the

rafters. A bare bulb caked with dust glowed dimly above him. His shadow lengthened and shortened as he moved about.

Bending over McComb's wrecked bike, he caressed it like a woman's body, running his hands carefully over it, exploring, probing for its secrets.

The bike did not respond like a woman, though, and he was about to give up when his fingers touched the face of the speedometer.

Seventy-five, it read. Seventy-five?

Outside the thunder rumbled, an ominous reminder of where he was. The presence of the crashing rumble here in this storage yard of death was all too appropriate. Violent as was its sound, the booming concussion in itself was only a response to a conflict of positives and negatives, the quintessence of violence. Those who lay interred around the shed had been part of the tensions that comprise living. Death was only the response, the resolution of conflict, as inevitable as thunder after lightning.

To Hawk the predictability of man's end made it no more acceptable, especially when it came at the hands of other human beings. In many ways the ancient religions had dealt with the subject more coherently than today's monotheism. To name a god "Mors" and make him responsible for death seemed more logical than to attribute both life and untimely death to a single deity whose name theologians and bumper stickers make synonymous with love.

Hawk had seen so many people dead and dying in his violence-splotched life that he detested death. It offended his sense of reason. A creature as complex as a human being should not be built to survive so briefly. Nature did not seem to give a damn as long as there were new seeds to sprout in the spring.

But Hawk cared. Fate had forced him to walk close to the abyss so often that he resented the execution order every man, woman, and child was handed at birth. Life was only a string of daily reprieves. His cyclist friend had been cheated by whoever it was that had altered the odds in favor of death. In Hawk's book that was an act that demanded retribution. Mors needed no allies.

And the lone survivor there in the storm-tossed cemetery did not fool himself. He might well have bought a plot next to the stunt man. Obviously a killer was loose, one with a significant advantage: unlike Michael Hawk he knew who his next target was.

Hawk was dealing with a question mark, but the speedometer cupped in his hand breathed life into the ugly images taking form in his head.

The instrument had read eighty-five miles per hour shortly after the accident. Of that he was sure. The figure checked with what Yankee Horn had told him.

McComb had to be traveling eighty-five to clear the open space over the bed of nails.

Of course, the indicator could have been pushed back while it was being carted to the cemetery. The speed shown on the dial meant nothing. Hawk could have been mistaken when he read it the first time; McComb could also have misread it. There were explanations for the change, no doubt about that. Still it bothered the pragmatic Hawk.

He followed the cable to the center of the front wheel. There might be a bend, a break, or a flattening of the coiled metal cover that would prove the speedometer drive had been damaged. He found nothing.

Then he checked the grooved speedometer drive gear on the magnesium wheel. A plastic screw tip on the end of the shaft rode in the grooves turning the cable which subsequently rotated a magnet inside the speedometer. The magnet moved a speed cup and pointer on the dial, the pointer designed to stop when a hairspring balanced the force of the magnet.

Although it was simple and old-fashioned, the system was highly accurate, exactly what Hawk would have expected McComb to build into his customized bike. The mechanism had been tested and proved. A man could trust his life to it.

Hawk's fingers next tried the nut that held the serrated disk to the wheel. It was loose to his touch, only finger tight.

Christ! he thought. Had Whip McComb's death been that simple? A nut loose enough so that the disk would not rotate properly with the wheel?

Life was a thread thin as spider's web waiting to be broken.

His mind backed up.

If that cable had been slipping, it would have caused the speedometer to show a slower speed than the bike was actually traveling. McComb would have cleared the bed of nails with room to spare if he had been traveling faster than he thought. Although the crowd would have been disappointed because the stunt looked too easy and Whip might have spilled going down the landing platform, one thing was sure: he wouldn't have fallen short.

Then what . . .

Mike stared at the mechanism again. Was the disk different than the one he had seen when he checked immediately after the accident?

Yes. It was smaller in diameter.

That was it. Damnit, he was sure, but he would never be able to prove it.

But why? Had it been switched after the accident? Again why? Because the first disk had been oversized.

Of course. The extra diameter had given McComb a false reading. He had been going slower than the speedometer indicated.

And what was it Yankee Horn had said? Whip trusted his instruments, not his instincts. A logical strategy. Drugged nearly senseless for whatever reason, he could not ride by feel. He had to rely on his instruments. It fit his engineer's approach to the entire sport as well.

But why was the nut only finger tight?

Mike bent closer and looked at the short screw section extending from the cable. The outermost threads were still intact. The threads closest to the wheel were stripped.

His theory was taking shape. During the accident, or afterward, the inner threads had been stripped. When the regular pieces were replaced, the nut couldn't be securely tightened down. The stripped thread had prevented it.

Someone had tinkered with McComb's speedometer, deliberately misleading him as to his speed.

And the regular gear had been replaced later. That's what Billy had been doing when he worked on the motorcycle after delivering it to the cemetery for burial. Having failed to make the switch because of Mike's interruption in the stadium, the retarded boy had brought the bike here and replaced the original drive gear before the funeral.

Again the thinking was beyond that of a boy with limited intelligence. The oversized, substitute gear had not been new. A used one had been taken from another bike or from spare parts and installed so that no one would notice the change during the confusion following the crash.

Hawk had missed it himself. Although he had considered the gear as a possible cause of the accident, he had missed a detail.

"Damn," he said bitterly.

He rose, forcing himself to accept what he had only suspected until now: his friend had been murdered. It jibed with the clumsy attack on St. Lucia.

And only Hawk knew. Hawk and the killer.

He heard a noise behind him, a sound that was not part of the storm. He whirled and quickly switched off the light.

Lightning flashed beyond the door where shadows of vertical tombstones came and went, animated by the swaying bushes and dripping trees. The movement had to be illusion; tombstones don't move, nor do their shadows.

# 12

The second flash of light came immediately after the first.

Thunder roared.

A figure loomed in the shed door. It slid around the edge cautiously; the lightning glistened off the metal object held in a man's hand.

Hawk concentrated on the gun.

He had a fraction of a second to decide who was coming after him. The gun was his only clue.

He knew the type well, a Browning 9 mm High Power. A nickel-plated, engraved Renaissance.

It was an expensive showpiece that a police officer wouldn't be carrying.

Hawk's instincts sent him rolling to the floor, tugging the .38 Special from his leg holster as he ducked behind the wrecked motorcycle.

He yelled. "Stop. Don't move."

The eerie shadow heard the order and reacted like a trained killer.

The figure dived for the floor, swinging the Renaissance toward the sound.

Mike squeezed the trigger, the barrel moving smoothly with the target. He would not miss. Less than six feet separated him from his mark.

The .38 popped like a cap pistol.

Hawk was torn between caution and overreaction. He knew what had happened. The primer had gone off in the shell, but not the powder. The slug might never have left the barrel. If he fired again, the wedged bullet could cause the gun to burst, possibly severing his hand at the wrist.

He gambled. He pulled the trigger again. It didn't move. The first slug had not cleared the forcing cone. The cylinder was jammed.

Lightning flashed again, and this time it was Michael Hawk who was the illuminated target. He started to rise, ready to use his futile last chance. His only hope was to jump the intruder before he could get off the killing shot.

Hawk measured the rest of his life in fractions of a second. His body tingled, tensed against the invasion of seering hot lead.

He leaped. Midair he heard the figure shouting.

There was no stopping; he came down hard on the intruder; raising his useless gun, ready to club it into the enemy's head when he could find it.

"Hawk, it's me," the voice squeaked from beneath him. "George Pollock."

The gun was near shoulder height when the ex-newsman stopped it.

"Pollock?" he muttered. "What the hell . . ."

"Roll off me, you big shit, or are you turning gay?"

Hawk stood. He shivered as he realized he could have killed a man who had saved his life.

His reaction to relief was to bully the CIA agent. "You prissy-assed bureaucrat. What the hell do you think you were doing, sneaking in on me?"

"I called to you," Pollock grumbled. Lightning revealed an expensive business suit, soiled by the dirt floor of the shack. He reholstered his gun. "You must not have heard me."

"There's a storm out there. Or hadn't you noticed?" Hawk said.

"What are you doing here?" George asked.

"*Faute de mieux*," Hawk replied.

"Nothing better to do? So you go to a graveyard."

"How did you find me?"

"Followed your motorcycle from your hotel. You're getting easier to track than a fish wagon on a summer day. Must be old age creeping up on you, dad."

"Don't 'dad' me, junior. You almost didn't get any older, sneaking up on me like that."

"What the devil were you shooting? Caps?"

Hawk pondered the gun in his hand.

"Nothing went off but the primer," he said.

"You reloading these days? A man with your money?"

Mike shook his head. "No, these were factory loads." Curious, he tipped up the revolver and shook out the one shell that would fall from the jammed gun. It was impossible to tell by weight alone, but he was willing to guess that shell too was void of powder.

He tugged on the light chain again. Pollock pressed closer to study the bullet in his associate's fingers. They both squinted, searching for tiny marks on the slug and the shell itself.

"Looks like a kinetic bullet puller was used," Pollock observed. "Can't be sure, of course. Might even be set deeper in the casing than she should be."

"Bell mouther die," Hawk added. "Somebody using a seater pushed her back in a bit deeper than usual before he put her on the crimper."

"All of the bullets like that?"

Hawk said, "I imagine."

"I thought you said they were factory loads."

"They were."

Mike sorted through the possibilities quickly.

The gun had been loaded with reliable shells when he spent the night with Jinx and Noon in the motor home at the Superdome. He hadn't carried it to the funeral. There was only one explanation. Between the time he had last handled the gun and the delivery of his saddlebags to the hotel in the French Quarter, someone had removed the slugs, dumped out the powder, and put the lead slugs back in the cartridge.

Someone had rendered him impotent as far as weapons were concerned. The possibilities were obvious: Husky Blackwell had the equipment in his motor home; Billy knew how to use it.

The act had saved Pollock the pain of a serious wound, possibly his life, but Hawk couldn't help but wonder what the two had in mind for him, once his .38 was useless.

"You got enemies again, I take it," Pollock said.

"Or damned poor friends," Mike observed.

He switched off the light and stayed clear of the door. He felt like a fox still in his cage somewhere in Britain, waiting for the huntsmen to release him in front of the hounds.

He watched the cemetery through the open door, waiting for a sign of movement, but the grave sites outside remained stark, immobile scarecrows, nothing more.

"What did you learn about St. Lucia?" he asked Pollock.

"You're in the clear," the CIA man said. "Although the authorities wondered why the hell you ran off when the girl was shot."

"She dead?"

"No. She'll make it, only she isn't going to look too good topless anymore."

"Too bad. She isn't a bad kid really. Not your average kid-sister type maybe, but she had her assets. Her brains just never quite kept up with her hormones, that's all."

Pollock continued. "The police version is that the first biker just went over the cliff. They didn't connect him with the one who shot the girl. He was a local boy, one the authorities are glad to see gone. They figured he had a thing for the stewardess, saw her in your arms, and tried to kill her."

"Case closed?"

"Yeah. They found enough of him and his bike in the crater to write him off as a suicide. Is that the way it happened?"

Hawk let the question pass. "What about the letter?"

"Apparently somebody paid the two bikers to pick up Jinx McComb's letter before you received it. When they failed, they tried to play rough."

"Who paid them?"

"If you'd let a few of your enemies live awhile, I might be able to question them."

"Meaning you don't know who wanted to keep me from getting that letter?"

"Meaning I don't know. But there are some interesting tidbits. The guy who received it in Chicago and forwarded it to New York got held up while he was putting the letter in a mailbox. Nothing rough, just a couple of kids with Saturday-night specials. But they held one up your friend's nose until he told them what he had just mailed and whom it was addressed to. They pretended they weren't interested after he told them, said they were after something else. They ran when a police car cruised by."

"And New York?"

"The news bureau office was broken into the night after the chief sent the letter on to Italy. He figures they took the Italian address from his desk pad. He'd written it down."

"Venice too?"

"Your old editor, Ceperley, was mugged when he went out to mail the letter. The muggers had his wallet and your letter until he got mad and beat the shit out of the two kids who took him on."

"So they saw the St. Lucia address?"

"Possibly. Ceperley had a few choice words to relay to you. Want to hear them?"

"No, they'd probably strike me deaf."

"Somebody got more desperate the closer that letter got to you, somebody with international connections."

Hawk pondered a moment. The Whip McComb Thrill Circus toured the States and Europe. The performers were heroes to bikers everywhere. It wasn't too surprising one of them would have connections wherever the letter traveled. There was no question why somebody had been so anxious to stop the letter from reaching its addressee. Whoever had killed Whip McComb wasn't anxious to have an investigative reporter poking around the show.

"What's it all about?" Pollock asked. "Another big crusade?"

"Nothing you boys would be interested in. No international intrigue this time."

"Doesn't matter. I got my orders. Stick with you, keep you alive so we can use you again. You're too valuable to be wasting yourself on anything insignificant."

"Somebody kills a friend, that's not insignificant."

"A private crusade."

"Yes. One nobody can fight except me. I'm not handcuffed by professional ethics, Supreme Court rulings, or . . ."

". . . or cost."

Hawk put the useless gun in its holster. He had his thoughts in order before he spoke.

"My friend Whip McComb was killing himself. Drugs and stretching himself to the limits. Somebody liked the idea. They were willing to wait until he did it on his own. Then they got worried I'd come along and hog-tie him if he didn't knock off the shit."

"So they tried to stop you from getting the letter."

"When the amateurs didn't stop me and the stewardess on St. Lucia was shot, our somebody figured he might as well go all the way." Mike made a motion with his head toward the bike. "Whip's speedo was rigged. By the time he figured it wasn't in sync with his tachometer, it was too late. He fell short and we bought him a little six-foot-deep pad where it's quiet."

"You told all of this to the police, of course?"

"They had their chance."

"Give them another."

"Too late. The original equipment has been replaced on the bike."

"So nobody knows but you," Pollock observed.

"And you," Hawk reminded him.

"Aw, no!" Pollock's voice reflected disgust. "Why did you tell me? I'm liable to get killed right along with you."

"What are friends for?"

"Friends! Who ever said we were friends? Look, damnit, a lot of weirdos are into this bike thing."

"And nice people too," Mike corrected him.

"Sure, millions of nice people, but . . ."

"I knew a whore on the Greek Island of Mykanos once," Mike interrupted. "She rode a donkey around half the island. She made some bread so she bought a bike and pedals her ass all over town. Increased her income so much she's thinking of buying a cruise ship so she can go international."

"Jee-zus, Hawk," Pollock said disgustedly. "Be serious."

Mike touched Pollock's arm.

They had both heard the sound outside. It had the deep rumble of thunder, but it didn't stop. It increased in intensity, coming from all four directions.

"Let's get out of here," Hawk snapped.

He preferred to face the attack he expected in the open rather than in the caged area of the shed. Pollock silently concurred. Mike stepped out into the storm.

He sensed the danger. His was not an imagination that inflated the eerie threat of a cemetery, but this was about as mean a night as he could remember.

Angry spears of lightning sizzled among the tall statuary on the knoll. Gusts of wind cast showers of spray from sodden, low-hanging willows. Ancient, gnarled wisteria vines bent and snapped; even the tombstones shuddered in the sporadic blasts.

The rumbling that underscored the storm was louder now—and closing in on them.

Mike knew the sound and its meaning.

Pollock laid a restraining hand on his arm.

The figures he saw were grotesque in the intermittent lightning. A meaty hand on the left. A black skull with sockets for the eyes and mouth to his right. A beefy bare arm with a tatooed gargoyle stretched across its muscular bicep.

A yard-long length of chain glistened in the storm's pyrotechnics. A tire iron waited at waist height no more than a dozen paces away. The invisible form wielding it was slapping the heavy end into the open palm of his left hand. There was a switchblade knife; a plumber's wrench moved in closer.

The weapons seemed to float in the sheets of rain.

A single powerful beam of light burst into the darkness, boring into Hawk's and Pollock's eyes. Momentarily they were blind.

The CIA man's hand slid toward his holster. Hawk stopped him with a touch.

Mike could guess who confronted them. They were bikers, an outlaw bunch, he guessed. He let his hunch go further. They idolized Whip McComb, he was willing to bet.

The stunt man had detested the few gangs that left bloody red stains on an otherwise decent sport, but he had no control over his fans.

The band's bizarre presence in the cemetery would be no coincidence. Undoubtedly they had been sent to stop any investigation before it went too far. No telling what the goons had been told, but their objective was clear enough: by whatever method, stop Michael Hawk.

On a hunch he walked directly toward the light. It was possible his idea might be more successful in getting him and the CIA man out with recognizable faces than would the one operating gun they had between them.

"All right," he said as he took a pace. "I know why you came here." He spoke directly to an unseen man behind the light.

The engine growled louder; others joined in the chorus. It was supposed to frighten Hawk.

Mike stopped. "You admired Whip McComb. So did I."

He took another step.

The engines roared. A few bikes started closing in. The chain made slow swishing circles. The tire iron rose.

The figures became more visible. Most of the bikes were choppers; their wheels were stretched in the machine equivalent of a swagger. But the customized bikes were crude, far removed from the magnificent creations of true lovers of the sport.

Even the engines were poorly maintained. They idled with a ragged sputtering that required frequent throttling to keep them alive.

This gang was a bunch of goons.

He could see some of them. God, they were ugly. In silhouette, one was a Quasimoto hunchback, but the tire chain dangling from a disfigured arm discouraged sympathy. Another looked like a robust transvestite, with hairy legs extending from tight, white shorts. One twisted face must have survived some terrible accident. It was permanently constricted in the deep shiny scar tissue that burns create. The eyes were slits in a misshapen mask.

A flash of light illuminated the torso of a rider whose open vest revealed a giant tarantula tattoed or painted on the hairless flesh.

"You want me to stop investigating," he said loud enough to overpower the storm and engines.

The misfits on the bikes muttered unintelligibly.

"Mike, no farther," Pollock whispered. "They'll beat us to death."

Hawk ignored him.

"You're afraid I'll find out that Whip McComb was a drug addict?" he said aloud.

A voice, thick and guttural, spoke from behind the light. "You'll ruin him like they tried to do with Elvis Presley," it said.

The growls grew louder. The engines snarled. The shapes moved closer.

"That's not what I want to know," Hawk shouted. "I want to know who killed him. So do you."

The suggestion of murder had the desired effect. Engines throttled back.

"Yeah, your friend, my friend, was murdered."

The extension of the silence proved what he had suspected. The cyclists were not out to cover up a killing. Under their own code of honor, they had come to protect Whip's image. But for them success would be measured in blood, a human sacrifice to a dead hero.

"No," the leader shouted. "He lies."

In the darkness under their riders' hands, the bikes were like living animals. They growled and strained at the leash, attack dogs, thirsty for blood. They eased in, shrinking the circle, ready to leap.

"Get a bike," Hawk yelled at Pollock.

It was the only tip he could give his associate. Having yelled, he leaped straight forward and over the blinding headlight. His legs skinned the handlebars and the instruments, but his momentum carried him forward against a block of solid, muscular flesh. The bike and the two men crashed to the wet paved road.

Bedlam broke loose. The headlights of a dozen bikes came on, glaring in the driving rain. Hawk stared briefly into bloodshot eyes peering from a face covered with matted wet beard still flecked with bits of garbage and tobacco-juice stains.

"Who sent you?" he shouted as big hands dug into his throat.

He ignored the pain. Gagging, he dug his thumbs directly under his opponents eyeballs. He made a slight shifting movement that could pop the fleshy balls from their hollow insets.

The hands left his throat and tried to dislodge the torturous thumbs. The movement only increased the threat of blindness.

The leader shrieked like a wounded rabbit, forming two words in spite of the pain. He repeated them when the pressure continued.

"Yankee Horn. Yankee Horn."

Hawk's contemplation of the response was short-lived. He had no idea who had sent the assailants, but the dwarf was probably last on his list of suspects.

"Hawk!" Pollock cried. Mike looked up to see a tire iron swinging at his head.

Mike jerked his thumb from the eyes, fell aside, and took part of the blow on his shoulder. The iron glanced off and smacked the gang's leader a stunning blow on the forehead. The attacker, a bear in a dirty fur coat, fell forward with his own blow. Mike's left-handed chop at the top of the spinal column left him stunned and paralyzed where he lay.

At the same time a chain swung from the other side, and Hawk allowed it to coil painfully around his arm in preference to letting it circle his neck. Yanking the chain loose, he used it to whip its owner across the kidneys.

Three down, but it was a fight he couldn't win. Escape was the only solution. He hoped Pollock had come to the same conclusion.

Kicking the inverted V between the legs of a shadow charging toward him with a knife, he won time to right the fallen chopper. The engine was still on and he kicked at the clutch even before he mounted. Knocking another form aside, he mounted with the bike moving, like a cowboy in the Saturday matinees he had loved as a kid.

The wheels bumped over a body; he hoped it wasn't Pollock. He didn't wait to check. He gunned the engine of the unfamiliar chopper and wobbled off across the graves and between the headstones.

A second bike pulled alongside.

Pollock shouted from the saddle, "It's me."

Behind them, a procession was forming. Headlights bathed the pair heading for the open gate. Rain stung their faces; wheels skated on the matted grass; low branches flailed their chests. Still they continued along a route between the aboveground crypts and out of the cemetery.

On the street their troubles did not end. They whisked to the nearest freeway to find it nearly deserted. Pushing the choppers to their maximum, they drove wildly in hope of attracting attention.

They succeeded only in arousing the ire of drivers already squeamish in the downpour. Accustomed to storms as they were, this one, sweeping up from the Gulf, a hundred miles south past Lake Salvador and Barataria Bay, was unusually violent.

Hawk swore through clenched teeth. "Damn. You never see a cop when you want one."

His complaint was tempered with mixed desires. He would welcome someone who could take the gang of goons off his tail, but he dreaded involvement with the authorities.

In desperation he took an off ramp from the freeway and turned into the narrow streets of Vieux Carré, the Old Square of New Orleans.

He headed for the heart of the French Quarter, hoping to find the famous tourist attraction filled with intrepid voyeurs. But the rain had taken its toll.

The area, with its historic Spanish and French Provincial architecture, was a chunk cut from history. Old apartment houses with louvered shutters and narrow balconies were packed together with common walls. Intricate wrought-iron fences, some with cornstalk designs in the uprights, marched along the sidewalks. Streetlamps in the shape of gaslights broadcast blurry beams in the pelting rain. Grilled gates provided views into open gardens and tree-shaded restaurants behind the buildings' facades.

But it was not the gourmet meals of the famous Antoine's restaurant or the atmosphere of the old Absinthe House, patronized centuries before by the pirate Jean Laffite, that the two hunted men sought. They wanted the sleazy, raucous ambience of Bourbon Street.

In particular Mike aimed for the blocks that were cordoned off to vehicular traffic after dark when pedestrians usually swarmed curb to curb after overflowing the sidewalks.

Skidding into a sliding turn, he ducked and let the chopper's front wheel crash through the wooden barricade.

"Aw, shit!" he groaned as Pollock's bike plowed up beside him.

The famous street was virtually deserted. Here and there girls in skimpy, tight skirts and low-cut blouses peered from massage parlors and doorways. Jazz music blared from half a dozen taverns, pouring out into the streets where thunder and splattering rain blended with bass and drums.

"Topless and Bottomless," declared a litany of signs. "French Style Entertainment." "Pleasure Palace . . . Your Satisfaction Is Our Pleasure." "Swedish and Oriental Massage." "Rent-a-Girl." "Fresh Popcorn." "Your Portrait Painted in 20 Minutes."

Although the attractions spanned an array of human cravings, the crowd had taken cover.

A bearded man in a suit made of colorful patches, like a homemade quilt, strummed a guitar beneath an awning; a black and white dog sat at his side, holding a cap by its brim. Man and dog waited for tips that would be scarce to nonexistent in the downpour. An organ grinder and his monkey huddled two doors away.

Farther along, T-shirt shops with suggested obscenities displayed for imprinting were empty; so too were the souvenir stores. The street bands were gone and only a few teen-agers stood beneath the swinging doors of a tavern advertising "Male-Female . . . Topless—Bottomless."

"Mike!" Pollock called behind him as they raced past a horse-drawn carriage. He continued to yell, the words lost in the rumble of their pursuers.

The gang was about to turn onto Bourbon Street.

Mike made a decision and went with it. He braked, throttled down some, swung off the bike, took a couple of steps alongside, and freed the machine. It scooted up the street, wobbling and smashing against the curb. He darted to the next male-female show, flung open the door, and bulled his way in. Pollock was directly behind him.

Atop the long, old-fashioned bar a boy in his late teens or early twenties was bumping and grinding to an old burlesque beat. A sparse audience of women and effeminate men cheered him on.

They stopped when Mike pulled the useless .38 Special from its holster and waved it menacingly. The arc of the muzzle took in the bartender and the male waiters wearing only jockstraps.

"Everybody keep calm," he ordered. "Go on with the show. We need a place to hide. Stay easy and nobody gets hurt."

He vaulted the bar and aimed the gun at the proprietor. The dancer started again, less sure of himself than before. A few of the voices from the audience verged on panic.

The sputtering of chopper engines poured in from outside.

A nervous crowd could easily tip off the bikers.

"Hide," Hawk yelled at the CIA man, but as Pollock started for the men's room, the audience rebelled.

"Take it off," one woman cried. "Take it off." The fear of guns gave way to good-natured ribbing of the government agent. "Dance. Come on, handsome."

The shouting jumbled the words; however, the message was clear. For a price the women in the crowd were willing to go along with the pair's need for a place to hide. They wanted the self-conscious Pollock to join the naked dancer on the bar.

"Strip!" Mike ordered.

"No way," George resisted.

"No choice," his associate told him. "Shag it, or those bikers will be running tailpipes up our asses."

"Damn you." Those were the last words Hawk heard before he stooped behind the bar. His gun pointed at the hefty man with the apron.

Approving screams filled the area of tables and chairs, and Pollock leaped to the bar top, assisted by middle-aged ladies whose sedate dresses belied their lusty natures.

Pollock was dancing. His suntanned legs, glistening with blond hair, were visible from behind the bar. He was trying to match the beat of the recorded music, while the naked boy bumped and ground his way nearer and nearer.

The audience turned ugly.

Its friendly disposition returned only when a pair of flowered boxer shorts dropped on top of the other clothes.

Seconds later Mike heard male voices, rough and crude. In his fertile imagination he visualized the scene. Expecting to terrorize the women while they searched the building, the bikers had come in looking for the two men who had escaped them in the cemetery. Instead the interruption unleashed the wrath of the audience; catcalls and the tinkle of breaking glass suggested the women would tolerate no intrusion on their entertainment.

Above Hawk, Pollock danced with his bare rear to the door: nakedness too was a disguise of sorts.

"You sonofabitch, you dirty sonofabitch," George hissed down at his choking friend.

In an effort to contain the laughter boiling up inside him, Mike clapped a hand tight across his mouth and held it there, his gut taut with swallowed mirth, until the bottles stopped flying and the ladies were happy again.

When the danger had passed, George jumped down and snatched up his clothes. The women sighed "Aw," in disappointment.

"Those hoods gone?" Mike asked.

"I swear, Hawk, I'm going to kill you. I'm going to chop you up for dog food. No! No self-respecting mongrel would touch you even if he was starving."

The tirade ended when a homosexual and two admiring matrons approached from around the bar to plant kisses on Pollock, who was still only partially clothed.

Darting his eyes around the room in search of an escape

route, Mike discovered an unexpected ally: a cigar box tucked behind a row of liquor bottles under the counter. As he reached for it, the bartender lunged, then pulled up short when Mike waved the barrel of the .38 at him.

Lifting the box lid far enough to raise the first layer of cigars, Mike uncovered a fruit salad of pills, capsules, and a few crude cigarettes. They were the leverage he needed.

"You forget I came in here with a gun and I'll forget I saw that shit. Okay?"

The bartender nodded.

On impulse Mike pulled a stack of bills from the roll in his pocket and spread it on the mahogany bar top. "Drinks on the house," he said, "for the ladies, the gays, and the two ways."

The crowd applauded as Mike and Pollock moved to the door and peered into the rain. The bikers were parked outside a discotheque down the street.

From the distance came the too-familiar paean of police sirens, a frequent overture to Michael Hawk's departures. He had spent a good number of his days and nights making hasty exits ahead of the arriving officials.

He crossed the street casually, climbed into a horsedrawn carriage with a red canvas top, and motioned to the liveried driver huddled on the front seat.

"Hey." Pollock was climbing aboard. "Where are we going?"

"Me?" Mike placed a hand across his upper chest. "I'm going to bed." He gave the name of his hotel to the driver and then turned back to Pollock. "You were beautiful up there, Georgy Girl. If the government cuts back, you've found yourself a whole new career. The least you could do is thank me for opening new horizons. Think of it. 'Georgy Pollock—Nude Disco Champion of the World!' In bright pink lights . . ."

"Fuck you."

"No, thanks, sweetheart. Like the song says, I do it my way."

# 13

The hotel was three stories high, fronted with balconies—exquisite wrought-iron lacework of white enamel acorns and oak leaves. Twin lamps glowed on either side of the entrance.

Mike checked his watch. For ten minutes he had watched the place from the opposite side of the street. Nothing seemed amiss; he crossed the street and entered.

He was cautious walking past the night clerk and he took the service stairs to his floor instead of the open-grilled elevator. The bikers might know where he was staying. Jinx could have awakened and called her stepmother; the girl would make no secret of where they were.

Reaching his room without incident, he went inside, pausing in the dark by the door until he was confident he was alone. Then he crossed to the connecting door and unlocked it.

Inside, Jinx stirred in her sleep. He closed the door again, switched on a light, and turned to survey his luxurious surroundings: gold and white French Provincial furnishings, white silk brocade on the giant bed repeated at the swagged windows and on the paneled walls; creamy deep plush underfoot. On the valet near the bathroom were the results of Pollock's long-distance shopping—a suit, shirts, shoes, and a new leather bag on the bench. Never had a wardrobe been so welcome; the filthy, sodden clothes he wore were distinctly uncomfortable and completely out of place at Le Richelieu.

The hot shower stinging in the cuts and scrapes on his

limbs and body made him feel good. He was alive—gratefully so.

Minutes later he had turned out the light and was ready to slip naked into bed when Jinx spoke softly from beyond the adjoining door. The knob turned tentatively.

"Uncle Mike . . . Mike, are you all right? I've been so worried. Can I come in?"

He dived for the robe he'd thrown over the chair, pulling it on as he spoke.

"Be right there." He pulled the door open for her. Haloed in the dim light from the streets, she was something a man might fantasize standing in his doorway. The sleep-tousled hair; the slender shapely body silhouetted in something diaphanous and white; the long tapering legs below the short gown.

God, did she know what she looked like, what she could do to a man? Yeah, she knew; women did.

"Hi, little one," he said, leading her to the Louis XIV loveseat. He flicked on the table lamp behind it. "How goes it?"

"What happened to you?" she asked. "You were gone so long."

"Well . . . I had an . . . interesting evening. Did the town, in a manner of speaking. I'll have to tell you about it sometime. But how about you? You okay?"

She nodded. "Now that you're back. I don't like being alone." She looked down quickly.

"You're not alone, Jinx honey. I'm right here. Next-door neighbor," he said lightly. He laid a comforting arm across her shoulder. Keep it avuncular, he warned himself, even if it's an act.

Almost imperceptibly she settled closer, head against his arm.

"What am I going to do when you're gone, though?" she asked sadly.

"Can you go on with the show?"

"Yes, it will go on somehow. It's a corporation, sort of. Whip was president because he could figure stunts the others couldn't."

"The others?"

"Husky Blackwell, Noon, and I."

"You're a stockholder?"

"Yes, but I might lose control. Husky and Noon are almost

as good as Dad. Husky just about killed himself once trying to jump farther than Whip."

"Then you think Husky will gain control?"

"Unless Noon tries to beat him. Or I do it, or maybe I could hire someone better. It's all down on paper. There's a contract." She read Hawk's quizzical expression and continued, almost defensively. "I suppose it sounds a little crazy, but a contest is the only way really. Otherwise the best rider would leave and start his own show anyway. There aren't enough cycle buffs to support two competing shows as big as Whip's."

"You could hire someone to take Whip's place and still retain control? Where would you get someone like that?"

"It wouldn't be too difficult. Dad was an engineer. He had everything figured in his black book. The angle and length of the launching ramp, the distance, the speed, everything for each stunt. I jumped as far as he could once. There weren't any of those hideous spikes beneath me, of course, and I was padded. He had jumps planned he had never used. He figured out how to leap ravines, rivers, all sorts of places around the country. He used some of them for special events and to drum up business for the show."

"They weren't calculated using his customized bike, his weight, were they?"

"No problem," she said. "There are two clones identical to his, just in case his broke down. The weight you can adjust in the saddlebags."

"He wasn't going to attempt the Grand Canyon using jet propulsion, was he?"

She smiled. "No. He did all his stunts on a regular bike—customized, but no jets or wings or parachutes." She sighed and for a while she was quiet. "I'll lose control in two weeks," she said finally.

"That soon?"

"Husky will challenge me when we get to California. I know he will."

"And your stepmother?"

"Maybe. One of them will set up a leap. Then it's follow the leader. If I don't try or if I fail . . . then it's his . . . or hers. I hope one of them doesn't die trying. It'll have to be something rather spectacular. You saw . . . they both made the jump Whip had been using as the high point of the show

111

lately. One of them will have to do something terribly dangerous."

"Control of the show is worth risking a life for?"

"It's not just the gate-receipts. There's the tie-ins. The product endorsements, the advertising commercials. I'll lose a fortune there."

"You think you could take your father's place?"

"In time. I would have eventually. But Dad would have been alive to help me take on the challengers. His book contains leaps that no one else knows how to make. If I were in shape . . ."

"Your shape looks great to me," he kidded.

She smiled. "You know what I mean. If I had two months to exercise . . ."

"But you don't have two months," her reminded her unnecessarily.

She sighed again. "No, I suppose I'll try to save the show anyway."

She sat away from him and looked into his eyes. She was so hurt, so vulnerable, he wanted to gather her into his arms, to comfort her. But to do so, he knew, would be to risk adding to the hurt later. He waited.

"Do you think one of them could have . . ." She left the sentence for Mike to finish.

". . . killed your dad? If there's money involved—enough of it—sure."

"Oh, God," she whispered. "I can't bear to think either of them will profit by killing Dad. An accident is bad enough. I mean, Whip was getting reckless. He'd have killed himself sooner or later. He even started training me to take his place. He didn't want to at first, but I insisted. He said I could have his black book. I've been studying it. I knew Dad was going to get hurt . . . bad . . . or killed. That's why I wrote you."

The drugs, Mike thought. The drugs must have been ruining the man's reflexes.

"Which explains why someone worked so hard to keep me from getting a chance to talk to Whip," Mike mused.

"What?" she said.

He made no effort to explain about the running battle on St. Lucia. The fewer people who knew the better.

What she had told him, however, did explain the attack on the island. Murder wasn't the original plan, in all likelihood.

Given time, Whip McComb would have done himself in. If Hawk had arrived earlier, he might have talked his old friend into semiretirement. McComb could have retained control by letting his daughter take his place.

"Mike, if Husky or Noon deliberately killed him . . ." Her voice trailed off. "Well, I'll have to fight them," she said at last. "I'll challenge them first. In California. I know a canyon Dad had all staked out for a spectacular leap. It's in the book. He never used it. I came across it the other day."

"A particularly dangerous jump?"

She settled back against his arm, as if to absorb part of his strength. "They won't dare to follow. There are only two ways across, along an entire mile of desert. All the speed they can get out of a bike won't carry them the distance."

"They'll just follow your lead."

He felt her shake her head. "I issue the challenge, I set up the rules. I'll stake out a hundred yards and make them pick their own crossing points. We all have to leap at the same time. They will never make it."

"You'd let them die?"

"Of course not. They won't try. And they won't be able to challenge me for two years. That's in the contract too . . . if I make it."

"Shit!" Mike muttered.

"What's wrong?" she asked, sitting up straight.

"You're not going to make that jump. There's no way I can let Whip's kid take that chance. I'll do it."

"You? Oh, I couldn't let you do that! You're no stunt rider."

"Your dad taught me enough. I've got two weeks to brush up, right?"

"Yes, but . . ."

"Then issue your challenge tomorrow." So here we go again, he thought, committed to something potentially self-destructive. Tomorrow, when this long, stormy night was over and the soothing light of day brought reality into focus, he would curse himself for the damned fool he was. But now, with Whip McComb's lovely daughter relaxed, almost asleep, against him, what could he do? In a way her dad was back; the responsibility had been lifted from her slender shoulders.

Despite the consequences Michael Hawk would make the jump. The decision came less out of valor than helplessness.

What else could he do? he asked himself again. He had already failed Whip. If he had arrived a day earlier, the star of the stunt riders might be alive. Could he let McComb's daughter down too?

His pain-in-the-ass, self-imposed code of ethics demanded he take the girl's place, even though she was more experienced in riding than he was.

He could only hope she was right about the jump. Maybe the leap over the gorge in California didn't require an expert. Whip McComb always attacked his stunts as engineering problems.

"Doesn't matter who's in the saddle," Whip had said once. "If they follow the formula and watch their instruments, practically anybody can duplicate what I do. Of course, an amateur might get pretty well messed up when he comes down, but there's nothing much to do in the air except to keep the bike from tilting."

Hell, Mike thought. He had money and a good life ahead. He didn't want to be messed up—or wind up a cripple. But he looked down at Whip McComb's daughter, her head cradled in the curve of his arm. She was sleeping, her firm, lovely breasts rising and falling in slow, regular rhythm. She trusted him, depended on him . . .

A wry smile pulled at his lips. Life is a crock, Michael Hawk philosophized. The gods, jealous reactionaries that they are, will not long tolerate contentment in their creation, man. If he loves his wife, they take her away; if he has money, they make him a fugitive; when he begins to enjoy his freedom, they give him responsibility, even if it belonged to another man.

Switching off the light, he sat for a while with the girl in his arms, his thoughts on Lisa, missing her more than he had in a long time.

Then he picked Jinx up, carried her to her bed, went back to his room, and closed the door.

He fell asleep at once, too tired to dream.

# 14

In the hotel's gift shop Hawk bought a roll of film, took it from its package, and stuffed it in his pocket. He grinned when he considered the leverage a couple of dollars had bought him.

Later, in a pawnshop, he asked the questions that would provide his most urgent need—a gun. He bought it in a witchcraft supply shop two blocks off Bourbon Street. Displays of tiny wax figures spiked with pins, bottles of blood-red potions, and brooms made of hand-tied stalks of grain concealed the gnarled old warlock who ran the place. Like some manifestation of wizardry, he appeared in front of a curtain on which a goat's face was superimposed on a circled star.

After the customary ritual during which the man persisted in his claims that he sold nothing more harmful than evil eyes and black cats, Hawk talked him into offering a "Baby Nambu." A 7 mm semiautomatic weighing less than a pound and a half, it kicked its bullets from beneath the Barleycorn front sights at a fair velocity. Unfortunately the shopkeeper had no shells except those in the detachable box magazine.

"Looks like I can't kill more than seven people," Hawk observed to the discomfort of the bearded proprietor. The holster fit on the inside of Hawk's ankle, its grip creating a telltale lump under his trouser leg when he walked. The gray slacks were a good choice with the expensive white sports jacket and the blue shirt that he wore open at the neck, but Pollock or the haberdasher had not taken the gun into account. Nevertheless the bulge on his leg was an accessory he would not be without.

He emerged on Chartres Street and strolled past the sidewalk artists displaying their wares around Jackson Square. Shaded by one of the block-long balconies on the old Pontalba apartment buildings, George Pollock tossed the last of the popcorn he had been feeding the pigeons and fell into step behind Hawk.

To the casual observer they would have appeared strangers. Mike seemed interested only in the line of people waiting to enter Brennan's, a spacious old home which had been converted into a restaurant and won renown for its lavish breakfasts.

"Where's the girl?" the CIA man asked.

"She took our things to the Superdome," Mike answered. He switched his attention to searching for a cab. "Did you find my bike at the cemetery?"

"I didn't look."

"Probably one of those freaks took it." Mike dismissed the loss without regret. The bike had not been registered in his name and the financial loss didn't matter. "I need some information," he continued. "A dwarf known as Yankee Horn, a stunt rider called Husky Blackwell, and McComb's widow. Maiden name Pu Noon, claims to be empress of China."

"I'm not your personal legman," Pollock objected.

"Get the information or I'll tell everybody you get your jollies dancing bare-assed for a bunch of horny old biddies." He hailed a slowing cab and spoke over his shoulder. "I'll be with the show. Keep in touch."

"Damn you, Hawk."

"Uh-uh, Georgy, mustn't ruin your image now that you're a star." He waited until his friend took a step off the curb. "Oh, Georgy Girl, one other thing."

"What now?"

"You think I could scare a confession out of somebody?"

"For murder, no." Pollock considered the question. "You could try drugs. How soon do you need them?"

Hawk shook his head. "Too heavy-handed. I'd have to kidnap them."

"Two of them?"

"Three actually."

"You have a hunch."

"Yeah. Probably couldn't get all three of them together at once. They'd have the law on me fast."

"Can't scare a killer into a confession," Pollock insisted. "Unless, possibly, you really took him by surprise."

"At some tense moment. Right? I mean really tense. If he were on the verge . . . backed into a corner."

"It could work, I suppose. What do you have in mind?"

"I'm not sure yet. But do me a favor, will you?"

"What this time?"

"Go out to the cemetery. There's a bike in the shed."

"I saw it."

"Look for a beveled plate slightly larger than the one on the front wheel. The speedometer plate drive gear, I think it's called. Look in the trash."

"In the trash?"

"Where would you toss a piece of evidence if you were almost caught with it in your hands?"

"Any fingerprints? Any way to tie it to me?"

"No."

"I'd throw it in the trash."

Hawk slapped him on the back. "Good thinking. You'll go far. See you later."

"Hey!" Pollock called. "What if somebody catches me?"

"Tell 'em you're looking for your best friend."

"In a trash can?"

"For you, where else?"

He rode through a sparkling, rain-washed morning to the paved desert of parking space surrounding the indoor stadium. The imposing structure had been built in the shape of a puffball mushroom, except that the stem was nearly as broad as the cap.

Inside, hammers echoed through the hollow chamber; crews were tearing down ramps and props. On the playing field, Billy, the skinny kid with the waxen face, was riding bikes up a board into the van of a truck.

When he saw Hawk, the boy's foolish grin soured; he was a deer in the woods, puzzling over whether to run or freeze before an approaching hunter.

"The show moving out?" Hawk asked.

The boy's eyes flip-flopped like unsteady windshield wipers. He seemed unsure of the reason he was loading the motorcycles for transport.

"Huh?" he managed finally.

Hawk smiled. "Never mind, Billy. You're rather important around here, aren't you?"

"Me?"

"You take care of the bikes, right?"

"Yeah, I guess so." The voice was a flat monotone, the words thick-tongued and slow.

"Check the fuel tanks, the oil, that sort of thing."

Billy's eyes brightened. "Yeah."

"Whip McComb's bike too?"

The lower jaw slackened and the eyes focused somewhere off to the left. "He's dead, I think." His limited memory was working to the maximum.

"You checked over his bike for him the day he died."

The boy's brow creased. "I guess so." He straightened, indignant. "I always do. I fix things. I do like I'm told. I ain't so dumb."

"Of course you're not. But who told you to check the bikes that night? Whip?"

"Naw, he done his own checking . . . in the mornings. Yeah, in the morning."

"But you worked on it later."

"Did I? Yeah, sure I did. I took good care of Mr. McComb's bikes."

"Who told you to work on it that night? Husky Blackwell?"

The youth blinked, the eyelids working deliberately. "I don't know."

"What did he have you do? Some repairs?"

"Yeah. I repair things."

"What did you repair on Whip's bike."

The frown returned. "I don't know." He turned and headed for his van, Hawk close behind. "How about a cup of coffee, Billy? I'd like to see your place. Can I come in?"

"No! You stay away, you hear? Stay out of my van. Mr. Horn! Mr. Horn!"

"Got a question, Mr. Hawk?" Yankee strolled around the truck. The interruption was all the boy needed; he opened the door of his van and popped inside. Immediately the faded curtains slid closer across the side windows. "Don't bother Billy. You'll confuse him."

"You, you bastard," Mike snapped. "You sent those wacko bikers after me. If you weren't such a little sonofabitch, I'd kick you in the balls."

"Go ahead. I don't ask any favors on account of my size. Whip McComb taught me that." The little man lifted his pudgy fists, ready to defend himself. "And I don't apologize for trying to keep you from nosing around."

"Investigating Whip's death, you mean?"

The fists lowered. "What did you expect to find? That somebody killed Whip?"

"Maybe."

"You wouldn't find that. He killed himself."

"The drugs, you mean."

"Yes, the drugs. You want his daughter to know her old man couldn't swing a leg over a saddle for a ride to the grocery store anymore unless he had his fix? That's why he didn't give the crowd the big buildup like he used to. That's why Billy checked the instruments. Whip couldn't stay upright for more than a few minutes at a time."

"You're saying he was an addict."

"Not like you mean. McComb had cracked up so often his body was a junk heap of pain. He took anything to ease the agony, but he didn't want Jinx to know."

"The rest of you knew?"

"Yes. We knew he was dying. He asked us to keep it from his daughter."

"Somebody killed him," Mike said flatly.

"Murder? Why would anybody bother? He was half dead anyway."

"What about Billy?"

"Oh, come on, the kid wouldn't hurt Whip. He does what he's told."

Mike nodded. "Then why did he go wild when I wanted a cup of coffee?"

"He collects things."

"Like what?"

"How should I know? Nobody gets in there. I just know he collects things."

"Things about Jinx?"

"Who said it's a girl?"

Hawk weighed the question before he asked another. "How long before McComb would have had Jinx ready to take his place?"

The dwarf cocked his oversized head to one side. "She's been in college. She needs to rebuild her strength is all."

Long enough for the girl to lose control of the show, Mike thought.

He changed the subject. "You're moving, I take it."

"Got kicked out by the Superdome management. Court order. We have to be in California soon anyway. Saddleback. Do you know that area?"

Mike nodded, his interest elsewhere—on the couple he saw standing outside Whip McComb's motor home. He walked toward them, but Husky Blackwell, his dark brows drawn together in anger, strode away. Noon McComb, however, waited, almond eyes glinting. In the look was a sensuality unbecoming a widow.

"Mr. Hawk." She greeted him with a Midwestern accent.

He used what Cantonese he knew. *"Jo sun,* Empress."

*"Dor jeh,"* she smiled. "Call me Noon. The empress bit is good for show business, but the Communists had taken over before I was born. Won't you come in?"

She stepped ahead of him into the home's living room which included a long white leather couch and a matched pair of recliners. Wearing jeans and a plain white blouse tied at the front to reveal a slender bare midriff, she was as appealing as her stepdaughter. She poured two cups of tea and handed one to Mike before settling on the couch and metioning him to a chair.

"You'll be leaving us now?" she asked.

He said "No," without offering any explanation.

"Oh." There was a mixture of both pleasure and its opposite in her expression. Teacup in hand, she leaned back on the expensive bleached leather, staring thoughtfully into space. "This is the end of an era, Mr. Hawk," she said sadly. "My husband was a very dynamic man, as you know. I am not sure where we will go without him." She seemed to want to talk.

"I'd like to hear about you and him," Mike encouraged gently.

She had been fascinated with him from the beginning, she

remembered. He was a gentle man, totally lacking in fear, much like her stoic father had been. "I was into motocross then," she said. Whip had trained her in stunt work, then married her. She became a part of the show immediately, finding the excitement of performing much preferable to the predictability of teaching.

"It scandalized my family," she smiled again. "Most of them escaped the Communists, although I have a very old Uncle Jie who returned to China after the war. Believe it or not, he lives there now quite comfortably in a sixteen-room house. A cousin of mine visited him in Peking. Armies of blue-clad bicyclists were riding past the old house. Sand and bricks were scattered about in front. Next door a grocer was piling up vegetables and across the street a fast-food stand had customers lined up for noodles and steamed buns. But Jie is the oldest male of the Manchu clan that ruled China as the Ching dynasty, beginning in the mid-1700s. Now he's a drop of water in a vast ocean of peasants. I digress—but it is fascinating, isn't it?"

And so are you, Mike thought, but he didn't say it. Centuries of plutocracy flowed in her veins, diluted now by life in a twentieth-century democracy. How would that affect her thinking? he wondered.

"Yes, it is," he responded. "You might have ruled all China had events arranged themselves differently."

She shook her head. "Not unless my uncle's daughter were dead or didn't claim the throne. She lives in Japan, married to a factory worker." She set down her cup and straightened. "But that's not what you want to talk about, is it?"

He drained the last of the tea and looked over the rim into the compact kitchen, complete with food processor and a bowl of fresh fruit that stood like a three-dimensional still life against a backdrop of walnut paneling. Hovering in the doorway, eavesdropping, was Jinx McComb holding a pocket-size black notebook.

"No, it isn't." He set the teacup aside and shook his head when Noon moved to fill it again. "Actually I was wondering if I could see Whip's notebook?"

Noon pretended ignorance. "Notebook?"

"The one in which he kept the calculations for all his stunts."

"Really, Mr. Hawk . . ."

"Mike," he corrected.

"Michael, then. I'm afraid I don't know where it is, offhand. Even if I did . . ."

"I have it," Jinx said, entering the room and offering the notebook to Mike.

"Jinx!" Her stepmother frowned. "Do you think it's wise to give away all your father's calculations?"

"Mike's going to ride with us," Jinx answered defensively.

He took the book and thumbed the pages. There were numerous drawings and calculations. Although they were not immediately comprehensible, with time he would probably understand them. He tucked the book in his pocket and rose. "Is there some place I could make a call—a personal one?" he asked.

"My room," Jinx said quickly. "The phone will be connected for another hour while the men are loading equipment."

"And away we go to Saddleback," Mike said.

"Yes." Noon stood up, slender and rather tall in her high-heeled boots and sleek-fitting jeans. "Are you certain you want to go along, Michael? We're having difficulties with the show, you know. We have to do away with the spikes and come up with something equally dangerous. The people at Saddleback are as squeamish as the management of the Superdome. And we'll be performing outside, after dark."

"Got nothing else to do. Besides, I have a good story going here."

"Especially if someone else gets killed?" Noon asked cynically.

"Only if it isn't me," Hawk shrugged.

He strolled into the first bedroom, closing the door behind himself. Noon's voice was audible through the door.

"You gave away years of your father's work," an angry Noon McComb chastised her stepdaughter. Jinx responded, and the exchange continued in lowered voices as Hawk settled on the bed and studied the notebook's pages.

Each stunt was so carefully calculated—angle, speed, ramp length, and height, bike weight, compensating formula for various weather conditions, everything spelled out to the last detail—that Hawk could almost believe Whip's theory: an amateur could be programmed into championship jumping.

Despite the fact that he had done no serious stunts for several years, it was possible that he could follow Whip McComb's instructions with a couple of weeks practice.

He glanced through the proposed exhibitions, the plans that had been fermenting in his mind beginning to take shape. If, like Whip, he calculated right, it could work: even a cool, calculating killer could be tricked into a confession, not one that would hold up in court, perhaps, but proof enough to satisfy himself that he had the right man.

There was a chance he would have to be the only juror and the only judge; he hoped he wouldn't have to be the executioner as well.

Thumbing through the pages of the black book, he came upon a familiar name: the Jungfrau. It was a hill near Saddleback in southern California, forming a backdrop for the show ring where the McComb circus would be performing next.

Mike had been there before with the circus. The Jungfrau was a steep wall of earth streaked nearly to the top with the tracks of the bikers who had attempted to climb her the way they had conquered that other challenge of the hill-climbing crowd, the Matterhorn. Only top bikers beat the Matterhorn, but the Jungfrau had been taken by no one, at least not yet. Whip McComb's notebook suggested a path to the top, complete with every detail, including where to shift gears. A diagram of the hill, spotting outcroppings of rock and scraggly trees, listed the tachometer readings a bike like Whip's, carrying his exact weight, would have to show at each benchmark. It even indicated how and where the rider would have to move forward and back in the saddle to change the center of gravity.

Mike felt better than he had for days. He finally had an idea how he might lure his friend's killer into the open. He would use himself as bait, then goad the piranha who had killed Whip into swallowing the hook.

Still scanning the pages, he came upon a title that stopped him. "Devil's Jaw Ravine." A crude map showed where it was located, in the desert southeast of Los Angeles near Borrego, an area where the ground was bone dry and the temperature rose above a hundred and twenty on a summer day. It was rugged country, tough on a bike and tougher on a man.

Apparently the ravine was a barrier, a hopelessly wide slash through the desert wasteland. This had to be the jump Jinx had mentioned; she had said she would challenge Husky and Noon to a jump no one had ever made before. It was all laid out for him.

A drawing showed an approach through the rock and cactus-strewn desert, along with a formula and details necessary to make the leap.

A long ramp, at least ten feet tall, was required, in addition to a sixty-foot landing platform on the far side. Both were surprisingly narrow; otherwise they were not unlike the ones used in the show.

With no wind, the equation required a speed of ninety-eight point five miles per hour.

There were two possible launch points, each a pinhead-sized dot measured from several landmarks. Evidently Whip had found the ways to master the seemingly insurmountable obstacle. Logically he would have searched out sites where the gorge was narrow, perhaps with one side slightly higher than the other. Whip had designed a key to a challenge that no other rider had ever dared try.

On the next few pages were more notes. How to direct the traffic to the scene. Where to place the grandstands. Hints on how to scrape the desert bare for parking, and estimates of the financial take based on several possible advertising and promotion budgets.

The bottom line was a gold mine.

Why hadn't McComb attempted the ravine before? But there was no reading a dead man's mind.

Should he trust his old friend, though? The ravine was tempting. The leap, potentially deadly, was exactly what he needed for a clincher if he hoped to drive the killer into some incriminating act or admission.

It was a gamble.

He wasn't a fearful man, nor was he needlessly reckless. When a precaution occurred to him, he picked up the phone and called George Pollock's hotel room.

"Georgy Porgy, been auditioning yet?" he asked after Pollock picked up the receiver.

"Go to hell."

"No thanks. You'll be there sooner or later. I couldn't bear to watch you dancing naked up to your balls in fire. Have you been to the cemetery yet?"

"Have I been to the cemetery? I could have been arrested for vagrancy."

"You find anything in the trash?"

"No."

"Damn."

"The gardener found it."

"The speedometer drive gear?"

"Yes, I think your friend sailed it like a Frisbee."

"It's oversized?" Hawk asked. Blood surged in quickening thrusts through his veins. He was certain who had changed the gears. Billy. But the retarded boy wasn't a murderer. He did as he was told.

"Yes. You want the evidence, or do I turn it in to the police?" Pollock asked.

"Neither. Keep it with you."

"Why?"

"Because I might get killed if the wrong person thought I had it."

"And me?"

"Oh, well." Hawk dismissed the worry flippantly. "See you in California."

"Don't hang up," Pollock said. "I have a few tidbits for you. Husky Blackwell did a stretch for killing a man while he was riding in a cycle gang a few years ago."

"Murder one?"

"Yes. He was released early because of his age. That empress of yours . . ."

"Phony?"

"No. She's part of the Manchu clan. Her uncle still lives in China."

"I heard."

"Yeah, well, did you also hear she spends time in Japan occasionally?"

"So?"

"She had trouble getting her final U.S. citizenship papers."

"Why?"

"The Japanese thought she was tied in with the Red Army."

Mike whistled. "The terrorists?"

"Yes. It could explain how she got help in Venice and the Caribbean. These terrorists groups are loosely tied together. An Italian Communist might be willing to help her. Also she's engaged in litigation with the branch of her family who escaped from China to Taiwan with maybe twenty million dollars. If she can afford to keep the lawyers appealing, she stands a chance to come out a millionairess from that alone."

"How did you discover that?"

"The bureau keeps tabs on the pretenders of every throne. The flake in the White House has an Orwellian view of international politics. He's practically paranoid over the fear that one of the Pu family might use their wealth to stir up trouble in Red China when we need it to keep Russian troops tied up protecting Siberia."

"That 'flake' is a personal friend," Mike told him.

"Sorry."

"But the Red Army terrorists are Communists," Hawk said, rejecting Pollock's line of reasoning.

"They're Stalinists. They'd like to throw out China's present government. It's possible they might help Pu Noon in hopes she'll finance their crackpot schemes. But that's all conjecture."

"You think she's tied in with the Red Army?"

"No. Whoever runs Whip McComb's show will be rich enough, but the conjecture gives the agency a reason for me to help you."

"Hm."

The problem was Hawk was not certain he wanted Pollock in California. The guy got in the way occasionally. But this much was sure: he needed Pollock's connections now.

"Okay, we're headed for Saddleback Park outside Los Angeles. We'll be there the day after tomorrow. In the meantime I have some data for you to check. I want you to run two programs on your computers. One is on climbing the Jungfrau." Overriding Pollock's objections, he continued, "Wait until I finish. The second is a way—two ways actually—to leap Devil's Jaw ravine."

"You don't put problems like that through a government machine. They have to be programmed."

"I know, Georgy, and there's more involved than algebra. Surveyors have to map the terrain both at the Jungfrau and Devil's Jaw. Pay that with money from the Hong Kong

Traders account too. Have them survey every inch."

"I can't do that."

"What if I told you one of the ladies took pictures last night?"

Pollock squealed. "They didn't!"

"Cost me two hundred dollars for the film. I could get it developed and prints made. You can tack them on bulletin boards all over Washington. You'll be mobbed with women."

"I don't believe you."

"All right, I'll have the film developed and one print made for proof."

"No! Give me the raw film, Hawk. I saved your life, remember?"

"Sure, buddy, at Devil's Jaw ravine. After I make the jump, I'll have the film on me."

"Hawk, you idiot. If you crash, the police will go through your pockets. They'll . . ."

"So be sure I don't crash."

He began to dictate, reading the formulas and describing the maps. It took more than an hour. There were men waiting outside to disconnect the telephone when he finally hung up and sat back to examine the black book again.

Once more a detail caught his attention. The speed for the jump over the bed of nails was shown as eighty-three miles per hour, not the eighty-five everyone seemed to think McComb used for the performance. Why the discrepancy? Hawk wondered. Not that it mattered. The leap at two miles per hour faster would push the landing point ahead about a foot or more. It would make the show slightly less dangerous, slightly less thrilling for the sanguinary crowd.

Something else about the page bothered him: there was an unexplained date at the bottom, perhaps scribbled on as an afterthought.

April. The day and year were not indicated.

He flipped a few more pages. Most had a month written in. No day, no year.

On an otherwise blank page he found a formula: $S + \frac{1}{2} M = RS$.

S meant speed, he thought. M might mean month. But how did you cut a month in half? And what did a month have to do with motorcycling?

Still thumbing through the pages, he noticed the lightly

penciled-in dates on the plans for Devil's Jaw ravine. One was dated "Wednesday, December 28," and the other "Easter, October 30." Easter in October? Whip must have been stoned the day he wrote that. What did that suggest about the accuracy of the other instructions in the book? Was it something you'd want to risk your life on?

He was still lying on the bed, puzzling over the formulas, when the bedroom door opened. Noon McComb entered on lotus-blossom feet, as if afraid to awaken him.

*"Doy um geeh,"* she said.

"It's all right, come in." She sat on the edge of the bed and studied him.

"I want you to know that I am pleased you're going with us—that my concern was for your safety," she said, smiling.

"And you're very . . . how do you say it? *Ho ian?*"

She nodded appreciation of the compliment. *"Dor jeh."*

When he sat up, ready to leave, she laid a restraining hand on his leg—at just the right distance above the knee to make it interesting, he thought, glancing down at the carefully manicured nails—and switched to English.

"I hope you didn't misunderstand my misgivings about Jinx giving the notebook to you. Whip was secretive about it. I never was allowed to see it myself. I hope you were not offended."

He shook his head. "Not at all."

She smiled up at him.

Hell, he thought, he was getting the old female come on. She wasn't even subtle.

"Where's Jinx?" he asked.

"At the airport." Was there a deliberate tinge of Oriental mystique in her tone? "She's flying to California with Yankee to do some advance work."

"Did she challenge you before she left?" he asked.

"You know about that?"

"Yes."

"Silly child. Devil's Jaw is madness. And neither Husky nor I, I think, would have tried to control the show. We could have been equal partners."

"But you accepted the challenge?"

"Tentatively, yes. But I'm sure she'll change her mind. She's not ready for that—physically or mentally."

"I'll jump for her," he said.

"Oh!"

Mike sat up straighter, the motion pulling his trousers tight over the bulge at his ankle. She noticed; her surprise was natural enough.

"A gun?"

There was no denying it. "Yes."

"Why?"

What was an acceptable answer? The truth? "Because I think Whip was murdered."

She glanced sharply at him; her response was surprising. "Then Jinx and I aren't alone."

"You don't think it was an accident either?"

"No. Whip had made that jump a hundred times. Husky and I had practiced it ourselves as stand-ins. It wasn't that difficult."

"You fell short too," he reminded her.

"True. Could somebody have moved the ramps?"

The conversation ended abruptly when the powerful engine of the motor home rumbled to life. Hawk felt the big home on wheels begin to move.

Noon was not surprised. "You're riding to California with me!" she laughed. "We have a driver, as you can see."

"Oh!" He closed his mouth and pulled his eyebrows down in to place.

"You don't object? Being with me for a couple of days and nights?"

"With the bereaved widow?" he deadpanned.

She stood and went to the mirror. Brushing the long, black hair free of her neck, she eyed him in the mirror and said matter-of-factly, "I'm not a hypocrite, Michael. I loved Whip, but he ceased to be a man better than a year ago."

"The drugs?"

"Yes. But please don't tell Jinx. It's hard enough losing your entire family without knowing your father's courage was shot into his veins with a hypodermic needle or swallowed as a pill. She idolized him as I did. Once. Toward the end, though . . ."

"You lost respect for him," Mike suggested.

"In the end I realized Whip McComb died months ago. He had become a hypothecary jar with a devil's brew of potions scrambled together inside his head."

"You didn't pity him?"

"Yes. But as I say, he died months ago. Ceased being a man long before that. And I'm still a woman, a young woman."

Hawk watched her, wondering if she really wanted more from him than the black notebook.

He could guess the price she was willing to pay for its contents, the formulas that could make her a star in her own right. To her the book was worth millions. That put her far above the two-hundred-dollar-a-night call-girl class. It also made her dangerous.

## 15

The motor home eased through the performers' gate of the old Saddleback raceway near Los Angeles, lumbered to the parking area set inside the fencing, and braked to a stop in a row of trucks, vans, and campers.

Wearing his jump suit, Mike stepped into warm California sun filtered through a thin veil of smog. He was amazed at the activity. Painters were changing signs on the vehicle exteriors and unfurling new banners to extend over the entrance. "The World's Greatest Motorcycle Circus," everything read. Whip was being painted out of existence, and three names of equal billing were taking his place. "Starring: Husky Blackwell, Pu Noon, and Jinx McComb."

In a few weeks they would be repainting again. As soon as one gained supremacy over the others or did them in, the losers would be brushed away just as Whip had been written off the original advertising.

The thought provoked Hawk. He detested the idea that somebody was mimicking his friend, stealing the products of Whip's brain, as well as his life; Whip deserved better than that, Hawk told himself as he strode toward the activity in front of the stands.

Noon McComb remained asleep in the motor home. He had given her reason to sleep during the trip from New Orleans. Engrossing though it was, the act had not satisfied him.

Subconsciously he was looking for Jinx, as he watched the

men building the launching ramp and the landing platform across the track from the wooden bleachers. Performers, drivers, and local workmen were building other props and testing the lights on tall steel standards.

Yankee Horn was directing work inside the track. No chromium spikes were being installed between the two wooden platforms. Instead white plywood flooring had been laid flush with the ground. Foot-tall walls of glass were installed down either side, forming what looked like a sandbox more than a hundred feet long.

Hawk wondered what the gigantic box was for. Whatever it was, the glass siding showed they wanted the audience to see it easily. It had to be dangerous, something no one would care to fall into, any more than Whip had wanted to drop into the bed of nails. He would ask Yankee, Mike decided.

To the east of the track, at the base of a steep hill, wooden steps and bleachers had been constructed. The upper area of the hill had been left in its natural state. That part of the hardpan earth and jutting rocks was gashed with rough parallel cuts worn deep by the spinning wheels of the cyclists who attempted to climb it every weekend.

The higher he looked, the shallower the cuts. Twenty-five feet from the top, the last tread mark stopped.

It was the Jungfrau, a challenge that had yet to be beaten.

Whip McComb, though, had figured a technique to conquer it. Mike had the notebook in his pocket although he had copied the formulas and diagrams for the stunts that interested him most.

He had not allowed Noon to see the book.

He had borrowed it from Jinx, and it was to her he would return it.

Still thinking about the girl, he saw her on the track. Tomboyish and slim in beige coveralls, she mounted one of the clones to her father's favorite cycle.

She was pulling on white gloves when he approached her.

"Hi," he said.

Helmet in her hands, she twisted and looked at him. There was no welcoming smile. Her eyes showed more hurt than angry.

"Go away," she said. "And give me my father's notebook." She snatched it from his breast pocket and dropped it down the neck of her own suit. She shook the front of the tough gabardine until the notebook made its way to the belted, narrow waist.

"Wait!" he demanded.

She drew the helmet down over her head and meant to shut him out by drawing the full-faced visor into place.

He caught her wrist tight in his fingers. "What's this all about?"

"You let me go ahead by plane alone so you could be with her."

"Noon?"

"You wanted to be alone with her on the ride out here."

"Will you wait a minute?"

She twisted loose and started the engine. "You probably showed her the book too. I forgot it until I was on the plane."

"I didn't show it to anybody," he objected. "I didn't ask you to take the plane. Riding out with Noon was her idea. I thought it was the way you wanted it."

"You were supposed to meet me at the airport." He could see the tears start. "You never came," she cried, turning away.

"How was I supposed to know? Noon didn't mention my flying with you." He recognized and regretted the pain he had caused her.

"I don't know who to believe," she said. "There isn't anybody I can trust."

"Jinx, I . . ."

She didn't wait to hear more. The powerful engine sprang into action, and the visor came down. Releasing the clutch, she roared away from him, the wheels spitting fine bits of dirt into his face.

"I wish you were smaller, you sonofabitch," Yankee snarled. "I'd beat the crap out of you."

Hawk looked down. "Not you too."

"You fuckwad, you not only dumped the kid for that whore Whip married, but you probably showed her everything Whip took a lifetime to develop."

"The hell I did."

Jinx had rounded the far turn and was speeding along the straightaway.

"McComb wanted the show to go to his kid," the dwarf was saying. "It was the only inheritance he could leave her."

Mike stepped around the dwarf and watched Jinx bank into

the last turn. The bike leaned almost to its right foot peg, yet she did not extend a leg to aid with her balance. She was good, better than he expected. Although the bike was tipped at less than a forty-five-degree angle to the ground, she was getting no skid from the tires.

"What's she doing?" Hawk asked.

"Going for the jump. She needs the practice. We put on our first performance in two days."

The clone was streaking forward in front of the stands, and the men around the platforms had stepped aside.

"She's going a helluva lot faster than her father," Mike observed.

"Ninety-three mph. The jump's longer than what we had in New Orleans. We figured we'd have to outdo ourselves to drag in the best crowd without Whip."

"How far?"

"A hundred and thirty feet. She'll make it. Noon and Husky have done it in practice themselves. Whip had it all plotted out for their bikes as well as his own. It's how she'll come down that worries me."

Mike was tempted to stop her, but the dwarf objected.

"Let her go, Hawk. She needs the practice."

The bike reached the launching ramp with the girl surprisingly upright in the saddle, leaning slightly backward to bring up the front. It climbed the painted wooden planks and launched itself off the end.

She was amazingly graceful. The wheels were steady; the bike didn't tilt an inch, and before the rear end touched down, she thrust her upper body forward to lower the front end as quickly as possible.

She hit with a thud, ran a few feet on the rear wheel alone, and then let the other touch lightly.

"Like a kiss on the cheek!" Yankee exulted.

It was a perfect jump. Some of the workers had begun to applaud when the front wheel started to wobble. She lost control too quickly for Mike to follow with his eyes, but he was sure the wheel fluttered in spite of her firm grip on the bars. Then the rear end was trying to catch up with the front end and she went into an uncontrollable sideways skid down the inclined platform.

Momentum flung her off like a rock from a slingshot. She folded her arms and legs for the roll, but when she hit the dirt, the bike caught up with her. It smashed her foot hard.

She rolled and skidded across the track, coming to a stop on her back, the helmet twisted as if her neck were broken. Her arms were outstretched, her legs tangled like the start of a pretzel.

Workers ran for her. A cry went up. "Ambulance, get the ambulance."

The cry was relayed the way a bucket brigade passes forward the water.

Mike vaulted the railing and reached her before the show people could encircle her.

Husky Blackwell and the retarded boy Billy were there.

The kid tried to rip off the helmet. Mike pushed him aside. Kneeling, Hawk raised the visor without moving the girl's head.

She stared at him with wet eyes. "Oh, God, Mike, it hurts."

"Where?"

"All over. My ankle. Oh, no! It isn't broken? Tell me it isn't."

He had only to glance at the way her boot was twisted to come up with a fairly sound guess.

"You'll have to go to the hospital. How's your neck?"

"It's all right. Take off the helmet, please?"

"No, let the doctor do that."

"My chest, Mike. Ribs, I think."

He unzipped the front of her outfit. There was no sign of blood on the white blouse, but the stiff covers of her father's notebook were bent back. The fall might have broken several of her ribs.

A hairy, masculine hand reached for the notebook. Hawk's fingers encircled Husky Blackwell's wrist like a rat trap.

Husky Blackwell glowered at him.

"I don't think so," Mike growled.

"Fuck off," the answer came back.

Mike twisted the wrist and watched the other man grimace. Blackwell tried to use his left hand to free himself, but Hawk's grip held until the notebook was deep in his pocket.

The duel of wills ended, but not before the glowing coals of hatred between the two men had been ignited.

Then the aid men were pushing through the crowd with their stretcher. They gently, expertly lifted the girl onto the white canvas slung between the two long poles.

"Mike, I can't go to the hospital," Jinx cried. "The show! I'll lose the show!"

"You just hired yourself a stand-in," he whispered. "Don't worry."

"You? No, Mike. You'll kill yourself. Mike?"

They had the rear doors of the van open and were sliding her in. When it rolled through the exit, Mike saw the sign, the paint still fresh, emblazoned across the side.

"AMBULANCE. World's Greatest Motorcycle Show."

Mike shook his head. "Money-hungry ghouls," he muttered.

Yankee Horn caught his meaning and tried to explain the logic.

"We drive the ambulance through the nearby cities with the siren going, and we get a ten-percent boost in ticket sales. If Jinx is actually hurt, we'll get extra publicity."

"You freaks," Mike snarled. "First Whip, now Jinx. You're cashing in on their bodies."

"Our own too," Noon McComb said from a few feet away.

The cold almond eyes stared at him over the shoulders of another rider.

Husky Blackwell agreed. "That's what we sell. Thrills and spills. Broken bones and wrecked bikes. The broken bones bring in the biggest gate."

"You have got to be crazy. Jinx is just a kid."

"She's of age," Noon countered. "Nobody forced her to join the circus."

"She's through," Husky said. "My name is going on top where it belongs."

"First you clear Devil's Jaw ravine," Mike reminded him.

Husky shook his head and laughed. "Don't have to. With Jinx in a cast, and not able to try the leap herself, there's no contest. The show's mine. I've been waiting for years to take top billing. Soon as we get a report from the hospital, we start repainting again."

"Can't," Yankee interrupted. "We have ads scheduled. We already changed the copy once."

"All right, but I'm top rider at the next stop on the schedule."

Horn jutted out his jaw thoughtfully. "Then you and Noon aren't going to jump the ravine?"

Blackwell smirked. "Hell, no. Why should I?"

"Because I was figuring on a big gate. I could have built it up like you were going to fly your bikes over the Grand Canyon. We wouldn't need all the other performers."

Hawk waited for a pause. "Count me in," he said.

Heads turned toward him.

"What?" Blackwell said suspiciously.

"I said I'm taking the girl's place."

"Not in my show, you're not."

Noon interrupted gently. "It's not your show yet."

"You mean he's going to jump the ravine?" Blackwell scoffed. "Hell, he hasn't jumped anything higher than a worm in years."

"I'll get practice during the show."

"I'll be damned if you will."

He turned on his heels and strode toward the area where the motor homes were parked. Noon went with him.

"Why doesn't he want me in the circus?" Mike asked Yankee. "I should be good for ticket sales. I'd undoubtedly take more spills than the rest of them put together."

The dwarf answered, "I heard him talking. He remembers a couple of years back when you were damned good. Whip would have taken you on, if you weren't already doing what you wanted. Blackwell's afraid you might get in enough bike time to improve yourself. If you actually jumped the ravine, he might have to try it too."

"So I get myself killed . . ."

"And he might join you at the bottom." Horn drew a scrap of paper from his pocket. "Did you hear the specifications Jinx gave us? Takeoff ramp, ten-foot-tall maximum. Landing ramp, nine-foot minimum. You hear that? Nine-foot minimum. Width, four-foot maximum for both structures. No parachutes, no nylon ropes, no net, and no safety ramps extended beyond the edge of either cliff."

"And she picks her site last," Mike smiled. Jinx had read her father's plan too.

"We'll have to build the ramps on retractable wheels. She's not designating her takeoff point until the last minute. Along a hundred-yard stretch of desert. That's suicide."

"I told you. I'll jump for her."

Horn studied him. "Then I set up the performance today? We'll need every hour we have left to get advertising on the air and in the newspapers. It won't take much to draw a crowd; lynchings always attract a big audience. I'll go on TV tomorrow. I called several L.A. stations yesterday."

"Get on it then."

The dwarf grinned. "You big bag of . . . wind," he said, censoring his words. "You're really going to do it?"

"Yes."

"For Whip?"

"Sure."

"Or the girl?"

"Both."

"Why?"

Hawk breathed in deeply. "Because nobody else can."

Yankee shook his head. "I have to give it to you. I liked Whip. But I wouldn't die for him. Husky liked him too . . ."

"Did he?"

"He was a loyal partner. A faithful friend."

Mike said, "You're the one that's full of shit. He couldn't wait for Whip to die."

Yankee contradicted him. "You don't know this business. We don't weep for the dead. Husky is saluting Whip McComb in the only way he knows how. So's Noon. And Jinx. Billy. All of us."

"One of you ends up with a million-dollar business."

"Not me."

"Noon or Husky then."

"Yes. They'll have to settle it between themselves."

Mike ran his hand over the bike that Jinx had ridden to her downfall. The damage was minor. Dents, scratches, and the front wheel wiggled under his touch.

Had it been that way before the accident? Loosened slightly, the wheel would not have held steady after the extra strain of impact.

"Bolts aren't tight," he said to Yankee.

The smaller man checked for himself. His lips folded in, but he made no comment.

"When did Billy get in?" Mike said. Rage was building inside him. A killer was loose and aiming now at the girl.

"Three or four hours ahead of you." Horn studied his watch. "Billy has to follow Husky. The kid doesn't read road maps and he doesn't have a driver's license. We're paying fines for him all the time."

138

Three or four hours. The pair had time to rig the bike Jinx had been riding.

Mike slammed a fist into his open palm, trying to vent his growing rage. He ought to beat a confession out of Blackwell, he thought. Or kill him.

Tempting as the idea was, he knew it was not the answer.

He vowed he would get a confession. He'd trick the phony cowboy into admitting he had used Billy to kill McComb and send Jinx crashing into the dirt.

Then he would . . .

Would what?

Kill him? Or turn him over to the police?

Right now, Hawk didn't know which. He was not a murderer, however. He killed in self-defense or not at all.

But how did he prove his suspicions? He had no evidence that would stand up in court; he couldn't stay around for a trial if he did have proof.

Yet he couldn't leave. If he had reason to stay before—to avenge Whip's death—it was far more imperative that he find the killer now. Obviously Jinx would not be safe until he was stopped.

He had only his vague plan to trick the killer into giving himself away. It wasn't much.

"How long will we be here?" he asked.

Yankee replied, "We booked two full weeks. We can lop off the last Sunday and refund the preordered tickets or let the holders opt for the Devil's Jaw performance instead. We don't get much advance in ticket sales, but this is motorcycle country. We'll gross more here than we would in New York."

"Teach me," Mike said thoughtfully.

"Huh?"

"Give me a quick brush-up course. I want to go up against Blackwell, say the Friday before the desert show—in front of the audience."

"Why?"

"To make him madder than hell before we try the ravine."

Yankee started to walk away. "You're crazy."

Hawk reached down to the humped shoulder. "Do it for McComb and his kid."

"Whip's dead."

"Then for Jinx."

Horn laughed bitterly. "For a woman, any woman? You

have any idea how a woman treats a runt like me? As if I don't have any balls. As if I don't have any feelings either. Oh, they're sweet to me. Jinx in particular. I'm cute and cuddly, but will one of them shack up with me? Hell, no. They act like I'm contagious. Three college degrees, a big bankroll, and I can't hire a whore half the time. So don't ask me to risk what little I have in the world—my job—for a woman, any woman. I have to live with Blackwell if he wins."

"You want that? Working for Blackwell?"

"No."

"Help me then. Help me rub Husky Blackwell's nose in the nearest, freshest cow turd. That Friday before the big event. I think I can make Husky go for broke at the ravine or get laughed off the circuit."

"Make it a grudge match?"

"Yes."

"That always draws well."

"Then you'll help me?"

"No. I'm not risking my position with Husky for money or anybody."

"Do it to stay alive then," Mike changed his tactics. Threats worked better than promises. "If I spread the word that you know who killed Whip McComb, how long do you think you'll survive around here?"

"Hey, I don't even think McComb was murdered."

"That won't count for much if I pass the word and support it with evidence."

"You motherfucker!"

"I've been called that before." Mike smiled pleasantly. "But while you're all trying to forget, I'm going to run Whip's killer into the ground and see to it his kid has a chance to own the show."

"Husky could gamble that you won't make the jump," Yankee said cynically. "He'll show up, abort the leap at the last second, and let you take the big plunge. If you're not there, he'll carry a chute or extend a safety ramp from the other side just far enough to be certain he doesn't get killed. Then he'll give the grandstand performance and walk off with control. He's no fool. That leap can't be made."

"I'll make it," Hawk said firmly. He held up the notebook: "Whip figured it out."

The smaller man rolled back his eyes. "You'd risk your life on that," he said. "What makes you so certain he didn't do his calculations when he was drugged out of his mind? He had the bed-of-nails deal calculated and you saw where that got him."

Reality splashed over Hawk like cold water. The dwarf had a point. The calculations could be worthless. He had no way of discovering whether they had been made before McComb had heavily sedated himself or not.

"I'll have to trust Whip," he said finally. "The book is all I have."

Yankee's eyes glistened. He looked up at Hawk with something close to respect. "Who are you, Hawk? A hurricane with a mouth instead of an eye?"

"Try me."

Horn kicked the dirt. "Okay. I'll help you set up the deal for Friday. For Whip and the kid. Not because I'm afraid. Now what's in it for you?"

Mike shrugged.

Maybe he was just plain madder than hell. His senses watered for the taste of revenge, and he was bitter with himself too for riding with the girl's stepmother from Louisiana.

Why had Noon set him up? Was she a horny bitch or was she trying to douse the fire smoldering between him and Jinx?

The girl's too young for you, Mike chided himself. But was that a reason for him to humiliate her by sleeping with Noon? Whip's widow wasn't good enough in the sack to warrant hurting the girl.

He'd make it up to Jinx, somehow. Maybe by turning the show back to her where it belonged.

And there was still Whip to think about.

They were worth the risks.

He looked to the Jungfrau, the hill named by local bikers after one of Switzerland's highest mountains.

"I'll goad Husky Blackwell so damned much he'll have to meet me Sunday."

"You think Husky killed Whip?" Yankee wanted to know.

"Who else?" Mike asked.

But then he wondered. Who else indeed?

# 16

His body ached. His spinal column felt as if the impacts of the hundreds of jumps he had made in the last eight days had permanently fused the vertebrae in his lower back. But the practice was paying off. Already he had regained his confidence and was jumping as well as either Blackwell or Noon McComb. Riding Whip's old bike—neither of the others wanted it—was a psychological asset to him; if the expert could trust it, so could Hawk.

Whenever he thought his body could take another beating, he tackled the Jungfrau. At first he had planned to deliberately stop short of the top. He wouldn't want Noon or Husky to see how he managed it.

But there was no need to sandbag.

The grade was murderous. The best way up was on your hands and knees, playing amateur mountain climber. The show people laughed whenever Mike made an attempt on the bike.

The path worn through the chaparral proved hundreds had tried and failed. All the wheel tracks came to a telltale end twenty-five feet from the top, where the incline rose to a wall-like eighty degrees.

"You go any higher," Yankee warned him, "and you'll come down with the bike riding you."

The dwarf was right. Even when he was alone and free to use the plan from McComb's book, he could no higher; or if he did gain a foot more, the bike threatened to crush him.

He measured the hill repeatedly according to McComb's calculations. Having located the landmarks, he approached at the right speed and shifted at exactly the indicated points. He had even weighed the bike and added several pounds to bring it up to his dead friend's weight.

Pollock still hadn't come up with computer verification of McComb's formula for beating the hill.

Each time Hawk called him, the answer was always the same. "We're working on it."

"Damnit," Mike stormed. "Time is running out."

"So forget the whole deal," Pollock replied.

"If I make it up the hill and the other two can't, they're going to be embarrassed. Five minutes later I'm going to make them both look like has-beens. They'll be convinced I'll make it across the ravine on Sunday. They won't dare sit on their duffs and hope I get killed."

"So you beat the Jungfrau, embarrass them with whatever else you have planned. Are you going to take on Devil's Jaw without computer verification?"

Hawk waved the problem aside. "I'll face that later. First, I have to play king of the mountain. Get a computer printout for Christ's sake. Tell me what I'm doing wrong."

"You know, don't you, that if your half-assed plan, whatever it is, doesn't work, you're going to wind up looking more like a turkey than a Hawk—and a wounded one at that. You need a helluva lot more than a computer, pal. Some common sense would help . . ."

"Now watch it, Georgy dear. You'll make me hostile and . . ."

"Hostile, shit." George was warming up to his anger. "I'm getting sick and tired of being jerked around on a string because you want to pop wheelies like some show-off kid—"

Hawk might not have heard. "I'll be waiting to hear from you, go-go gal," he said. Then he slammed down the receiver.

Every call seemed to end that way.

Beating the Jungfrau was an essential part of the plan to draw Whip's killer out into the open where Hawk would have a crack at him . . . or her.

If he could humiliate the two prime suspects publicly and often enough, one of them . . . the one who already faced a potential murder rap . . . would have few qualms about finishing off the embarrassing amateur.

Hawk would take his chances on surviving.

The Jungfrau alone might not do the trick, so he was preparing another surprise. He'd been practicing the second phase for a week and he knew it would work. Although he hadn't used a McComb formula, he had seen the old pro do exactly what he had in mind several times before.

For the second surprise there was one prime requirement: he needed every bit of speed the bike could give him.

He ticked off the days on a mental calendar. The show was still drawing crowds, but the ex-newsman was growing nervous. Then shortly before dark on a Friday, the telephone call came through from Pollock's nearby hotel.

The parking lot was filled, and the performers were revving their engines to build excitement.

Mike had the call switched to a phone booth and stood with his back to the crowd. After cursing Pollock with his customary disdain, he let the CIA man report.

"The computer says Whip McComb is off on all his calculations," Pollock reported, "as far as the Jungfrau is concerned. We're still working on the ravine."

"What?" Mike bellowed. "You sure your people aren't using an abacus instead of a computer? McComb was the best in the business."

"Was," came the verbal jab over the phone line. "He's dead, and his calculations stink. I had three top-notch surveyors there the morning after you called. We evaluated every angle, every rise on that hill, and I tell you it can't be done McComb's way."

"You're wrong."

"You try it by any chance?"

Hawk lowered his voice. "Yeah!" he admitted reluctantly.

"You came down on your ass. I was watching you."

"You telling me the Jungfrau can't be beat?"

Pollock said, "No, I'm saying you'll never beat it using that system. Add four to everything and you'll sail over the top."

"Four?"

"You heard me. Add four. Hit the rise at four miles per hour faster, add four pounds to your weight, make each gear shift four feet higher and start four feet to the left of the old path. Do that and you'll go over the top."

"Who says?"

"The computer."

Hawk puzzled. He felt uncomfortable where computers were concerned. He knew he was buried in their memories all over the world. Bits of information had been fed in by police, the CIA, the FBI, the IRS, Interpol, the KGB, and an alphabet soup of other agencies. Whoever pushed the right buttons on a display terminal might get back the profile, name, and address of a guy who had more money than most small governments. A computer could make him a target for assassins and do-gooders alike.

So he didn't appreciate the necessity of trusting a computer now.

"You realize what happens if I make it halfway up that last thirty feet and don't go all the way?" he asked. "I'll tell you. I get my guts scrambled and my bones pulverized."

"So you're an idiot like I said," Pollock ventured. "You have any idea how many kids have been busted up on that damn hill? Forget it."

Hawk grumbled, "No." He disliked changing his plans. He disliked even more the prospect of getting hurt, but he had this damned stubborn streak that wouldn't let go. As a newspaper man he could never leave a promising lead until he had the story, regardless of the dangers involved. He felt the same way now about finding McComb's killer. But he was torn. This was twice Whip's book had proven wrong. He would have to go with the computer. "What about Devil's Jaw?" he asked. "Got anything on that yet?"

"Nothing concrete," Pollock said. "Except it seems to be off too. We can't figure how much. I've had surveyors there too, and programmers working equations into the banks."

"Shit! That's coming up soon, you know?"

"Yeah. Oh, and Mike. Don't try the ravine until we check it out. Promise."

"Cross my heart and hope to die."

"Be serious. You can get hurt on the Jungfrau. If you miss on the ravine trick, you're dead."

"Yeah, yeah."

"You doing anything I don't know about?" Pollock asked.

"Remember it's my job. You get killed. I get fired. So be honest. You doing any other stunts?"

"Just the big leap. Noon and Husky Blackwell are doing it every night."

"They're letting you take part in the show?"

"No. I've been doing it in practice so far, that's all. Tonight I join them. Only they don't know it just yet."

"Watch those spikes."

"No spikes. Snakes."

"Snakes?"

"Rattlesnakes," Mike answered. "They fill the pit between the two ramps with barrels full of rattlesnakes. The management is raising hell, but the audience loves it. They can't wait for somebody to fall into the snake pit."

"Jesus, Mike. Is the girl worth all this?"

"What girl? I'm doing this for Whip."

"Bullshit you are. Only a woman could make you risk your neck so often."

Hawk replaced the phone without replying. He wondered if Pollock was right for a change.

# 17

The final notes of the national anthem crackling from the overused recording died away in the cool of early evening as Hawk left the phone booth and went through the performer's entrance. Lights high on wooden poles carved a sphere of illumination that cut the bleachers and raceway apart from the surrounding night.

Beyond the sphere, smaller lights created satellites of visibility around the gates and the mobile living quarters of the show people.

Hawk picked up the customized bike where he had parked it minutes before, next to Noon's vehicle, so he could see it from the phone booth. He had not stayed with Noon since he arrived in California; instead he had taken a motel suite close to the suburbs. Since it was near the hospital, he had visited Jinx often—when he wasn't bruising himself on the Jungfrau.

He felt safer keeping his bike at the motel away from Blackwell and Billy.

A few yards away Yankee Horn was approaching his mini bike.

Struggling to get his leg over, he called to Hawk. "Tonight's the night," he reminded the bigger man.

Mike nodded and continued to study the motorcycle. He could allow nothing to fail him as the original copy had failed his friend.

"Remember," the dwarf said. "Don't move until Noon and Husky are halfway around their first swing for the big jump. I'll be at the microphone. Make it look spontaneous."

"You'll have the lights on the hill?" Mike asked.

"Yes. Not that you'll make it to the top, but be careful. Jumping the snakes is the important part. That we know you can do."

"I'm doing that 'no hands,' " Mike added as an afterthought.

"You're what?"

"Soon as I clear the ramp, I'm holding my hands above my head."

"Don't be a fool . . . You'll never get them down again before you land."

"I've done it," Mike replied.

"But if the wheel shifts . . ."

"It won't. I've been practicing early in the morning when the rest of you were sleeping. It looks great. And I'm coming the other way."

"Aw, no."

"I saw Whip do it, so I gave it a try. I spilled a lot, but the crowd will love it. Husky and Noon better see me coming. I'll need room between them or there's going to be one hell of an aerial show that's not on the program."

"Why didn't you tell me?" Yankee demanded.

"Because I don't trust you. Just get a light on me coming around the track in the wrong direction. Make a big deal of it so the other two can take to the edges of the ramp."

"God, Hawk, I don't know if there's room."

"There is, providing they hug the edges."

"You're crazy."

"One other thing. Play the mystery-challenger game. I won't take off my helmet or lift my face mask. I won't be sticking around for the accolades. Next time you see me will be at Devil's Jaw ravine."

"Holy shit," Yankee muttered.

"Places," a call came from the track. "Places, everybody."

Yankee added his bike to the guttural rumble of the parade. The crowd stirred, then laughed when Horn appeared, waving wildly until he smashed into a hay bale and flew over the handlebars like a clown. A second later he was up and wheeling his mount with the skill of a rodeo rider.

Other performers stood on their pegs. They formed into

148

colorful columns, all of them in the same bright costumes they had worn in New Orleans. They pumped their fingers on the clutch levers like nervous percussionists.

They were all younger than Hawk, more experienced. Yet, foolishly perhaps, he was attempting maneuvers none of them had ever accomplished.

A wave of doubt gripped him; for a moment he wanted to shrink from his self-imposed commitment.

Then he saw Blackwell—in all likelihood, Whip's killer.

Resolve replaced the doubt.

Blackwell sat his bike with the pride of a champion. His scrawny figure was clad in a black cowboy outfit, the heavy boots, and the ten-gallon hat. In deference to the warmth of early evening, he had dispensed with the fleece-lined jacket. He was a smug, self-satisfied actor making the grand entrance.

Watching Blackwell's pompous demeanor, Mike was sent twenty years into the past to the classroom where his English teacher wrote her daily bit of philosophy on the chalkboard. Mrs. Jennings had written in round, carefully formed letters, "Conceit is God's gift to little men." It applied to the Husky Blackwells in the world, and a lot more.

The main lighting faded and a spot picked out the brash sidekick of the late champion of the stunt riders.

"And Husky Blackwell, ladies and gentlemen," the loudspeaker system announced dramatically. "The star of our show."

The crowd applauded while Billy appeared from the shadows with a pair of gloves. In an overdramatic display Blackwell, eyes straight ahead, let the fawning boy tug on one glove. The kid darted to the other side to repeat the operation.

Like a doctor before surgery, Husky held up both hands, considered the gloves, and snugged each tighter over his fingers. Then he pulled down the brim of his hat.

The crowd liked it. They had a new star.

From the sidelines Hawk could catch their hero berating the slow-witted boy.

"Tell the MC to get on with it," Husky demanded. "We ain't makin' gas money sittin' here in the lights, you know."

"Yes, sir, Mr. Blackwell." The subservient boy ran for the speaker's stand.

Another light came on, not quite as bright as the one still

encircling Blackwell. The second spot took in Noon McComb, regally sitting on a bike a few paces back.

"And that brave little lady of motorcycling's greatest thrill circus, Miss Pu Noon, empress of China."

The crowd applauded again.

"Now on with the show." The main lights came on again.

Not a mention of Whip, Mike thought. How quickly the dead were forgotten.

The caravan began to roll. The music picked up the tempo, and the audience squirmed in the bleachers. Like matadors at the corrida, the daredevils showed themselves to the crowd. It was part of the pageant. Blood in the afternoon. Blood in the lights and the glitter of chromium-trimmed bikes.

When the column had completed the first lap of the track, the riders broke into separate columns. They returned in pairs, cutting back and forth in front of each other, creating formations that dazzled onlookers with the precision and the flowing colors of the uniforms and the machines.

The preliminaries did not interest Michael Hawk, and he had turned back to his own bike when he saw Jinx McComb coming toward him on crutches. Although her ankle remained in a cast, makeup covered the facial bruises and she looked stronger than any day since her accident.

"Mike," she said.

"Hey," he tried to smile. "You supposed to be out of the hospital so soon? I thought they were keeping you a few extra days."

"I heard what you're planning for tonight," she said. "You can't do it, Mike. I won't permit it. You're running too many risks for me."

He studied her. She was younger than Lisa, of course, but she reminded him of his dead wife. Jinx was beautiful; so was his wife before he took her into an African dictator's domain and returned with nothing except her ashes. Jinx was smart, too, as Lisa had been.

What was it he used to say about Lisa?

Together they were Adam and Eve. Wherever she was, that was Eden.

He had never done enough for Lisa. Perhaps by helping Whip's daughter, he could pay to the living some of his debt to the dead.

The girl took his hand. He brushed his lips lightly over her forehead.

"There was nothing between me and Noon. You know that, don't you?" he asked. "Nothing that meant so much as an Italian centime." He had told her this in the hospital, but it bore repeating.

"I know," she said, "It's just . . ." She shook off the thought. "You could stay on with the show," she said hopefully. "Yankee says you're great on a bike, a born athlete. You could take dad's place."

"As your father?" he joked.

"No, silly," she blushed. "As my . . ."

"Husband?"

"Maybe. If that's what you want. You'll stay, won't you? That's what tonight is all about. That's why you want to show Husky and Noon you can do everything they can do on a bike."

"And more," he added, quietly evading the answer she wanted.

He was about to turn away when she lifted one hand from her crutches to touch the lapel of his riding outfit. It bore McComb's familiar purple, black, and yellow colors, though, and would attract attention when he made his reverse jump.

"You will stay, Michael, please, say you will," she pleaded wistfully.

Off-balance on the crutches, she swayed toward him and he caught her in his arms. The vulnerable lips were so close, and the eyes deep enough to drown in. He bent and kissed her hard and quick.

"See you after the show," he said.

He straddled his bike, kicked it into life, and rode to the far end of the track. He waited there while a pickup truck backed up to the glass-sided box between the two ramps. Several men in safari outfits raised and tipped the first of a half-dozen wooden boxes.

From the audience came a groan of anticipation and revulsion as the first of the huge snakes fell into the pit.

Its long, heavy body landed with a thump that Mike heard over the murmur of his own engine. Instantly the deadly reptile went into a tightening coil. Its flat head jerked from side to side searching for the enemy who had uprooted him from his environment.

Another slid from the box. Then a third.

Several more emerged tangled together.

The men worked more quickly now, emptying box after box until the pit was a writhing mass. Angry and frightened, the creatures coiled and stretched and slithered against the glass walls, lunging for freedom. A few flat-topped heads poked over the rim hissing and darting lethal tongues toward the fascinated spectators.

In the front section people retreated from the railing. The men in the safari jackets pushed the snakes back inside with gingerly thrusts of their long-forked sticks.

Yankee had been right. The snakes were even more frightening—and therefore more crowd pleasing—than the spikes had been. The reptiles were living, moving things that would strike at a man. They wouldn't just wait inanimately to claim a victim. They were primed to kill.

Hawk did not like snakes. Even as a boy, when other kids hunted garter snakes to terrorize their little sisters with, he had begged off. Nor did he enjoy seeing them probing around glass enclosures in the zoo. When Lisa teased him to go with her through the reptile section, he went, but not without a little chill of abhorrence playing along his spine.

He felt it now, that familiar skin-crawling sensation. He shook it off. Of itself, fear could inject a kind of venom into a man's veins, especially when his performance hung on confidence. With so much depending on the next few minutes, he must not lose his concentration.

Between the audience and the snake pit Hawk could see Husky and Noon beginning their first slow ride. They waved and smiled their appreciation to the cheering stands. They had the audience enthralled.

Yet one of the two was a murderer, Hawk thought. One had killed his friend. That one must be revealed and made to pay. It was that simple.

The only amateur on the field pulled down his visor, released the clutch, and picked up speed when he hit the dirt track and started around the far side.

With the helmet on, he could barely hear the announcer. Yankee Horn had taken over the microphone. The dwarf was an actor.

He sounded genuinely surprised. "Hey, wait, who's that on the track?" he was saying. "Guards, get that fool out of there. Husky. Noon. Hold your places."

There was more but Mike was concentrating on gaining

speed. This part was easy. He enjoyed every second as he bore down on the two other riders.

Noon and Husky still had their face masks up, and in the spotlights he caught a glimpse of their expressions. Shock. Anger. Hate.

They were grip to grip, but they had to split when he sped between them, spitting obscenities into the wind. Crew members ran onto the track, trying to force or wave him off.

Nothing stopped him. The moment he sent Noon and Husky swerving for safety, he braked hard, let the rear of the bike slide completely around and gunned between them again, this time waving them to follow.

"A challenger!" Yankee's voice was booming from the loudspeakers. "A mystery challenger. Follow him, Husky. Don't take that from anybody, Noon. You're the champions of the world. There's nothing he can do that you can't."

The crowd was on its feet; they were caught up in the mood.

"Follow him! Follow him!" the people chanted.

Hawk grinned. Horn had done a magnificent job of stirring up the competitive excitement. Noon and Husky had no choice. They might guess who was on the bike ahead of them, but they couldn't let an apparent amateur go undefeated.

With the pair on his tail Hawk left the track and aimed at the hill. Floodlights came on, lighting the entire area for him.

The Jungfrau rose skyward, a defiant wall that Mike had not yet conquered. In his mind, though, was every benchmark and instruction Whip McComb had left as his legacy. Each calculation had been corrected to suit Pollock's computer printout. He drove four feet to the left of the worn trail that led most of the way up the ridge.

He checked his speed, actually throttling up slightly to match the computer's directions. It had to work, Hawk told himself. If it didn't he would come tumbling down with the bike on top of him, making an ass of himself, and blowing his chance to draw the killer into the web he was attempting to weave.

Confidently he dialed the throttle and watched the needle whip to eighty-six on the speedometer. Exactly eighty-six, no more, no less.

"You'd better be right, Pollock," he said aloud. "Or I

may be joining Whip sooner than I care to."

He hit the rise with a thud before he carefully poured more gas to the engine. The bike arched upward. The engine screamed. The saddle bucked, and he had to bend low over the gas tank to control his center of gravity.

The customized cycle faltered slightly, losing speed gradually as he zipped past the halfway mark on the worn part of the trail. Fifty feet below the highest point cleared by other bikes, he reached the big rock designated on the diagram. That was the secret to mastering the hill.

He had held off until his rear wheel cleared the rock, although his instincts told him to shift sooner while he still had plenty of momentum. When the bike was ready to surrender, he bang-shifted and hoped.

The rear wheel spun. Dirt spit like flame from an exhaust. His feet spread from the pegs for balance. When he hit the final rise, he was sure he would plunge from the seat. Instinct told him to leap free while he could still make a controlled dismount.

"Idiots!" he yelled. They were crazy—first Whip, now Pollock. Still, without recourse, he followed the calculations.

On the edge of a precipice the tires clawed for a hold.

His own shadow covered the dirt and stone ahead. Only by feel could he tell that he had climbed beyond the ruts. He was higher than anyone else had ever come.

The crowd was screaming below.

They were pulling for him. Or hoping he would come tumbling backward. He didn't care which.

There was no stopping, no retreating. He had passed the last chance to abandon the bike with any degree of safety.

Man and machine agonized together. He hung, suddenly positive the computer calculations were wrong. Maybe the Jungfrau couldn't be mastered.

With one last thrust of energy, the front wheel cleared the rim at the top. Then as if to take flight, it rose from the turf. The bike reared on its haunches, poised briefly on its spinning rear wheel, and hung there, undecided.

Hawk could lean no farther forward. There was nothing he could do to shift the center of gravity.

Backward down the hill or forward to success? For what seemed an eternity, the bike hesitated.

"Please," he begged. "One more foot."

In answer the big bike coughed and fell forward. It came down hard. Hawk held his seat and rolled onto the flat surface on top.

He let out a rebel yell and spun the bike around the narrow flat surface on top. He rolled to the edge, braked where the searchlight could display him, and poised for the cheering audience.

Then he watched, smiling as the other two bikes tried to follow.

They didn't have a chance. Even with all the speed they could muster, neither Noon nor Husky made it to the top of the worn trail. They had to dismount and try to keep their cycles from sliding down without them.

The crowd went wild. Their latest hero was on top of the hill, a monarch on his dusty throne.

People started to run for the hill. They wanted to touch the victor, but Hawk couldn't permit it.

In spite of the risk he pointed the bike down and began the dangerous descent, skidding directly between his two pursuers.

They were after him immediately. The chase was on again. Now his challenge wasn't hard-packed earth.

It was live, slithering snakes, dozens of them, each with enough venom to kill. If the victim were susceptible or if he were struck so close to the central nervous system that the antivenin would not have time to work, death could come within a few hours.

He forced his thoughts away from the snakes. With his two opponents tailing him, he rode past the stands, both hands lifted over his head triumphantly, an arrogant salute to an adoring audience.

Passing a set of speakers, he could hear Yankee Horn building suspense.

"The ghost of Whip McComb," he was calling the unknown champion of the Jungfrau. "It has to be, folks. It has to be the ghost of Whip McComb."

Then Mike throttled up the engine again, Noon and Husky still far behind him; and started for the launching ramp and the deadly snake pit he had to clear.

155

## 18

The crowd cheered, expecting Hawk to make the jump, and they waved at the show stars trailing him at a distance. The people in the stands wanted them to catch up, to make the jump with the mystery man who had bested them on the Jungfrau.

Now Hawk braced for the second gambit in his plot to thoroughly humiliate Whip's killer, thereby forcing him to show his hand, be it a winning one or not.

As he approached the launching ramp, Mike deliberately pretended to lose his courage. At the last second he swerved, avoided the launch ramp, and cruised past as if he were heading for some distant exit.

He could hear the catcalls from the stands, the boos: "Come on back, yellow!" "Outta gas or guts?" "Lose yer balls?"

"Chicken," Yankee Horn, warming up to his role in Hawk's parlous scheme, was shouting over the loudspeakers. "Come on, Husky. Come on, Noon. Show the fink how a real pro does it. Jump, you two, jump!"

Hawk disappeared into an unlighted area at the edge of the park. He braked and swung around in time to see his two opponents pulling down their visors. Were they grateful their humiliation had been so brief?

With a dramatic show of determination, they set their visors and began the sweep around the entire perimeter of the track. Once again they were the favorites of the fickle audience.

Hawk judged their speed, waiting until they were into the final curve before the ramp. Then he unleashed his own mechanical steed and roared toward the snake pit.

"What's this?" Yankee Horn cried. "The ghost is back. My God, he's heading for the wrong ramp. Noon, Husky—make room. I think he's going to jump between you. Is there room? Folks, is there room?"

The clone of Whip McComb's bike stayed to the right of the platforms long enough to match its distance to that of the others. From that position he could also see the pit alive with writhing snakes. Hawk breathed deeply and swerved onto the path that would take him up the very center of the landing platform. He was heading directly at the other two riders. He could only hope they continued to stay along the far edges; he couldn't see them.

A drum roll began, underscoring the danger that lay ahead. A few fascinated onlookers in the bleachers moved forward. Others leaped to their feet. Soon no one remained seated.

Mike bent low over the tank. The platform rushed toward him. Last chance to change his mind, he thought. Last chance to run. Faster, he told himself.

He checked the speedometer. The bike wasn't accelerating as fast as he thought it should be.

"Move!" The cry was a plea.

He could no longer look down. The front wheel had hit the planks and was rattling straight up the center. Upward, upward. He wished the ramp would never end. The snakes were beyond the edge. Then, airborne, he forced himself to yank his hands from the bars. He sat upright, arms spread like wings, his eyes drawn downward as if by a magnet.

Snakes below.

Blackwell coming at him on the left. Noon on the right.

A moment of pleasure, the thrill of escape. Not even gravity held him. He was flying.

Then the lights went out.

A blink and he was staring into the blackness.

Panic struck.

The handlebars jerked. In midair something on one of the other bikes had nicked his cycle. A hand, he thought.

He gasped, trying to grab the steering mechanism before it was too late.

The bike canted under him, tipping to one side; the front wheel was turning.

He was losing control. The lights came back on. They had scarcely winked.

In a frantic grab for the bars he lost his balance. There was time to guess the truth. He was going to crash against the leading edge of the landing platform. There was no way a tilted bike could complete the proper trajectory.

There was nothing he could do.

The impact jarred his entire body. He flew forward, his shoulder hitting unyielding wood. The crack of metal and the roar of the engine deafened him. His vision blurred, and he recoiled from a weird collection of images. He saw the spokes of the front wheel, first round and in perfect shape, then twisting, bending. He saw the tire pop. Rubber slapped his knees.

His cheek socked against metal.

He was falling. His fingers clutched at the edge of the ramp. They held briefly, then slowly, pried straight by an invisible force, they slid loose.

The bike was below, dragging him down by the ankle. He screamed, but the voice seemed to come from a distance.

It wasn't like him to scream.

Just before he hit the dirt, he thought of the snakes. He caught a glimpse of them, writhing, coiling, crawling over each other.

His body struck the hard plywood floor of the pit. Pain spiraled up his leg. It began at his ankle and jolted like a bolt of electricity along the bone to his thigh.

His helmet twisted his neck. His teeth slammed together, his tongue caught between. Stunned, he couldn't move.

His eyes were closed.

He opened them reluctantly. Snakes were all around him, writhing, hissing. Their tails were lifted, the true sign of a rattler. Most had upward of ten segments to their rattles, each hollow ring partially fitting over the one behind it.

Sidewinders. The horned rattlers were found in the desert regions. Although they were not particularly large snakes, their mouths were opened wide. The two long hollow teeth which were normally folded back in the mouth were now thrust forward from the upper jaws.

Poison formed in a pair of glands gushed into the fangs.

Some struck; the fangs darted at him. One hit his helmet, others struck his boots. One sank its teeth into his suit, staining the fabric with its poison.

If he screamed, it went unheard among the shrieking spectators.

A few of the rattlers drew back on themselves, returning to their protective coils, but one was trapped beneath the bike. With its spine crushed, its big head whipped wildly to and fro. Inch by inch it stretched toward him; the forked tongue fluttered like hummingbird wings between the fangs.

The teeth aimed at Hawk's leg.

Two more coiled between him and the wall formed by the leading edge of the ramp. Trapped and dangerous, they would strike at the least provocation.

Mike tried to crawl away, his scraped and bleeding hands clawing at the wood flooring.

His foot held. His leg was tangled with the engine. The hot metal burned through his suit. Ignoring the pain, he tried to reach the gun tucked in his ankle holster, but the snakes snapped for his hand when he moved.

He pulled and tore at his knee. Still the bike held him.

Through his blurred vision he could see the audience and the crewmen, all safely outside the glass-walled pit. Dumbfounded, none of them moved. They were staring, frozen in horror.

"Do something!" he raged, as much out of anger as panic.

The men on the fringes of his vision came to life. They ran, sprinted, and leaped for the pit. The snake handlers came first, then the mechanics. The handlers worked with sticks, lifting the snakes away. The regular showmen attacked with tire irons. Yankee Horn tumbled his short body into the enclosure too, dancing and darting about. Using a long stick, he flayed the vipers and leaped outside when they turned on him and attacked.

The mentally retarded boy Billy also helped. Mike hadn't expected that, but he joined the offensive with the others. He tried to stomp the squirming bodies with his boot. His mouth hung open and his eyes bugged—he didn't seem to comprehend the danger. He was just part of the crew fighting the alien things in the pit.

Miraculously the snakes missed him. Like someone charmed and thus impervious to the reptiles, the slow boy ran for

Mike, stopping just short of the pinned millionaire. First he looked at the twisted bike, next the trapped rattler, its head only inches from his own leg. Then, although his entire body shook with fear, he reached down to lift the bike.

"Back off!" Mike yelled when he recognized what was about to happen.

There was no indication that the boy heard. Muscles strained, he lifted.

"*No!*" Hawk warned.

The bike came up. The trapped leg pulled free. So did the snake.

"A-w-w-w!" Billy cried. The boy convulsed as the rattler struck the bare flesh on his left hand.

The snake hung on.

Billy toppled backward.

Hawk rose and grasped the first rattler behind the head and tore it from the boy's hand. With crushing force he hurtled it against the wood wall of the ramp.

Then he was dragging Billy away while other men killed the snakes beneath the boy.

Hawk stumbled over the glass side of the pit. He and the boy fell outside.

As he sank to the ground, he felt the blackness rushing in. Then Billy and the men attending him faded into the void.

# 19

Jinx stood on crutches at the foot of the bed, slowly coming into focus, like a figure approaching from a London fog.

"Michael." She said it several times before he opened his eyes and smiled weakly.

She came around the bed in a wobbly rush. A female doctor Hawk had not seen before tried to stop her, but she slipped past and bent over him. Her lips were enough to rouse him from the comfort of unconsciousness.

"Thank God," she was saying. "Oh, thank God, you're going to be all right."

The doctor had her way, gently easing Jinx to the foot of the bed. More of the room came into focus. It was typical hospital decor. Soft pastel colors, TV set leering down from a wall bracket, pull-over table with plastic water decanter and glass with flexible straw, a blood-pressure device near his right arm, and one plastic chair for visitors. The lights were on and it was dark beyond the venetian blinds, so he must not have been out for long.

The doctor, although young, and attractive, had a stern, disapproving look about her. Either she didn't accept that he was ready for visitors or she had had a bad day.

Beyond her the second figure was a surprise to Hawk.

It was George Pollock.

"This is Mr. Pollock," Jinx introduced him. "He says he is an old friend of yours."

"He's old anyway," Mike managed to mumble through lips that hurt when he spoke.

Pollock leaned against the wall, his arms folded, weight on one foot, the other leg crossed in the most casual pose Hawk had ever seen him assume. He was not dressed casually, though. Even in California he still wore the suit and tie of a 1920's Harvard Business School graduate.

"How's Billy?" Mike remembered suddenly. As he tried to sit up, he found new places that ached.

Jinx looked from him to the nurse.

"He's not dead," Mike snapped. "Damnit, he saved my life."

"He's in terrible condition, Mike," Jinx answered. "He was bitten several times. It was awful. Swollen and purple around the fang marks. They injected antivenin immediately. He was so pale and weak when they took him away. I felt his pulse. It was weak and fast, and he vomited."

Mike glanced at the doctor.

"I can't tell you whether he'll make it or not," the young woman said. "The antivenin was injected almost immediately, but he has other physical problems, and some of the bites were close to the heart."

"And I didn't get a single bite," Hawk said, almost in disbelief.

"Pitch a lucky fool into the Nile and he will come up with a fish in his mouth," Pollock said softly.

"Billy keeps calling for you, Mike," Jinx said.

"Me?"

Pollock assumed a new position. "He wants to tell you he's sorry."

"Tell me he's sorry?" Mike was incredulous. "He saved my life. If he hadn't lifted that bike, he wouldn't have been hurt. Why the hell does he want to tell *me* he's sorry for risking his own neck for me?"

"I don't think that's what he means," Pollock answered.

"Then what?"

Jinx said, "I don't know, darling. Nobody does. He's out of his head."

"He has moments of coherency," the woman doctor objected. "Now I think you'd better rest, Mr. Hawk. There are friends outside, but I think you'd better send them away until tomorrow."

"Who?" Mike asked.

"Yankee Horn, Husky, and Noon. Others wanted to come, but I wouldn't let them," Jinx explained. "I told them no. You've suffered a slight concussion."

"Contusions and lacerations over seventy-five percent of your body," the doctor corrected Jinx. "So I think . . ."

"No, send them in."

"Mr. Hawk . . ."

"I said, send them in."

Pollock opened the door. The doctor exited in a huff, and the three people from the show came cautiously into the room.

"Is he awake?" Noon McComb asked obsequiously.

Mike barked directly at Yankee. "You told them, didn't you, you money-hungry little runt!"

"Me?"

"You."

Yankee shrugged. "Yeah." He said it again with more assurance. "Yeah, I told Noon and Husky you were going to jump against them."

"You pocket-sized weasel. I told you in confidence."

Yankee stood tall. His head poked just above the foot of the bed.

"You think I was going to let two friends come riding up the center of that ramp and meet you head on over those snakes? The hell with your confidences."

"But you let it go on."

"It was good show business. Spontaneous. The ghost of Whip McComb. We still haven't given your name to the newspapers. I'd do it again."

"You turn off the lights too?" Hawk demanded. "Just before I passed between them?"

"No! What do you think I am? Any one of you could have lost your orientation in the dark. The audience missed the big moment too."

"Then who did?"

Yankee looked around.

Jinx answered. "We don't know, Mike. A power failure maybe."

"Bullshit!" the angry man in the bed retorted. "Those lights were off just long enough for one of you to give my handlebars a nudge as you passed." He looked from Noon to Husky Blackwell.

163

"Fuck you!" Blackwell sneered. "I came in here feeling sorry for you; now you're accusing us of trying to kill you. Go to hell, you asshole!"

"Well, one or both of you did."

Noon sounded hurt. "Mike, you can't think I'd try to hurt you."

"I can and I do." Hawk glowered at Noon. "Which one of you made the worst landing?"

She said, "I don't understand."

"Whoever touched me up there in the darkness must have lost some of his—or her—own balance too. Did one of them crack up or come down hard, front wheel wobbling maybe?"

"No, well, I mean . . ." Jinx tried to answer.

"Who was watching them?" Yankee snorted. "You were the one falling into the snake pit."

"We made perfect landings," Husky insisted. "I did anyway."

Noon became indignant. "So did I. I didn't touch you, Michael, deliberately or accidentally. Ask anybody in the crowd. I made a perfect landing."

"Nobody is going to remember how you landed," Pollock put in from the wall.

The three newcomers faced the CIA man. "Who's he?" Husky demanded.

"A detective," Hawk lied. "He's having my bike dusted for fingerprints. If any of your prints show up on it, you'll be up on attempted-murder charges. Murder one if Billy dies. I wiped that bike clean before I mounted."

"You're out of your mind," Husky snorted. "Let's split, Noon. I've had enough of this shit."

"You'll see me again," Hawk said after them.

They turned.

"You forget? We've got a date at Devil's Jaw ravine."

"You!" Husky sneered. "You going to spring clear out of bed and straight over the ravine?"

"Mike, you can't," Jinx cut in. "You almost got killed going a hundred and thirty off a ramp. I made the challenge, so I'll keep it."

"With a cast on your foot?"

"I'm not going to walk across."

"When is the challenge set for, Yankee?" Hawk asked.

"Four P.M. Sunday," the dwarf answered. "The performance should draw a mob. Don't chicken out on me."

"I'll be there."

"No, Mike," Jinx said firmly. "I have Dad's notebook. I'll be all right."

"Neither one of you will be there," Husky said. "The show's mine from now on."

"Or mine," Noon added coolly.

Husky laughed. "You, Empress? That's a joke."

"What makes you think you'll make it across that ravine and not me?"

He aimed a finger at her. "Because you never tried anything that Whip didn't have all figured out beforehand, and he never let you see his little black book, so you ain't jumpin' nothin'. Me, I take a look and I go for the brass ring."

"You miss the ring this time and you'll be dead," Jinx responded.

Husky stalked out and Noon faced her stepdaughter. "Neither of us should attempt it, Jinx. Let Husky kill himself. I'm sure you and I could come to some more sensible way of settling this."

"Jinx isn't jumping," Hawk said. "I'm going for her."

"Then I suggest you talk to Mr. Hawk, Jinx. I see no reason for any of us to risk our lives."

"Think of the take, though. This time we can fill a whole desert with cars and paying customers," Yankee reminded them.

"Get the hell out of here, Scrooge," Mike ordered.

The small man spread his arms. "Okay. See you at the ravine Sunday, four P.M. It's a BYOC party. Bring your own casket." He chuckled, then followed Noon to the door.

When they were gone, Jinx came around the bed again. She started to plead, but Mike kissed her, stopping the words.

"Oh, Mike, I love you. It'll be wonderful. Our own show. You're good. So am I. Can we use Whip's name for a while?"

"Sure, kid." He patted her affectionately on the rear. "Better get out of here; I want to talk to this Pollock dude for a minute before I pass out again."

"Is he really a detective?"

"Naw, he's a photographer. Wants to buy some dirty pictures from me. See you in the morning, honey."

"At your motel?" she asked.

He hesitated. Giving in was easy. "Yeah, of course. You wouldn't want to stay with Noon any longer."

"We'll buy our own motor home. We can afford it."

"Sure."

She was at the door before he spoke once more. "Oh, Jinx, a little detail has been bothering me. If your dad kept his notebook so secret, how come that first night in New Orleans Yankee Horn knew exactly how fast Whip had to be going to clear the bed of nails?"

"Eighty-five?" she asked. "We all knew that, Mike. Dad kept the details secret when a trick was new. When he grew bored with one, he'd give all of us the figures; then we could understudy him if he got hurt or take over and do it ourselves while he introduced the new ideas. But now I have the book. It was the only legacy he could leave me. It's ours now, Michael darling. You can use it any time you want. But Sunday . . ."

"Later," he said. "Maybe I won't be out of bed after all."

"Then I'll see about the ravine. I'll win for both of us."

"We'll see," he said. "Meanwhile, stay off that foot."

She hobbled away on her crutches, and the door closed after her.

Mike stared at the heavy paneling for a long time. She was a kid, he reminded himself. He was a decade or more older than she was.

Yet she was honest. Too many people in his world, including himself, were liars, cheats, and scoundrels. She had a dream too; to have her own show, to sail through the air like a bird, a few seconds of utter freedom with every stunt.

It must have been that same sensation that drove her father on until he died—until someone killed him.

"This notebook you keep talking about . . ." Pollock began.

"Yeah, what about it?"

"Did Whip give it to his daughter?"

Mike rolled the question around in his head.

"Not exactly. She knew about it."

"So did his wife."

"So did everybody in the show."

Pollock ducked his head. "But he gave the book to his own daughter."

"I didn't say that. She took it from his pocket after he was dead. Why?"

"Nothing much," Pollock sounded nonchalant. "Except if

either of you follows any of those formulas of his, if you leap from either of the two spots he designated, you're going to get your necks broken no matter how fast you're traveling."

"That's stupid! He wouldn't do that to his own daughter."

"You just said he didn't give her the book."

"Well, he didn't."

"So he didn't expect her to follow the formulas."

"That what the computers tell you?"

"Indirectly, yes."

"Programmed by clerks getting minimum wage."

"Programmed by the best experts I could find. And we went to the site. Measured everything exactly."

"The spots I gave you."

"Yes."

Hawk puzzled briefly. "Your same computers said he could have made that jump at the Superdome going eighty-three miles per hour and everybody else said he took the ramp at eighty-five."

"Right."

"So the computer's wrong."

Pollock stroked his chin. "If you figured out stunts that competitors would kill to get, Hawk, would you write down the instructions in a book and carry it around in your pocket?"

"He had to write it down somewhere. Wait . . ."

"Yeah," George nodded.

"The formulas are fakes!" Hawk exclaimed.

"Yep."

"Anybody who stole them would get killed."

"Or hurt," Pollock said. "Near as we can tell, your friend Whip McComb wasn't the murdering type. He never recovered emotionally from the death of that kid who he felt he might be responsible for."

"Then why write them down?" Hawk asked and answered his own question. "Because he couldn't remember them. Too many details. Difficult for a genius. Impossible for a guy nearly stoned on heavy drugs."

Hawk stretched his arms painfully and interlocked his fingers behind his head.

He had to think. The formulas meant something. The computer couldn't decipher the meaning. It could only report whether the figures were right or not.

There had to be a key, a detail, a trick so the numbers would make sense. Like the leap in New Orleans. Something translated eighty-three miles into the necessary eighty-five-mile-per-hour approach. And the Jungfrau formula—that had to be altered by a factor of four. The computers were right that time.

But what was it?

He needed to know or there might be dead bodies at the bottom of Devil's Jaw ravine.

Husky Blackwell's. Noon McComb's.

His own.

Any of their bodies could be chewed to pieces by the Devil's Jaw.

168

# 20

George Pollock lounged in the Corvette, watching the figure limp away from the rear door of the hospital and into the beams of the headlights. The CIA agent could feel the aches and pains that went with every step. Solicitiously he swung open the door and let Michael Hawk take the passenger seat. The ex-newsman said nothing; he grasped the doorframe with his rigid hand, bending his big frame carefully, lowering it as though the seat were crushed glass instead of polyester velvet. Pollock winced inwardly while his friend used both hands to lift his right leg into the car. It might have been a piece of luggage.

The Corvette rolled down the drive, took a turn onto the parking lot, and adjusted to the legal speed limit. They headed for Saddleback Park.

Pollock admired the man beside him. He wouldn't have said it and he didn't understand, but he admired the gutsy fool. Hawk ought to be in bed. It was four A.M. The doctors had refused to release him officially.

Mike had smiled pleasantly, joked with the nurses, and left when he damned well pleased.

"You got it?" Hawk asked.

"Yes."

Pollock extracted the speedometer drive gear from his pocket. It was fastidiously wrapped in tissue.

Hawk opened the package and held it to the light which

fanned out from the last giant gooseneck streetlamp along the freeway.

"Good," he said.

The gear, larger than the one on McComb's bike at the cemetery in New Orleans, was exactly as he expected.

George read his mind. He was positive he could name the killer. He had known all along: Billy.

"You ruined that as evidence," the government man said piously. "I can't testify where I found it." There was no response. "You can't kill the kid," Pollock worried. "He's not responsible."

Hawk moved a hand, a gesture eloquent with disgust. "I could have killed him in the hospital," he said. "No trouble."

Pollock breathed easier. They were of the same opinion for a change. Billy had switched the gears, but he was no more than an inanimate weapon; Hawk wanted the real killer. "I still don't see . . ."

"Don't try," his wealthy confederate advised.

Hawk tucked the gear away and closed his eyes. He didn't rouse again until the sleek white car had driven to the rear of the raceway. When the cessation of motion alerted him, he slid stiffly from the car and hobbled to the chain link fence. He crawled up and dropped to the ground inside, his right leg dangerously close to buckling. Pollock followed.

Quietly they circled through the shadows to the caravan of trucks and motor homes. All the windows were dark; the performers would be up at dawn, moving their gear to the desert.

A single light on a power pole left dark corridors for them to hide their passing between vehicles to the old van.

Pollock stepped forward, ready to demonstrate his skill in breaking locks.

Hawk tried the handle first. It opened.

They stepped, crouching, into the rear compartment. George pulled the drapes tight, then switched on the overhead light.

To Pollock—the bon vivant—the scene was repugnant.

It was the sheer austerity of the quarters that disturbed him. The van contained only a pile of ragged blankets for a bed, a pail for water, and a plastic ice chest with a broken lid. The place was filthy, reaking of sweat, oil, and spoiled food. The floor was caked with mud and grease. A pile of dirty clothes was strewn at the foot of the makeshift bed.

Pollock felt remorse. They had violated the privacy of the boy. They had intruded into his most intimate sanctuary. Hawk felt it too; George could tell.

From the rubble on the metal floor, Mike picked up a single scrap of paper. It was a triangle no more than an inch on a side, two sides evenly cut, the third torn and ragged.

"Newsprint," Hawk announced. His eyes skimmed the side walls and ceiling of the van. There, cellophane tape told of pictures or news clippings ripped away. "He collected things," Mike said mostly to himself.

"He must have," Pollock agreed. "Every available inch must have been filled."

With a sense of inadequacy—the cryptic Hawk had not deigned to honor him with the objective of this breaking and entering—George surveyed the camper. Then he saw the built-in box at the rear of the van, noting the holes in the wood where a latch and padlock had been torn loose. He peered in: nothing.

"We're too late," he said. The place had already been thoroughly ransacked. It was all gone: the clippings of pictures from the walls and ceiling, the contents of what was probably a box of treasured mementos. Nothing remained except this bleak place that spoke volumes about a life impoverished by the uneven hand of fate. Pollock sighed, thrusting the lid shut; the box shifted to the right. Then in the lint and dust that lay in a dirty drift behind the box, Pollock saw a tiny glint of metal. He poked it loose and held it to the light.

A golden spur.

Pollock's mood improved. Minor as it was, he had scored a triumph, even if he didn't know what it was.

Hawk took it from him and studied it for a long moment without speaking. "Let's go," he said finally.

"Well, wait a minute," Pollock was confused. "You said the kid collected things. You're positive he switched gears on the bike. Right?"

"Right."

"And someone searched this place, stripped it bare of pictures, newspaper clippings. That must be significant."

Mike agreed. "It is."

"Then we have to discover what he was keeping that warranted a search."

"I know what it was," Hawk answered. "The kid kept souvenirs. He was in love."

"With whom, Jinx? Noon McComb? One of the show girls?"

Hawk held up the spur. "There's all kinds of love."

He switched off the light and crawled from the front door into the cool California predawn. Together they drove to the motel.

The newsman got out. "Damnit, Hawk," George complained. "What are you going to do?"

Mike leaned through the window. "I don't know yet. I might have to jump that damned ravine tomorrow after all."

"When the ever-present computer keeps telling us you can't make it?"

"McComb thought he could." Hawk pushed away from the car. He acted tired and older than his thirty-five years.

"You'll kill yourself for nothing, Mike. Let's call in the police."

"Buy me a pair of panty hose instead," Hawk replied.

Pollock gaped.

"Put a run in them. Bring them to the show tomorrow. Hand 'em to me just before the jump."

The agent swung his head slowly from side to side. "I don't believe it. Panty hose?"

"I forgot. You prefer dancing naked. See you tomorrow, Georgy Girl. You won't want to miss seeing me splatter my brains on that canyon floor."

"You act like you already have."

Hawk flipped the golden spur and whistled as he climbed the stairs to the motel suite. When he was gone, Pollock sat watching the door.

"Panty hose?" he said again. "With a run . . ."

# 21

Michael Hawk and Jinx McComb sat in the motel room, the notebook on the table between them. She still didn't believe him completely when he said the formulas were not accurate.

"I'll jump anyway," she said. "Husky says he's going to give it a try. Noon too, perhaps. I won't let all Dad's work go for nothing, maybe straight into the hands of whoever killed him." She glanced at her wristwatch and rose from the chair. "We'd better go, I mean, I'd better be going. Stay here, please, Mike. It would only make me nervous to know you were watching."

"Wait," he said.

Another thought had occurred to him, and he flipped back to the page laying out the specifics for the jump over the bed of nails.

"April," he said, reading the date at the bottom. "April," he said it again for his own benefit.

"Oh, Mike." Jinx had grown impatient. "We went over this for days while I was in the hospital. The date doesn't mean anything. It was probably the month in which dad did the calculations or the date he proved them or . . ."

"No," Hawk reached for the pencil and wrote the formula from the back of the book across the corner of the notebook. "$S + \frac{1}{2}M = RS$. 'M' equals 'month,' " he read aloud. "Oh, hell, of course. April, the fourth month." He slammed the heel of his right hand against his forehead as if to jar his sluggish mind into action.

"I don't understand," she said.

"M means month. The bed of nails trick was dated April, the fourth month. So substitute four in place of M and what do you get? Speed plus one-half four equals RS."

"RS . . . real speed?" she asked.

"Right," he jabbed a finger at the calculations for the jump. "Eighty-one miles per hour plus one half of four equals eighty-three. That's the speed your dad actually used, the speed he told each of you. At two miles less, you'd fall short."

She was unbelieving. "You mean he set it up so anyone who stole his book would be killed?"

Mike shook his head. "Not Whip. If any of you had stolen the information before he was ready to give it to anyone, he could have warned all of you. Or the thief would have tried the distance in practice with the spikes removed. Whip was no killer. He just knew how to hang onto his circus."

Jinx snatched the notebook from his hands, eyes bright with excitement. "Then we know how to jump the ravine!" She turned to the Devil's Jaw page and ran her finger to the date for the first launch site Whip had plotted. "December," she exulted. "The twelfth month. Add six miles per hour to the speed." She flipped to the next page. "Or this spot. October, the tenth month. Add five mph and I'm home free. Mike, my magnificent darling, you've done it! I can make it now. We're going to make it!"

She reached for her crutches, but he stopped her.

"There's more," he said. He pointed to the other information written in connection with the month given for the ravine plan. "Wednesday has to have some meaning. So does the 28th . . . Wednesday, December 28th . . . It's on the other plan too. Easter, October 30."

"Michael," she argued. "There isn't time. You've had days to figure out what the month meant. You used computers. We can't go through that again."

"Give me a minute," he said.

"No."

He pivoted in his chair and took up the crutches before she could hobble to them on her cast. Tucking the notebook in his

174

pocket, he stood the light aluminum crutches against the wall at an angle and raised his foot.

"Mike, don't, please."

She lurched for him, falling, while his left foot smashed down hard on the first crutch. The end bent under the weight and momentum of the stomping blow.

"Oh, please," the girl pleaded again.

"Sorry, sweetheart," he told her, rendering the second crutch useless. "If anybody crosses that ravine today, it will be me."

"Mike, don't leave me here. Mike . . ."

She was hopping across the room as he walked out onto the balcony of the motel and down to the last copy of Whip McComb's original bike. Before he mounted, he shouted to an elderly maid pushing her linen cart along the lower tier of rooms.

"The lady in 206 needs help," he told her. "Send the manager up."

Then he started the engine and rode toward the site of the desert show. Off the freeway the dirt road leading to the ravine was filled with cars, campers, and cycles. Both lanes headed in the same direction, and drivers honked or cursed when he wove in and out among them, occasionally taking to the gulleys to gain time.

He had to be prompt; Husky or Noon might claim victory by default. His mind, though, was not on the road. It was a turmoil of unsolved puzzles.

He could not be sure who had plotted Whip McComb's death. Logically it was Husky Blackwell. The scrofulous bastard was the type to kill by stealth. He had waited longer than anyone else for the starring position in the show.

Still there was that remote possibility that the braggart was innocent.

Someone else could have killed Whip.

There was Noon, his wife in name only.

And Yankee Horn was a suspect. Who knew what years of indignities might have done to the dwarf's mind? Conceivably the brusque Whip, obsessed as he was with success, had offended the proud little man. Yankee had made it obvious that he was inferior to no one except in size.

That left Billy—in all probability only a tool, whose nebulous mind made him fair game for exploitation. And Jinx, theoretically, but, whether because of his emotional involvement or not, Mike could not bring himself to consider her as capable of taking her father's, or anyone else's, life.

Temporarily it didn't matter. Mike only knew he had to stop the jump over Devil's Jaw. No one could be allowed to make the attempt.

The special notations around the dates on those two pages had to have meaning.

"Wednesday, the 28th. Easter, the 30th." He tumbled the arcane phrases around in his mind, trying to find slots for them, slots alongside other facts he had already deciphered.

He pictured the maps again, projecting the memorized illustrations before him like slides on a screen. The details had been complete. The two points of possible launching were clearly marked. Anyone seeing the map could pinpoint the spots on the terrain. They wouldn't know the speed McComb recommended but . . .

Hawk's brain cells sparked.

"Speed, speed," he said aloud.

Speed counted on some of the other stunts. In most cases it was calculated to make the leap look dangerous while leaving a margin for safety. Often it didn't even tax the motorcycle's capabilities. In other parts of the show the speed had to be exact so the bike would not land too far from the designated landing point. Mike remembered the importance of the leaps that ended just short of a solid barrier. The exact speed allowed Whip to land early enough so he had sufficient time and space to avoid crashing against the wall.

At Devil's Jaw, though, the extra speed called for in the coded message simply set the customized bike close to its maximum speed over semirough terrain.

The others in the show would know that. They had undoubtedly clocked Whip squeezing every mph out of his machine.

Husky and Noon would push their own bikes to the ultimate. If they couldn't equal Whip's speed, they wouldn't attempt the jump.

That left the takeoff points as the only secret, and those Whip had clearly identified. So why the code?

Suddenly Mike read the dead man's mind.

The locations on the map were wrong. That's what the

extra code meant. "Easter," he yelled with satisfaction. "E for east. Wednesday. W for west."

The ravine ran north to south.

The first coded site would be west of the designated launch points shown by the pinhole in the map. The other was farther east of the second mark.

"Wednesday, December 28th." The place he could make it across was twenty-eight feet to the west. "Easter, October 30th." Thirty feet east.

Feet?

He almost plowed into the car ahead of him.

How did he know Whip McComb was using feet?

Because all his other stunts were done in feet, he told himself.

But could he be sure? Was twenty-eight feet along the ravine that crucial? He doubted it. Maybe Whip meant yards.

There was no way of knowing. That was the one fact McComb had kept in his mind. Feet, meters, yards.

Just ahead of him the desert had turned into a parking lot. Around the hills encasing a natural bowl, boys were selling parking spaces at twice what anyone would pay in midtown Los Angeles. The entrance to the area had been roughly graded and outlined with a single strand of barbed-wire fence. The alternative for the drivers was to chance crossing the gulleys on either side of the narrow road. A few who had tried it were hung up, their vehicles lodged at rakish, awkward angles like whales tossed onto a beach. Their drivers, obviously frustrated by the results of their own poor judgment, spun ineffectual wheels for a while and then climbed out in disgust to curse themselves for trying to save a few dollars. Only motorcycles could traverse the gulleys, park in the open, and save money. Yankee Horn had thought of everything.

Hawk drove straight to the ticket gate, nodded at the attendant who recognized him, and rode over the circular row of hills.

The sight shocked him.

The natural bowl was packed with people. A show was already in progress. Latecomers were finding places so far away they had to use binoculars. A fortune in tickets had been sold.

The McComb performers were going through their routines. They drew only perfunctory attention from the crowd. The big attraction lay to the east.

There the ravine cut a wide ugly gash through the desert. From the hill Hawk could see the vertical walls that plunged straight down to a canyon floor which would spell sure death to a rider who failed to span the chasm.

His mouth went dry.

He could make out the two spots McComb had suggested as takeoff points. They were clear enough, but those locations alone were not enough. There were no obstructions forty feet or forty yards to the east or west. Forty feet, forty yards. There was no visible difference. Yet he was willing to bet the question was crucial.

Feet, meters, yards.

He would have to guess.

If he made the jump, his life would depend on an unfounded guess. The prospect was chilling.

## 22

Hawk stopped his cycle and craned his neck until he could see through the helmet visor to the edge of the ravine that ran a hundred yards or more along the northern edge of the half-moon-shaped natural bowl.

What he saw surprised him. A few feet in front of the rim, a white chalk line had been laid down by the type of device used to mark football fields. Tick marks of chalk indicated in increments of ten were chalked onto the flat hardpan surface.

At first it didn't make sense.

Then he realized the two possibilities. Either Noon or Husky had calculated a crossing point or one of them had seen Whip McComb's notebook and knew his recommendation. He should have suspected the latter, he thought. The stunt man had carried the book with him for years. Some time during that period his two main understudies could have found an opportunity to copy his calculations. He must have known it. That's why he had carefully coded the actual points.

He should stop Noon and Blackwell from killing themselves. It might not be easy.

Still on the bike he found the markers shown on the map and counted east from the farthest one and west from the other.

When he had the two chalk marks in sight, he made his choice. He would go with the point on the west. The corrected launch point was only twenty-eight feet from the marker shown on the map.

Feet? he asked himself. Or yards? God, I don't know.

He would try yards. Twenty-eight feet was too little. The terrain didn't change significantly in such a short distance.

Twenty-eight yards west then, he counted.

His eyes fixed on the new point. He forced the doubt from his mind. Doubt was no ally. You made a decision and you went with it; that was his credo. If he had to jump, he would do it without hesitation.

The corrected spot he had calculated from McComb's formula was no closer to the far side than any of the others, but there was an approach that appeared to dip and then rise again at the point he would have his launch ramp placed. The other side of the ravine might be slightly lower. The landing site was located at the beginning of a bend in the cut the infrequent rains had made through the centuries. The water flowed west. The curve would cut the north edge somewhat deeper. It was not much of an advantage, but it was all he had. Probably McComb had ascertained it was enough.

"Hawk!" Yankee Horn called to him. "Thank God you got here. Husky and Noon have their ramps in position. Husky's ready to go."

"And Noon?"

"She's over there." He pointed and Hawk followed his extended arm.

Noon McComb was nervously tugging at her gloves. Several mechanics were tinkering with her motorcycle, making a last check.

Her ramp was directly in front of her. It was lined up behind one of the two points suggested in Whip's map.

Did this mean she was the one who had plotted Whip's accident?

Not necessarily. It only showed that she had seen the notebook. It didn't prove that she killed her husband.

"Where's Blackwell?"

Horn pointed, aiming at yet another surprise for the rich crusader. Blackwell stood beside a bike exactly like the one Hawk was riding, one exactly like Whip's.

Hawk protested. "I thought there were only two clones. The one smashed up in the snake pit and the one I'm riding."

"There are," Horn confirmed. "Husky's men rebuilt the

one you left in the pit. He figures the only way across is to use the same machine Whip would have used."

"You'll have to stop them," Mike told him.

"Why?"

"Neither one is going to make it."

"So now you're the expert."

"It's not that. I'll be nothing but part of the machine, doing exactly what McComb would have done. The bike's balanced to the weight he specified."

"The tank filled?"

"Yeah."

"Good. He always started with a full tank. Kept his calculations easier, I think. And don't worry about those two. I have a hunch they know as much as you do about how the leap is supposed to be made."

Hawk knew better. Noon was pointed in the direction specified in the book. She'd never make it, if the ex-newsman's code reading was right. The same was true of Blackwell.

"Both of them will be killed if they go through with the challenge," Hawk warned.

Yankee sniffed. "That's your assumption."

True. Mike accepted the comment. He only assumed he had broken the code.

Shit! Mike cursed under his breath. He couldn't let them die; one of them was probably innocent. "Tell them the challenge is off," he told Yankee.

"No way," Horn answered. "This isn't just between you and them, you know. They're also riding against each other."

"Then tell them we'll schedule it another day, using parachutes or nylon safety ropes. If one of us falls short, we'll at least have a chance of surviving."

Yankee sneered. "Chicken. Drop out, and Blackwell intends to go alone with a parachute. Another cycle star used jet propulsion and parachutes for a leap years ago."

"And he survived."

"But the crowd came here to see you three idiots risk your necks. A parachute is like a net under a high-wire act. The zest is gone." Yankee paused. "Well, where do you want your ramp?"

Reluctantly Mike raised his hand and pointed. "Twenty-eight yards west of Noon's ramp," he said. "Exactly twenty-eight yards. The dwarf cupped his hands and shouted to the crew standing about the fork lift truck that would help the men move the wheeled triangle of painted boards into position.

"Twenty-eight yards west of Pu Noon," he repeated.

"Twenty-eight yards!" The man on the forklift confirmed the measurement and started his engine.

Hawk's stomach was a volcano of nervous energy. He was committed.

Was he right? Had he decoded the calculations correctly? Or would he die with the other two?

And where was Pollock?

"The crowd's about in," Yankee Horn smiled. "They're practically standing on each other's heads to see this."

Hawk looked across the canyon.

It seemed impossibly far, but was it?

Would Husky or Noon go through with the contest unless they were fairly sure they could do it? Noon, at least, felt certain; she was relying on calculations by a dead man who couldn't ride from the grave to stop her.

Blackwell saw the movement of the third set of ramps and paled. The motorcycle cowboy realized his bluff had been called. Hawk was going through with the jump without safety apparatus. So was Noon McComb.

Hawk grinned behind his visor. "Sweat, you cocky bastard," he said aloud.

Across the canyon, workers were moving his landing platform into position. They had a surveyor with electronic gear positioning the two wooden runways directly across from each other.

Behind them was a smaller crowd. They stood along a roped-off crescent where the victors were supposed to brake to a stop after the big event.

"How'd they get over there?" Mike asked.

Yankee laughed. "I didn't miss a trick. I rented four-wheel-drive vehicles and brought people twenty miles around from the north. Told them they were getting the best 'seats' in the house. They'll be demanding autographs . . . if you're going, that is."

Mike kicked the starter. He knew he was going through with it. He'd win for Jinx, but he still hadn't accomplished what he set out to do.

He still didn't know who had killed his friend. Noon or Blackwell, or both of them? Who had told Billy what to do?

Yankee clapped his hands. "I'll start closing down the other acts. Wait for the drum roll and the flagmen. And you'll have to move up parallel to the others. Remember, you all go together. You picked your spots. You stay with them. Any one of you turns chicken, you lose automatically."

"What if we all get killed?" Mike asked.

The dwarf shrugged. "There's always Jinx. And me. The split will be bigger, that's all. Five minutes, okay? And keep your mask down. I'm still calling you the ghost of Whip McComb." He paused before the afterthought: "And don't worry, we got an ambulance waiting over the hill."

"You sure it isn't a hearse?"

"It'll carry three passengers, dead or alive."

"Thanks! You're a great comfort. You'd probably throw an anchor to a drowning man."

"Comfort's not the name of the game, big shot."

Horn rejoined the show. Riders were finishing their acts. Workmen dismantled the props; the spectators wouldn't want their vision impaired.

Hawk twisted about in the seat. In this mass of people he was utterly alone. He grew uncommonly nervous. Pollock should be here by now, he grumbled to himself. Why had he let that idiot buy the last prop?

Finally, sighting the CIA man walking over the hill, his arm supporting Jinx, he exhaled heavily with relief. There was still a chance; maybe he would not be forced to trust his hunches about the code and the measurement.

"Mike, don't," Jinx tried to run with her ankle cast, nearly fell, and had to be helped again.

Mike didn't want her here. If anything went wrong, she should not watch him die. He had already failed her enough.

"George, take her away!" Mike yelled.

"Places," Yankee Horn said dramatically over the sound system. "This is it, folks. The greatest grudge match in the history of motorcycling. The unknown challenger, the ghost of Whip McComb, challenging the top two bike jumpers in the world."

Pollock and the girl kept coming, following as Mike moved his bike up on to line with the others.

"Mike!" There were tears in her voice. He waited. She—they—deserved that much.

183

She reached him and threw her arms around his neck. "Don't go, Mike. Let me, please," she begged.

Pollock made a motion with his head, indicating the entrance road.

"You have friends on the way," he said. "I picked up Jinx at the motel when they were inquiring about you."

"Two men in business suits, Orientals," Jinx said. "Probably newsmen or publicity men from the Japanese manufacturers of Noon's motorcycle. Oh, Mike, please, let me have the bike. I'm better than you. We'll have the whole show to ourselves."

Newsmen?

Not likely. Reporters wouldn't be late to the big event. They rarely traveled in pairs unless one carried a camera.

Newsmen, hell. He knew better. Red Army men maybe. Or IRS agents. Detectives from some of the places where he had been involved in bloodletting since he came into his fortune. Or a killer who wanted the vast wealth he controlled so tenuously.

It didn't matter. There was no retreat down the road.

"Mike, I think they're calling in a helicopter," Pollock said. "If that gets here while you're in the area . . ."

"Darling," Jinx was asking, "what's wrong?"

"Nothing." He raised his visor long enough to kiss her cheek and found it damp. "But what's wrong with you? Why the tears?"

He lowered the visor again.

"Just tears of joy," she lied. "Even though you have never said it, you must love me to even think of challenging Noon and Husky."

Pollock gave a better explanation for the tears. "Billy died this morning," he said.

Hawk felt his stomach go sour. A kid he hardly knew had died for him. He thought he knew why.

"Where was Billy when I crashed into the snake pit?" he asked.

Jinx withdrew. She couldn't believe what he was suggesting. "He was at the speaker's stand."

"Near the power switches?"

"No." Jinx insisted.

"Yes," Pollock answered. "The police got a partial print.

Not enough for evidence; it was blurred, but it was Billy's print all right."

"No," Jinx cried. "Billy wouldn't have done anything to hurt you. Or anybody."

"He would do as he was told," Mike suggested. "And he was told to turn off the lights before I passed between Husky and Noon. With my hands off the bars, I didn't stand a chance. The touch of a fingertip tilted my bike. You don't correct that in the air."

"But he died to save you."

"Yeah. I think he finally understood. He was being used."

Pollock took a small brown bag from his pocket and held it out. "Here's what you ordered. I hope you know what you're doing. I sure don't."

Hawk took the contents and let the bag drop to the ground. At least there wasn't any wind. Taking the golden spur and the speedometer drive gear from his pockets, he showed them to Jinx.

"Billy switched the gears on your dad's bike, Jinx."

"No, he wouldn't. Did you find that in his van?" Her brows knitted together. "He kept things, but why would he keep that?" She pointed at the offending gear. "He wouldn't be proud of it—of killing Dad."

Mike rolled the gear over in his hand and then showed her the spur from a cowboy boot. "Billy kept a lot of stuff. They were mementos of someone he loved, a person he would do anything for."

"Riders, are you ready?" The loudspeaker blared.

Noon and Blackwell signaled the affirmative. Hawk stared at the things in his hand.

"Are you ready?" the question was aimed at him alone.

"Go," the audience cried. "Go. Go. Go. Go."

He stalled, feeling the tension in his own body tightening like a noose around his neck.

"Go. Go. Go."

"I say, are you ready there?"

"Go. Go."

The gladiators were being called into the arena again. The jaws of the lions awaited.

Even Blackwell was growing worried. Hawk watched him raise his face mask and shout. The words weren't audible over the crowd but the meaning was clear. The man in the ten-gallon hat and the boots with silver spurs was a spring ready to snap.

The old daredevil was finally terrified.

"Go. Go."

Noon straddled her motorcycle. Her eyes had been fixed on the ramp. She twisted slowly, confused. She raised her face mask. What was happening? Why hadn't they gone? Like Husky, she was tensed to the point of breaking.

Crew members were running toward Mike.

"What's wrong?" they were shouting.

"Go! Go! Go!"

A drum roll began. Jinx leaned harder on Pollock. One of the mechanics arrived to take her arm. He screamed at Hawk through the visor.

The drum reverberated from the sound truck.

Hawk let the tension build. The bow of human patience must be bent to the snapping point. Perspiration coursed down his spine; still he sat immobile. The other two wouldn't go without him.

"Get over the hill, George," he told his friend. "There's an ambulance. Turn on the siren."

"What the hell for?"

"Maybe it'll sound like a police car."

"Mike, you're not making sense," Jinx argued.

"I rarely do." He pulled her close and held her face near his visor. "Love you, kid. Remember that."

"Mike, it's going to be all right, isn't it? I mean, you're certain of what dad meant with those formulas."

Hawk winked. "Sure, would I risk my life when I have you waiting for me? Georgy Girl, shag your ass. Get that siren going."

He eased Jinx away and put his hands on the bars. He revved the engine.

The chanting stopped.

The drums had stopped. They would start again soon. Timing was important.

Despite the tension Pu Noon sat her mount with the grace and self-assurance of the empress she pretended to be. Husky Blackwell was closer, dressed in a light fleece-lined jacket in spite of the heat simmering off the hard dirty-white clay.

The desert plateau grew quiet, except for the three engines poised along the canyon.

Mike turned toward the imitation cowboy, lifting the visor so that his voice would carry.

"Husky," he yelled, "you're not going to make it from there."

Blackwell gave him the finger.

"Are you ready?" Yankee Horn asked from the microphone.

Hawk lifted his fingers from the grip. Again he stalled.

There was the rustling of the crowd rising to their feet. One person stood, blocking the vision of several people behind him. More stood. Finally the entire audience was on its feet, straining and eager.

There was only the soft rumble of the idling perfectly tuned engines.

# 23

Michael Hawk turned the front wheel of his bike toward his opponents as if he were going to move closer.

His friend's young widow cried nervously at him, "Let's go! What are you waiting for?"

He stayed where he was to avoid frightening her. He enunciated clearly, his voice slicing through the purr of the idling engines.

"I talked to Billy this morning," he lied. "He told me everything. He showed me things he saved."

"I don't believe you!" she retorted, attempting to concentrate on the deadly task ahead.

"Cut the talk, Hawk. Let's roll," Blackwell urged. His voice crackled with nervous tension.

"The police are going to bother you a lot more than me."

"You lie," Noon jeered.

"Do I?" He held up the golden spur. He could see Blackwell lean forward in his saddle. His face showed his bewilderment. The spur had been deliberately planted in the van, Mike decided. "Billy saved lots of things," Hawk added. He held up the pair of panty hose and let the two legs dangle for a moment before he released them.

The crowd thought it was funny.

The drum roll started again.

"Strange things," Mike said over the laughter.

He raised his hand again, this time exhibiting the speedometer gear Pollock had found in the cemetery.

Noon McComb could no longer conceal the raw terror sweeping over her. The black almond eyes flared wide; her lips parted, trembling.

A siren wailed from over the hill.

To her it was proof. The police were coming—for her. Her worst fears had become reality. Panic and confusion swept across her face.

She was releasing the clutch.

"Don't!" Mike called. He tried to stop her. "You can't make it from there. The calculations are wrong!" The bike bolted for the ravine, shooting ahead like a rocket. With her powerful machine she just might make it and escape.

Hawk dropped the gear in the dirt. He kicked his own engine into action.

Yankee Horn was yelling at them to wait.

Blackwell was confused. His engine died. He started it again.

Hawk's bike reared, then bounded ahead. Hot wind slapped his face. He had not taken time to pull down his visor. Bits of dirt closed one eye. He aimed at the ramp.

It had to be right.

Then the ramp loomed ahead of him. There was no turning back now.

If he braked, he'd slide over the near edge of the ravine.

Noon was committed too.

Her bike reached the ramp before Hawk's. Like a graceful bird it sailed for the opposite bank. Then Mike was airborne too.

He was free; it was a thrill like no other he had known; almost worth the gamble.

He was aware of Noon off to his right. At the top of its low arc, her bike settled gently downward. It would be so close . . .

The front wheel did get across, but the stern was down. The rear tire hit the leading edge of the landing platform; the wheel spun, trying to lift the girl and the machine the last two inches. Instead the tread tore away the wood. It splintered the end of the planks, then began slipping backward. She tried to dismount. Men ran to grab her. Only inches separated her from their outstretched fingers as she and the bike paused in midair and then plummeted into the abyss.

The last Hawk saw, Noon and her bike were tumbling into

the ravine, cracking and rolling into the rocky bottom of the gorge.

He landed himself, his own rear tire striking no more than six inches onto the wood. As soon as he had the front down, he braked, left the incline for the dirt, took a foot off the left peg, and went into a sliding turn.

His landing went unheralded. On both sides of the ravine people were running to the edge, peering at the carnage.

Noon McComb had landed on the rocks below, the bike smashed down on top of her. At first the spectators were quiet, mute with shock; some turned away, sickened.

Gore was not as titillating in reality as it was in the imagination.

"She dead?" someone asked.

"You kidding?" an answer came back. "She ain't got an unbroken bone in her body. Yeah, she's dead."

Mike sighed.

It was over. He knew now it was Noon's pictures that Billy had kept in the walls of his lonely hovel. He must have idolized her. When she asked him to change the speedometer gears on her husband's bike, he had done so willingly, probably never connecting Whip's death with his own actions. Or maybe he did, and in his simple way had tried to make amends. He had given his life to save Whip's friend. It was the best the boy could do. It had to be that way. Billy could change a speedometer part; he could loosen a bolt or switch out the lights, but he couldn't arrange to track a letter across the continent, to Venice, and finally to the Caribbean.

A woman with brains and connections, though, could arrange all that.

Perhaps the Japanese government's suspicions about her were true. Maybe she did have international connections with terrorists. They would gladly have helped her to gain control of the profitable thrill show.

Or she might have used bike freaks in her attempt to intercept the letter Jinx had written seeking his help. Pu Noon would have fans wherever she went. She wouldn't mind a few muggings to please her. If they idolized her as Billy had, they would have gladly helped her in Chicago, New York, Venice, even a quiet Caribbean island.

How she managed that part no longer mattered.

Whip McComb's killer was dead.

He waited for some sense of satisfaction. He had done what he had set out to do. Why did he feel this way? Empty.

Once more he looked across the ravine. In the crowd it was easy to pick out Husky Blackwell. Still tangled in his bike, he had aborted his jump at the last moment after seeing Noon fall. Mechanics were helping him out of the twisted results of his panic stop.

He was favoring one leg; his left arm hung at a strange angle suggesting it was broken.

At least the egotistical bastard was still alive.

George Pollock also stood along the edge, his expression devoid of emotion. Mike knew what the CIA man wanted.

Pulling the roll of film out of his pocket, he ripped it from the cassette, exposing the emulsion to the light. He let it dangle the way he had the panty hose. He dropped it into the canyon before Pollock had faded into the crowd.

Finally Hawk saw Jinx. Yankee Horn was helping her stand. Another show rider supported her left shoulder.

She was waving. She was crying again; he could tell that without seeing the tears. Her words couldn't reach him over the din, but he knew what she was saying.

"Mike! Come back, Mike!"

Join her, he told himself. Live in the pleasant pool of her youth and exuberance. Love her. Enjoy her love. Share the show with her.

It wouldn't be a dull life. She was a little like his Lisa.

Stay.

The answer was always the same. Somewhere in that sea of faces—across the ravine and around the world—were the predators who sought to wrest from him the secret of his past and to use it for their own purposes.

Whoever the men Pollock had seen were—Red terrorists or government agents—they were bad news for Michael Hawk.

He couldn't stay. He couldn't take Jinx with him even if she would go.

Slowly he wheeled his bike around and pressed through the mob. On the other side Jinx would be waiting, but there had been enough farewells today.

Besides, he had to put distance between him and the stalkers. Lots of distance, fast. If they had a helicopter coming, he had to stay ahead of them until dark.

He couldn't go west toward the city.

He had to head into the desert. Out there by nightfall he would find a road. He had to or he'd be just as dead as the others. Without water, he would never survive a second day under the killer sun.

Where would he go? he asked himself.

Not back to the Caribbean. Not for a while. He would be too easy to track there.

He'd go north for a change, he decided. To Canada.

"Yeah," he said aloud. "Time to go fishing."

He knew an Indian guide north of Rainy Lake in Ontario. They used to share shore lunches. Bass and walleyes. Lake trout. Mike even liked northern pike the way the Indian filleted out the bones and fed the dark strip of meat to the gulls. Dipped in a batter of egg yolks and canned milk, then dredged in corn meal, even northerns were a delicacy when they were deep fried in an iron skillet held over an open fire.

Yes, Canada. He would like that.

But the loneliness was already beginning to seep in around this dream of pine trees, clear skies, cold lake water, and stillness broken only by the whine of mosquitoes and the call of the gulls.

## SPECIAL PREVIEW

Here are the opening scenes from

## *HAWK #8*
## *THE ENEMY WITHIN*

Coming in April!

# 1

The President of the United States, Warren Stone senior, stood at the window of the Lincoln bedroom, poised cautiously to the side, his back to the wall, one hand holding the drapery to allow a peephole view of the scene below. Rain splatted upon the glass and beat against the painted sandstone walls. Lightning sizzled, its candescence revealing ghostly snippets of Victorian furniture around him and deepening the impenetrable grave-black voids in the corners of the room.

The cannon fire of thunder rumbled and pounded. Wind whipped the Jacksonian trees in the President's Park below; a gnarled old elm planted by John Quincy Adams dipped and heaved in frantic paroxysms, her ancient limbs like rigged arms semaphoring distress into the storm.

Ordinarily the President's vantage point at the window would have offered an excellent view of the outside environs. Serving both security and aesthetics, moats of concealed lighting would have created artificial daylight in the area between the fence and the shrubbery surrounding the White House. Tonight, however, with the droplets of water diffusing and reflecting the light back upon its source, there was little comfort in the hidden illumination.

"Damn!" the President uttered. He despised nights like this.

The storm laid siege to his castle. The abrasive gale smashed the ramparts of greenery in the manicured yard. The Jacqueline Kennedy garden lay like flowered carpeting before the onslaught of driven rain.

Months before the famous Rose Garden had given way to the defense-minded military: beauty sacrificed to security. From the lawn a cleared field of fire had been created around the mansion, denying cover to would-be assailants who might try to dash past the barricades and into the building. Recent plantings, close to the structure itself, blocked trajectories from surrounding buildings to the windows the President used for his nightly watch. The precisely calculated combination of range and angle would keep the most expert marksman from striking panes unprotected by the greenery.

In the storm, though, wind whipped the screening cover, holding it aside like a coconspirator with death.

The President shivered. Never a coward before, he had recently suffered a shattering trauma; he had heard the click of a gun's firing pin less than a yard from his head.

It was a sound that would reverberate in his mind for a lifetime. Now, months after the incident, the secret service man's shout on that crucial day still echoed in his brain.

"Look out!" The words had sliced, laser sharp, into his nerve centers as he pressed through a crowd in New York. The shout stunned him. He looked into a 7.65 mm Luger with a 32-shot snail magazine aimed squarely at his forehead. His muscles had tightened into hard knots. He had seen the animal eyes of the stocky woman, watched her short, powerful forefinger ease the trigger smoothly backward, even thought he could see the hammer move forward in slow motion.

Life stood still, transfixed by shock. Onlookers, momentarily paralyzed, were unable to speak.

The scene froze into a Dali surrealism, painted in black and white, and blood. To the victim the woman's face was a mask of triumph, smiling and superior. In one brief pinpoint of time she had the power to explode the plans and work and dreams of a lifetime.

The click of the gun's hammer released the spring of life's clock; and time began moving again.

And then he had watched the woman's big ivory teeth disintegrate into splinters mixed in red muck. He felt fragments sting against his skin.

A bullet from an agent's weapon popped the woman's head like a firecracker. Other security men fell on the bloody mess, crushing it to the broad walk that stretched between the flags outside the United Nations building.

Stricken voices sought relief in screams.

His men had hustled him to the protection of the bullet-proof limousine, but he could no longer deny the raw facts. In spite of all the measures taken to guard him, the woman's long-barreled gun had been brought to bear on his face, the hammer had fallen before she could be stopped. Only a misfire had saved him. The next shell in the cylinder was live.

How many more like her were beyond the wrought-iron fence?

The shadows in the yard, thrusting and sidestepping, lunging and withdrawing, were quasi-humans parrying with swords of lightning.

Someday one of the shadows would lunge again. The next bullet might not misfire.

"Dad."

The President's tall, straight figure flinched at the sound of his son's reedy voice.

Warren Stone had not heard the door open behind him. Usually the hinges protested under the load of heavy paneling and the latch snapped like a breaking twig.

"Why are you standing in the dark, Dad?"

The lights flicked on. The deep shadows in the room disappeared, melting into the corners where the walls met the floor.

The President dropped the drapery back into place. "Just resting my eyes," he said, tapping the font of self-control that years of training had nurtured.

He summoned his campaign smile while his back was turned to his son. When he faced the younger man, he was once again in control.

Still youthful at sixty-five, Warren Stone was blessed with the physical characteristics that media demanded of a president: heavy dark hair touched with distinguished gray at the temples; beside his eyes, lines that deepened into crow's-feet when he smiled; good teeth and an easy grin; a low sonorous voice, honed for effective speaking—both public and private.

He was handsome, but just enough; without the appropriate blend of flaws, he might have made lesser men envious. An old football scar sliced his left cheekbone—his PR men maintained it was worth millions in campaign pledges. And the cleft in his chin lent him a vulnerability that was especially appealing to women. That, coupled with an innate trace of shyness, had inspired invaluable help along the climb upward; loyal supporters were eager to share his victories. But no one shared his anguish.

The people had chosen him overwhelmingly; they loved him and he loved in return. He loved being their President. There could never be a thrill to equal standing on the White House steps, taking the oath, or waving toward the panorama on Pennsylvania Avenue while he stood with his second wife and his son in the glass-enclosed observation booth.

He appreciated the social perquisites of rank, too. An expansive host, he had enjoyed the balls and parties before the attempted assassination. He would never forget dancing with jeweled women and drinking with powerful men in the East Room. He loved the room with its cheerful white enameled wood paneling and the cut-glass chandeliers dating from 1902 dangling from the ornate ceiling. The oak parquet floor was made for dancing; the world's elite had waltzed and tangoed and discoed there.

The Steinway concert piano, decorated with folk-dancing scenes and golden eagles, was made for the finest artists; he had reveled in their performances of both jazz and the classics.

The White House would always be his favorite home—the elliptically shaped Blue Room, the Lobby and the Cross Hall with the six classic columns of varicolored marble, and the State Floor where portraits of his predecessors looked down, inviting him to join them someday in the protective dust of history.

Unfortunately the people had chosen him but not his party. The voters cared not that they had left him isolated in an island prison surrounded by the unrelenting guards of Congress.

More and more he allowed himself to retreat to the lonely sanctuary of the third floor, where the attic had been turned into guest rooms that were seldom filled anymore.

After the shooting he began to lose touch with old friends. Suspicions haunted him and no one guessed the tenuous grip he held on reality. No one seemed to care.

The fear was more unbearable because it was new. It was anxiety a man should discuss with his family, but he could not share it. He was the father figure to a nation.

"Did you forget your meeting with the Iranian delegation?" his son asked.

"Iranians?" The President tried to visualize the day's agenda. The Iranians were not on the list. They were tomorrow.

"You did forget," Warren Stone junior said flatly. The edge of criticism in his voice cut deeply.

At thirty-seven, a natural-born citizen, Junior Stone qualified for the Presidency himself.

His brows, so shapely they had a plucked look about them, shaded pale blue eyes that could bore hypnotically into an audience. With those eyes he might have become a hypnotist or a trial lawyer—or a politician. Despite a demeanor that was misleadingly subservient, he could skewer an opponent with that gaze, and he did, with increasing frequency as a member of the First Family.

The son had his father's mouth, although he smiled less easily, and his skin was cratered with scars of teen-age pustules. Four inches under his father's commanding six feet two, he made himself shorter by hunching his shoulders like a man leaning into a winter wind, a stance that encouraged the paunch of indulgence which marred his silhouette.

The President recoiled visibly from the soft, uncallused hand that held the agenda. The boy had never seemed to grow up. He never left home. Perhaps he still sought the parental attention he had missed—a mother who had deserted him, a father who successfully pursued one political office after another.

Junior was a pallid substitute for a son. His father could muster no confidence or find any vestige of comfort in him.

As he had when his boy had come home from school with a report card, the President now groped on the table for his reading glasses. If he could not manifest interest, he could always fake concern. He disliked the unsavory ritual, but he had no time for more than laconic affection.

A shiver of panic lingered in his spine. He had placed the glasses on the Victorian dresser where a full-length mirror was braced between dark wood drawers with lathed round knobs. Flame-shaped bulbs burned in single brass candle holders on either side of the looking glass.

"I'd swear I . . ."

Lately he left sentences unfinished.

He was positive he had put the reading glasses on the dresser here in the Lincoln bedroom after he had retreated from a meeting with belligerent congressmen. He had not needed the glasses to stare into the moat of greenery and light that isolated him from the world.

"On the bed." Junior's brittle articulation sizzled with impatience. "Your glasses."

The plastic-framed glasses were there in the case on the Victorian bed, a purchase from the Civil War days.

He had not put them there. The President carried them about in his shirt pocket without the case. The plastic case added unnecessary weight and increased the bulge in his impeccably tailored jackets. He had not seen the case in the eleven months since his inauguration. He could not have put the glasses on the bed.

Yet he must have.

Doubt etched another flaw into his self-assurance.

He held the glasses indecisively, finally giving in to the need to express his inner feelings to someone.

"I heard pitiful sobbing last night," Stone said softly. "From the East Room. I went there. The lights didn't work, but I thought I could see mourners like pantomime demons in the darkness around an ornamental coffin-shaped structure.

"A catafaque," his son added.

"A what?"

"A catafaque. It's used sometimes for lying in state. There was a soldier too."

"How did you know that?"

Junior Stone smiled weakly. "And he said the President had been killed by an assassin."

"My God, you read my mind."

"No. It was a dream Abraham Lincoln described to his wife shortly before he was killed. It's in the history books about the White House."

Stone became indignant. "I wasn't dreaming. I was in the Red Room working."

"You called a guard, Dad."

"Yes."

"He found nothing."

The President grew cautious. "They must have gone out by the Entrance Hall."

"They?"

"The mourners," his irritability bordered on the irrational. "If the guard had moved fast enough, he would have caught them."

Junior corrected him. "If I hadn't caught him in time and convinced him you were pulling his leg, the story would have gone further. It may have been leaked to the press anyway."

"You don't believe me."

"You had a dream. You're working too hard. You ought to move up your fishing trip to Canada."

Stone drew deeper inside himself. He couldn't let himself become vulnerable, even to his son.

Quickly, before Junior could notice his consternation, the President pulled the glasses from the black case. He fitted them to his face and took the agenda to scan the list of times and names.

The print blurred.

He held the sheet farther out.

Thunder crashed outside. Wind rattled the window.

Even with the glasses, the print would not clear.

His irritation unnerved him. "These aren't mine," he said. Frustrated, he snatched the spectacles from his face and flung them at the bed.

His son watched him, then shifted his curiosity to the glasses. He cocked his head wordlessly and lifted the plastic bows.

The President saw the tiny gold-colored screw attaching the rim to the right bow. The screw did not match its silver counterpart on the opposite side of the frames. The replacement symbolized the frugality inbred in the President during childhood and the teen-aged years before money came easily.

The glasses *were* his.

"I'll get your other pair," Junior said amicably. He started for the door. "Oh, your wife called."

"Vanessa?" Warren Stone instantly regretted the ridiculous question. Who else could he mean? Junior could not be referring to his mother, the President's first wife. Neither of them had heard from her in more than thirty years. She might be dead by now, or she might be a drunken whore in some decaying slum. Even the evocative media, even his opponents in the campaign had never traced her whereabouts. Of course his son meant Vanessa. Junior had never known his real mother. "Do you have to say 'my wife'? Can't you call her by her name?"

Junior did not resist. "Vanessa called. She's in Chicago addressing a woman's group."

"When is she coming back?"

His son's rounded shoulders shrugged in dismissal. "You should know better than I."

Should.

The paths of Warren and Vanessa Stone crossed only when protocol absolutely required, when rumors surfaced periodically and had to be immediately squelched. Then they appeared in public to dispel the truth for the hundredth of a second it took a camera shutter to open and close, or in the thirty seconds a TV anchorman allowed the big eye to register the President and First Lady together. The czar and czarina were in their place, and all was well in the land.

The President never forgot that Vanessa could crush him; she had only to reveal that their marriage had been a charade from the beginning. But to destroy him, she would have to destroy herself. In that he found security.

"Ten minutes?" his son asked.

"What?" Warren Stone was snatched from his thoughts.

Again his son cocked his head. "I said, will you be down to speak to the Iranians in ten minutes or not?" he repeated in his pale reedy voice.

"Yes, yes, I'll be down." The President always thought of his son in pastel colors. "That was in the Oval Office, wasn't it?"

"No, the library."

"Yes, that's right. The library."

His memory was failing. He had been certain his next appointment was scheduled for the office.

Memory was a politician's stock in trade. But who could keep anything straight in a sprawling mansion of one hundred and thirty-two rooms plus a labyrinth of shelters, control rooms, and storage areas honeycombed beneath.

The job too was a continual, hydra-headed crisis that caused one problem to spin off and worsen while he tried to control another. Lately he often felt like somebody deciding seating arrangements for a state dinner while the kitchen burned and the chef resigned.

Right now he could not recall whether the Iranians were

here to discuss another oil boycott or to beg defense against further foreign intervention.

"On second thought, let the Secretary of State handle the meeting," he said. "I'll be down for the close. My presence would only overemphasize our needs." It was not a good excuse but he had come up with such a paucity of ideas lately that he needed reasons to avoid at least a few taxing conferences.

Junior silently disapproved. The latch of the door clicked and his son went out.

Warren Stone switched off the light and returned to the window. He pulled back the curtain and peered into the battle of the elements being waged in the President's Park. The thunder continued to cannonade the battlefield. Lightning exploded and flared over the whipping trees.

And through the bending tree limbs he could see a figure hovering across the park and beyond the gates.

It was the shape of a man in a great trench coat. It waited. Ominous. Foreboding. A silent threat.

What was he waiting for?

For the President to be driven into the open by the storm's machinations?

Or maybe the man was a gunfighter, like those who had stood outside western saloons, waiting for challengers to come for the inevitable showdown.

Stone shivered. He was as chilled and uncomfortable as the man in the street must feel.

Yet, drawn by a growing compulsion to have the confrontation over, decided, finished, he would like to have dashed out into the darkness and accosted his silent pursuer.

But he knew a showdown was impossible.

Crouching, the President crossed the window and picked up the telephone.

"Security," he said without waiting.

The diaphragm in the earpiece made metallic clicks until a familiar voice spoke in a deep masculine voice.

"Yes, Mr. President."

"He's there again."

"Sir?"

"That man, damnit. The one I told you about last week."

"I'll get right on it, Mr. President. Don't hang up. Stay away from the window."

Pulled by the subtle magnet of curiosity, the same one that makes a man examine an old memorized wound, the President took the phone with him. He pulled the drapes aside. Carefully he peered below.

There was no one on the sidewalk.